THE SCOT'S SECRET

BORDER SERIES BOOK FOUR

CECELIA MECCA

ALTIORA PRESS

To Terry and Carol

1

____

Bristol Manor, England, 1271
     "Alfred?"
Clara didn't flinch at the use of her boy's name. Over the past years, she had grown accustomed to answering to it.

"Where were you?" Toren handed the reins to a groom and lowered his voice as he approached. He knew that she was no squire at all, but a woman in disguise. She'd first come into the chief's acquaintance when he'd hired her—"Alfred"—to squire for him at a tournament designed to bring men from both sides of the border together in a peaceable display of skill. The chief had even offered her a position in his household.

"I. . . " She stumbled on her words. "I fled," she finally mumbled. But of course, he already knew as much, and he likely knew *why*. She'd run from the fear that he would spread her secret. She'd run even though he'd assured her that she still had a safe place in his household.

All along, she'd known she was playing a dangerous game, posing as a lad—one that could end badly—yet it was better than the alternative. It was better than getting caught.

A rustling sound reminded her that they were far from alone.

Everyone gathered in Bristol's courtyard was watching them, bearing witness to her shame. If only she could have sought the chief out privately. . . But by the time she'd learned that he would be here at Bristol Manor with Lady Juliette, Toren Kerr had already been preparing to leave for Scotland. And, despite everything, she dearly wished to go with them. The thought of making her way, alone, to the next tournament was nearly unbearable.

"Do you still wish to come to Brockburg with us?" Toren whispered for her alone to hear.

She peered up at his wife, Juliette, who was already mounted and prepared to leave for her new home.

"Come with us," Lady Juliette said. She looked as if she meant it.

Clara nodded, afraid to say too much. She had been a fool to run away. Toren and Juliette would help her. If nothing else, they would get her across the border safely.

"Come," he gestured toward her mare, and without assistance, she quickly mounted before he changed his mind.

This one would take her away from her homeland. A good thing under the circumstances. Any distance she could add between her and her past was welcome indeed.

"Fare thee well," called out the lady of the manor, Toren's sister.

Toren and Juliette waved in parting. With that, their small retinue, which included four of Bristol's men, began the journey that would bring them into Scotland.

Following a well-worn old Roman road north, they met no resistance other than the lack of clouds on an unusually hot day. Clara tried to push away thoughts of how she would remain in disguise at Brockburg. She'd simply make it work.

By the time they stopped to water the horses and eat a light repast, Clara was grateful for the splash of river water that served to cool her down, if only temporarily.

One of Bristol's men, a burly knight who had hardly spoken a word all day, brought a handful of water to his face.

"A small one, you are."

As was her custom, Clara nodded. Speaking little and deferring to all who didn't appear to be a threat was her primary means of survival. The more she spoke, the closer she came to people, the more likely they would realize the truth.

"You'd do well to use that water on your face," he said in parting.

She didn't dare. The smudges of dirt that she'd spent years perfecting were her only defense against exposure.

Clara stood, intending to blend into the countryside until their party continued their journey, when her savior approached from behind.

"Alfred?" the chief said in his deep, intimidating voice.

"Aye, my lord?"

Though she looked at him, Clara kept her head bowed and did not meet his gaze.

"I feared you were dead."

Not yet . . . and with any luck, the protection he offered would keep her alive longer than she expected.

"Nay, my lord."

He reached into the river once more, and Clara couldn't help but long for the same sweet relief. To remove the cap that hid her woman's locks and cool her face with the cold water. . .

"You were scared of something."

"Aye, my lord."

He ran his hands through his hair, clearly exasperated with her short responses. But Clara had learned to be short with words. Once, after Gilbert was killed, she'd attempted to play the mute. In the end, it had been too difficult to obtain employment without speaking, so she'd reverted back to speaking only when necessary.

"We need to discuss your position at Brockburg."

He glanced at the others and smiled at the beautiful woman

who stood at the center of the men. Clara was truly happy for the chief. She'd witnessed the beginnings of their courtship at the tournament. In all likelihood, she'd recognized he was in love before he himself had known.

And it was Lady Juliette who'd first discovered Clara's secret.

"Alfred," the chief said now, "when we return to Brockburg, we would like for you to stay with us. Serve Clan Kerr."

She whipped her head up to look at the battle-hardened Scot.

"Nay, my lord—"

"Before you refuse, as I suspected you might, think on it. I don't know your story or why you are so afraid to reveal yourself."

"I—"

"Nor do I care."

Clara exhaled. Was he really not going to ask?

"You served me well at the tournament, and my initial offer stands. When you disappeared . . ." He shrugged. "'Tis your right to keep your own counsel. We will not reveal you, and both Juliette and I will forever be grateful for what you've done for us."

She'd hardly done anything at all. Mayhap a push in the right direction. She'd seen their love for each other and had given them counsel.

"But I offered you training when I thought you a lad. My brother is unrelenting. The men, well, you hardly belong among such brutes. We would be happy to have you among us as a lady . . . mayhap as a lady in waiting to my wife."

Clara did not require any time to consider her options. She would not reveal herself.

"If that is a condition of my retention—"

The chief didn't allow her to finish. "It is not. The original offer still stands." The idea clearly made him uncomfortable, but she knew him to be a man of his word.

"Then I shall serve you and your brother well."

Clara meant it with all her heart and soul. She would do

anything not to worry about her next meal. Or wonder if she would be discovered by someone unscrupulous.

Toren Kerr nodded, but his expression remained skeptical. "I must at least tell my brother the truth."

"Nay!" she shouted, and all eyes turned toward them. "My apologies. I should not have—"

"Alex will know soon enough."

So he did not want her apologies. Clara had seen noblemen give servants black eyes for speaking thusly. The Scot was truly the man she thought him to be.

"He will not know," Clara rushed to explain. "Your wife is perceptive. I've learned to stay away from women." She belatedly realized how that sounded. "I mean no disrespect. That is to say—"

His laugh forced a smile from her. He was not insulted but merely amused.

"Then your secret shall remain safe." His gaze shifted from her to Lady Juliette, who was now making her way toward them. "Alex and his men care little for anything other than training and battle. But if you're intent on remaining a squire, I shall do my best to protect your secret."

As Lady Juliette approached the bank of the fast-moving river, her husband moved protectively toward her. "You will not consider becoming my lady in waiting, Alfred? Or. . . what shall I call you?"

"Alfred, my lady. Your offer is very kind, but I must respectfully decline."

She could say much more—and part of her longed to—but Clara had long since trained herself not to reveal more than necessary. She knew Lady Juliette was trying to protect her from the men. The gesture was appreciated, but she would be at a much greater risk if her secret was exposed, even in part.

"Then we will do more than *try* to keep your secret safe." Lady Juliette bent down by the river and thrust her hands into the water. Clara watched longingly as the cool water splashed her cheeks. The chief was all but standing atop of her now—prepared to catch her should she tumble into the river.

Lady Juliette's hands stilled suddenly as the chief leaned in even closer. What was she doing?

He jumped back abruptly as the splash of water reached his face, the lady laughing at her successful attempt at soaking him.

Clara watched their interactions and began to feel as if she was intruding. She had started to back away when Lady Juliette stopped her.

"I could not resist," she said. "But I do wish to ensure we are very clear, Alfred."

Clara froze, not sure what the lady meant by that.

"Toren told you he will do his best to keep your secret."

Lady Juliette paused, waiting for Clara to meet her eyes. Clara had to remind herself they already knew. There was no reason to avoid the lady's gaze.

The chief's wife was so lovely. Golden blonde hair streaked with brown and eyes so large their guileless expression was impossible to ignore.

"And as I said, we will do more than try. None will learn from Toren or I that you are not the young squire he hired at the tourney. I owe you that. *We* owe you as much and more. But know that if you ever change your mind, there will still be a place for you in a less. . . intimidating position. You need only speak your mind."

Their kindness reminded her of Gilbert, of the man who had kept her safe these past five years, until . . .

She would not think of him.

She would not cry. She had abundant experience in fighting tears. Biting the inside of her cheek, she looked down once again.

"Thank you," she finally managed. And before she embarrassed herself, Clara turned and fled for a thicket of trees nearby. The Scotsman and his wife had offered her protection, and Clara would not do anything to make them regret it.

2

---

*B*rockburg Castle, Scotland

"Get down, Reid."

Alex glowered at his younger brother, albeit by only one year. At five and twenty, Reid was every bit a man, although it was difficult to think of him as such at times like these. He sat high up in the oak tree beneath which Alex and the Brockburg men stood gathered, in the dense forest at the edge of Brockburg's northern border.

"I fear I'm unable, brother. You'll have to fetch me."

The other men looked at him and waited for his reaction.

Alex hesitated only briefly. As the chief's second, it was his job to ensure the men of Clan Kerr were always prepared both for counter-raids or full-scale battle. This close to the border, either could threaten at any moment. He took their training more seriously than anything, but they'd already finished for the day. Surely there would be no harm in. . .

He scaled the tree so quickly he almost caught Reid then and there. At the last possible moment, his brother ventured onto a thick branch of the oak and then swung himself onto the tree's leafy neighbor. Alex followed.

It was a game they'd played as children, which had the added benefit of toning their arms. As the trainer of Brockburg's men, Alex would take any opportunity to hone their skills and strength. Even if it meant chasing his damn fool brother from limb to limb high above the other men. By now the men were clapping and cheering.

Nimble for their large size, both he and Reid were evenly matched in most feats of strength. Save one: Alex was quicker, and Reid always seemed to forget that fact.

Taking advantage of Reid's position, perched precariously between the branches of two trees, Alex climbed too quickly for his brother to react. He touched Reid's arm and shouted in victory to the spectators down below.

Both men made their way to the ground amidst laughing and applause.

"Well done, Alex," someone said.

"You'll have to move quicker than that, lad," another added.

Alex laughed at Reid's expression, his younger brother not hiding his displeasure at the nickname meant to remind him of his status as the youngest Kerr brother.

"Do try to keep up," Alex shouted over his shoulder, already running toward the keep.

Giving the men one last challenge, he moved more quickly than usual, knowing none would be able to catch him. Slashing through branches, hardly noticing the cuts and scrapes appearing on his muscled arms, Alex chanced a look over his shoulder.

Only Reid was close.

Alex ran through the open field, past the training yard, and through the sole curtain wall that separated Brockburg Castle from the castleton below it. Built on a rocky crag that afforded spectacular views on a clear day, even into England at times, the ancient castle had been in his family for generations. It was both well-fortified and one hell of a climb, especially at this pace.

The guards hardly glanced at him. They were accustomed to

the sight of the middle Kerr brother putting his men through one final grueling exercise as the sun set over the mighty Brockburg Castle. By the time Alex arrived at the foot of the hill that gave the castle its impressive vantage point, he was far ahead of the others. He ran to the top, ensuring the men would curse him by the time they finished. Only a visiting merchant packing his goods looked his way.

The man and his assistant were about to say something, but Alex held a finger to his lips to silence them. Regaining the same brutal pace he'd set earlier, Alex moved toward the small building adjacent to the main keep. This was the realm of the most important member of Clan Kerr. . . their cook, a Frenchman who had been serving their family for longer than Alex had been alive.

He turned the corner and placed his back to the cold stone of the building behind him.

And then waited.

Reid should already have made it up the hill, and by now the other men should have also made their way to the castle grounds. But he was as patient as he was quick, so when no one appeared, he stayed in the same spot. His brother was hoping to sneak up on him, just as he'd suspected. With the delicious smells emanating from the building that lent him shelter, Alex suspected his brother would soon be pressured into giving up his game.

When he heard the old door of the kitchens creak open, Alex somehow knew, without looking, that Brockburg's priest would be joining him. Father Simon spent as much time in the kitchens as he did in the chapel, and the cook and his assistant and the maids would be too preoccupied preparing the evening meal to venture outside.

"You've the devil's look in your eye, Alex." As he'd suspected, it was Father Simon's brogue.

"How would you know, Father?"

Alex did turn then, not surprised by the man's bemused expression. Only a few years older than Toren, Alex's elder brother, Father Simon was more a member of the Kerr family than he was their priest.

"'Tis a common expression for you, Alex."

Alex put up his hand again, effectively stopping the father's next words.

Someone was coming.

"Damn you, Alex Kerr," Reid said, walking around the corner of the building.

Alex stepped away from the wall and walked toward his brother. "For the run or for effectively evading your not-so-subtle scouting party?"

Reid rolled his eyes. "Both. And pardon, Father."

While he'd enjoyed proving, yet again, his younger brother was no match for him, he was extremely hungry.

"Bernard is anxious to start the meal," Father Simon said.

Alex and his brother turned toward the priest.

"Bernard, is it?" More likely it was the priest, not the cook, who was eager for the repast. Father's appetite was legendary. Alex knew the castle inhabitants waited on them for the evening meal, but he'd been too eager to best Reid to concern himself with that.

"Aye, well. . ." Simon shrugged.

All three men laughed.

"It's a wonder to me that you stay so lean, Father," Alex said.

While he and Reid ate with an equal amount of enthusiasm, they spent the majority of their days in training, while Father Simon's habits were much more sedentary. Even so, it didn't take a toll on his looks—his lean frame, shoulder-length brown hair, and well-formed features made him the target of many sideways glances from women who seemed to forget he was not theirs for the taking.

He and Reid, however, had no such vows holding them back, and both enjoyed the attentions of the fairer sex. They'd often attempted to get Father Simon to admit he had made a grave error in taking his vow of celibacy, though he still had not admitted to any such thing.

Alex turned to his brother.

"So where are the men?"

Reid waved to the keep. "I ran them around back. Those who survived the heat and your pace, that is."

It had been an unusually warm week, but that meant nothing for the men's training. It was Alex's duty to ensure Clan Kerr was always prepared.

"When Toren returns—"

Both men looked at their trusted advisor, who cut himself off.

"Perhaps taking a wife will have improved his disposition," Reid suggested.

Alex frowned. "What an absurd idea."

"Now that the eldest Kerr is married. . ." Father Simon repeated a familiar tome. "Perhaps it is time for you to consider your choices more carefully, Alex."

This again. . . If only he could make his escape from the priest as easily as he'd run from his brother and his men.

"Hear me, men. The day I take a wife will be the same day I'll kneel to this man," he gestured at his brother, "and allow him to take my position here."

Both Toren and Reid had been attempting to convince him to defer the men's training to the youngest Kerr brother and take up residence at Dunmure Tower. It was his by right, but their holding just to the north reminded him too much of their mother. That tower was his mother's favorite residence. Many of those memories were good, but they were tainted by the memory of what came later—their mother had abandoned them immediately after the death of their father.

Because of that fact, Alex wanted nothing to do with his former home.

"'Tis enough talk of wives for the day," he said dismissively, walking toward the front of the keep. "More important matters await. Toren is expected," he tried to keep the bitterness from his voice, "with his English wife."

As their small travelling party entered the front gate of Brockburg Castle, Clara looked up and squinted. With the sun setting, she could not see anything save the outline of a large stone keep, which spread impressively to the edges of the crag where it was perched. The outbuildings were also impressive to the eye.

"The groom will see to our horses," the chief said to her and Lady Juliette after they dismounted. Meeting a young lad at the front of the thatched-roof stable, Toren spoke a few words to him, no doubt delivering instructions. Left alone with the new lady of Brockburg, Clara watched as Lady Juliette surveyed the keep.

"You will not reconsider?"

That Lady Juliette would worry about her at such a moment, when she was seeing her new home for the first time, reinforced what Clara already knew of the woman. She'd made the right decision to come with them.

"Nay, my lady."

"Then I have a plan."

Toren returned, so Lady Juliette could not elaborate, but curiosity drove her to follow the chief and his wife as they made their way into the keep. It seemed rather odd that no one had come out to greet them, though it was equally as out of character for Clara not to attempt to hide herself in the stables

As a squire for hire, Clara had grown accustomed to sleeping in the small tent she had bartered for with the last of Gilbert's belongings. When anyone started asking questions she could not answer, she disappeared. And although she wasn't as familiar with the customs here in Scotland, the borderlands and its people on both sides were notoriously faithful to their own families or clans, even at the expense of king and country. If she was to squire for

Alex Kerr, the man would certainly ask about her upbringing. The hierarchy among squires, in England at least, very much depended on one's family. Her duties and even where she resided would depend on the lies she concocted, though she hated to lie at all.

They entered the great hall together, and the clanging of cups and shouting of men ceased. All turned to look upon them, the lack of women noticeable.

"Where are my brothers?"

"Here," a voice called from behind them.

Clara did not turn around. She was unable to look away from the magnificent black stags woven into two royal blue banners hanging behind the high table. She clasped her hands together, attempting to stop them from shaking. The coat of arms was so startlingly familiar that she could not control her reaction to it. Just like her family's crest, it featured a stag and two swords—the only difference was that these swords were crossed. And, of course, the color. Her family's crest was yellow, a symbol of loyalty. Her father had died because of his misplaced loyalty.

Her hands refused to stop trembling.

"Alfred?"

How many times had Lady Juliette called to her? She turned and froze.

Three men stood alongside the chief. While two, obviously Toren Kerr's brothers, were as tall and broad as the chief, the third was a slightly older gentleman—a steward, perhaps? But it was the one in the middle who drew her attention. Unlike the others, he smiled, waiting for her to speak. Perhaps it was that smile that drew the eye. . . or the way he stood, so tall and proud, as if *he* were the chief, not his brother.

Though all three brothers were heavily muscled—she'd seen Toren's chest more than once since serving him at the tournament —this one was just slightly wider. His hair was darker than his elder brother's, a shade somewhere between dark and light brown, and shorter too. More dangerous yet, it capped the most perfect face she'd ever looked upon. The color of his eyes was masked by the lighting in the hall, even though there was an abundance of candles. His face was slightly square, and a few days' growth gave him a more ominous look than his clean-shaven brothers.

In a past life, Clara would have been appalled by her honest perusal of the man, but she'd seen much in the past year, and it seemed silly to pretend otherwise. He was finely built, and she was not ashamed to admit it, even to herself.

"Welcome to Brockburg, lad," the object of her admiration said. "I hear you'll be training with me."

Clara looked down just enough not to give insult. *This* was Alex? She could not train every day with this man. He was simply too distracting.

"Thank you, my lord," she said in a husky voice that she'd perfected. Clara couldn't even remember what her real voice sounded like.

"And as a son to a very prominent family in England, you will, of course, be given your own quarters here in the castle," Lady Juliette said firmly. She delivered the lie without flinching or giving herself away in any manner.

A prominent family in England? So that was Lady Juliette's plan. Clara tried not to appear surprised. The lady was extremely thoughtful. While it was true she'd helped bring Toren and Juliette together, the chief and his wife had already done more than enough to repay her. Bringing her here was repayment enough.

She nodded and peeked up again at Alex. He looked at her the way most did, as if she were a young boy and nothing more. The cap, the dirt, the loose, long-sleeved tunic. . . all Gilbert's creations to ensure she went overlooked. And all quite effective these past years. But suddenly, for the first time since they had run from home, Clara wanted to be herself. The girl whom everyone had said would grow up to be a beautiful woman "like her mother."

That was a dangerous thought indeed.

"Alex," the chief said, "so kind of you to send a greeting party for the new lady of Brockburg Manor."

Alex's attention turned from her as the Kerr brothers bantered back and forth in a manner that indicated they'd had plenty of practice. Lady Juliette glanced at her and winked. She smiled and then immediately bowed her head toward the ground.

Gilbert had warned her against smiling. She'd once thought him overly cautious, but his worries had proven quite practical. A knight who'd paid Gilbert to repair his sword during a small tourney had come to their tent to fetch it. A kindly man, he'd overpaid Gilbert, declaring his work worthy of a greater fee than had been asked.

The man had joked with Gilbert, and Clara had momentarily forgotten herself. She'd smiled, and the man had immediately walked toward her. He'd lifted her chin, turned to Gilbert, and then turned back to her. Clara had been discovered. Though they'd left immediately, and without incident, it had served as a much-needed reminder. She could never let her guard down.

"Your smile is your mother's," Gilbert had said. "As bright as the midday sun. Not the morning one just peekin' out, but one high in the sky, warming everyone in the land with its bright and beautiful rays."

She'd chided him for his poetic sensibility, something she'd actually come to love about the man who'd become like a second father to her. Though he couldn't read himself, Gilbert had loved to listen to troubadours' tales and often sought them out at tourneys, sometimes at the expense of coin he could be earning.

Clara pulled herself back to the conversation around her. The man who would be her master caught her eye and walked toward her.

"Toren says you are to be my squire."

Was he unhappy about the fact? The others moved toward the high table, but Clara was no longer hungry. Could she really stay disguised as this man's squire? He looked at her in a way that made her feel he could see straight through her.

"Aye, my lord."

"I've not had one before," he said and shrugged. "Tomorrow is soon enough to begin your training. But I'm sure you are hungry now."

"Nay," she said, too quickly. The thought of food roiled her stomach. She'd not been this nervous traveling alone in the dark.

"Then come. I'll show you to your rooms first."

She followed him from the hall down a winding staircase, through an arched wooden door, and out into the courtyard. Brockburg Castle was a contradiction in so many ways. While they walked through a cobblestone courtyard, a clear sign of wealth, the passageway that led to one of seven towers—if she'd counted correctly—was overgrown with weeds. Like most hilltop castles, its design was compact, every necessity fit within its outer curtain walls.

She concentrated on the uneven path beneath her feet rather than the Scotsman she followed. It would do no good to dwell on his appearance. Experience had taught her that a man's looks had little to do with his character. Besides, how was she to train with the man if she could not overcome her foolish attraction to him?

They entered a tower that contained, as far as she could tell, nothing more than sleeping quarters.

"There's a storeroom below," he said, gesturing for her to follow him up another set of winding stairs. "'Tis where they hide the bodies."

"The bodies?" She couldn't keep the alarm from her voice.

Alex barely broke a smile. "Of the squires who displease me, of course."

So serious was his tone, it took her a moment to realize he chided her. They passed through a small iron gate and climbed nearly to the top of the edifice.

"As you heard, Lady Juliette has requested that you receive

private chambers," he called back. "'Tis a luxury not provided to our servants," he said, arriving at a small platform and another wooden door. He lifted the iron handle and pushed inside. She followed him into a modest chamber devoid of any luxuries beyond a large bed without coverings and a single chair. It was clean, though a mite dusty, and she'd spied a wardrobe below in this same tower. If it was not already in use, it would prove most convenient.

Modest, aye, but much more than she'd expected. Lady Juliette had given her the invaluable gift of privacy.

"You can sit beside the arrow slit and see well beyond our borders."

She walked toward where he stood and peered out of the small opening. Indeed, a most spectacular view lay beyond, though an even more impressive one stood next to her. He filled the room, which had become quite warm, and Clara backed away.

"Shall we return to the meal?"

She needed to separate from him. "I can find my way back, my lord."

She placed the small sack of her belongings on the bed.

"Then I shall see you there. I don't require personal assistance, except on the training yard. Despite your size, you'll be treated the same as the others, so be sure to eat. You'll need the energy." He turned to leave. "Should you require anything, I am just above."

He pointed to the high, wood-beamed ceiling as he walked back through the door, and Clara's shoulders sank. Just above? She'd assumed his bedchamber was in the great hall. How could she possibly endure living so close to him?

You are his squire, Clara. What did you believe, that you'd never see the man?

"And Alfred," he called back from the other side of the entrance. "Take a bath."

3

A bath!

It should not have come as a surprising request. The well-placed smudges had saved her from being discovered, but they did not fit with her newly escalated status. Had she come as a lowly squire of no rank, her filth might have been accepted, even expected, but Lady Juliette's story indicated that she was a visiting knight, not a typical servant. She could even request a maidservant of her own, which, of course, she would not do. Clara could not possibly have someone attend to her; it was too dangerous. Which meant she'd need to find bed coverings and something to clean the cobwebs from this clearly unused bedchamber.

A bath.

She imagined her handmaiden at Barrington, who had oft chided her for taking so many baths that a tub had been permanently positioned in her bedchamber. If only she could see Clara now...

Of course, she would need to keep the dirt, however it antagonized her new master. "Master Alfred," a small voice called from behind the door.

It would seem her wish to remain without a maid was not to be granted.

"I am Ansley," the young girl said. No more than ten and two, she was well-kept and neatly presented. "My lady asked that I see to your needs."

From lady to servant to squire. Clara sighed.

She could do this.

"I've none, Ansley, save bed coverings and a clean chamber," she said. "And a basin of water, if you please."

She could not ask for a bath to be brought unless she wanted the servants to speak about her, which she did not. Filling a tub was no small matter, and until she learned how Alex cleaned himself, she'd not presume to request such a thing. And though they'd crossed a river not far from the castle before arriving, Clara was not yet prepared to follow it into the forest. She must first ensure it was, indeed, private.

With a small bow, Ansley left her. A short time later, she returned, and the two of them set to putting the chamber in order. It was only when she received a strange glance from the maid that Clara remember her newly altered status.

God's blood, this was going to be difficult.

"So *this* is where the new squire sleeps." Lady Juliette's voice jolted her out of her thoughts.

When her patroness entered the room, Ansley bowed deeply. "That will be all. Thank you, Ansley."

The servant startled, likely for being thanked for doing her duty. Or mayhap she was merely surprised that Lady Juliette, who had only just arrived to Brockburg, knew her name. Clara was not. Had circumstances been different, the new lady of the house was exactly the kind of woman whom she would have befriended.

Placing a small wooden tray on the bed, she closed the door behind her. Lady Juliette sat in the solo wooden chair against the circular stone wall and gestured for Clara to sit on the newly made bed. She did so, folding her hands on her lap.

"You've not yet eaten." Lady Juliette pointed to the tray, which was piled with bread and cheese. Clara eyed it hungrily, but she would wait for the lady to leave before partaking of the food.

"You only just arrived at your new home and have no need to care for me, my lady. Although I thank you for doing so."

Clara cursed herself. Though she'd succeeded in training herself to speak in a lower voice than was natural for her, she still struggled with her speech. Gilbert had often chided her for slipping back into the speech of a high-born lady, and she'd just done it again.

And Lady Juliette had noticed.

"When I told the men you're bred of a great family, a noble family, I was not far off the mark." She stated it as a fact, not a question. Adorned in a simple but elegant deep green gown fit for a queen, her long blonde hair flowing down her back, Lady Juliette embodied the noblewoman she had accused Clara of being.

Clara knew to secure the safety of living at Brockburg, she would be forced to reveal more than she was accustomed to the chief and his wife. But just how much was safe to share?

"At least tell me your name."

In this Clara was lucky. All who knew her, who would be looking for her, called her by her given name, Lady Clarissa.

"Clara."

"'Tis Lady Clara, I presume?"

She hesitated.

"We will start with Clara. And I insist you call me Juliette."

When she began to shake her head, Juliette amended, "In private, if it pleases you."

Clara tilted her head to the side.

"Do you remember the night we spoke last?" Juliette pressed. "The night I left Bristol?"

Neither of them were likely to forget it. It was the same night Lady Juliette had discovered that Toren had been sent to England to kill her father. The lady had been so upset at his duplicity, she'd left that very night, prompting Toren to go after her.

"Aye, and I'm sorry I was forced to share your secret with Toren."

"I understand. 'Twas necessary." Juliette leaned forward. "Do you remember what I told you? I said that you could trust him." She smiled. "I stand by my claim. You can trust us both to keep your secret as long as you wish it. Clara, you've nothing to fear from us. We will keep you safe, 'tis my promise as well as my husband's."

She so desperately wanted to believe it. And would have more easily if Gilbert's voice had not been whispering in her head ever since she'd agreed to come to Scotland. *Trust no one.* He had said it so many times Clara had often teased him about the refrain. Though he had never been amused.

"Perhaps. . ." Juliette shrugged. "Perhaps we can even be friends. I could certainly use one now."

Relieved that the conversation had shifted away from her secret, Clara said, "Your reception here has been a warm one."

Juliette scrunched her nose, as if she smelled rotten meat.

Clara amended, "With the exception of the lack of a greeting party."

"Even now Toren is arguing with his brothers about that. 'Tis just as well—I don't require a grand welcome. But. . ." She trailed off, her nose still scrunched prettily.

"Brockburg is a beautifully appointed castle."

"Of course," Juliette agreed.

"But there is a certain lack of—" She hesitated, not wanting to offend.

And then, at once, both exclaimed, "Women."

"You noticed too?" Clara asked.

"Aye, 'twas the first thing I commented to Toren as we walked into the hall. Chauncy Manor, where I am from, is rather isolated.

You already know my father is the English Warden, which means he knows of most of the crimes committed along the border."

As Warden, her father brought criminals to the monthly Day of Truce to meet the Scottish Warden, who did the same. Both attempted to keep peace along the border, a task that seemed to get harder, not easier, with time.

Juliette arched a perfectly formed eyebrow. Indeed, everything about the lady was perfect. "Unfortunately, that made him a bit. . . protective."

Clara knew of Chauncy Manor. She didn't think it was more than two or three days' ride from Barrington. Which made this conversation all the more dangerous. Lady Juliette might have known her father. . . or at least heard of him by reputation.

"So we may not have had an abundance of visitors, but certainly there were at least more female servants."

"'Tis odd," Clara agreed. "Well, there are at least two more females at Brockburg now."

Juliette crossed her arms.

"Well, of sorts." Clara's smirk was an acknowledgment that she understood her predicament well.

Juliette stood. "I will not ask again for you to share," she said more seriously. "But please do be careful. I wish you would agree to—"

"Nay," Clara said, softly but firmly. "I am a squire and must remain as such."

"But you will be Alex's own squire. Surely you realize what that means? How are you to conceal yourself from someone you see every day, all day?"

"I served your husband, and he was not aware," Clara reminded her.

"And I tease him about that even now," Juliette said. "How he could not have known. . ."

"'Twas my duty to ensure he did not."

My life depends on it.

But that was a thought Clara kept to herself.

Alex and Toren entered the heavily wooded area as they watched the men run ahead.

"Kind of you to finally join us, brother," Alex said. Nearly a week had passed since Toren's arrival, and he'd only seen his brother once—that first night, at the evening meal.

"I've been otherwise occupied," Toren replied.

"If by 'occupied' you mean enjoying the company of your beautiful English bride, then aye. I am sure you have been."

Dressed lightly without armor, the men entered the clearing Alex and Toren's father had designated as another list for training. Surrounded by trees and cut in half by a river strong enough to carry a man at its center, it afforded more obstacles than the artificial field housed inside the castle walls.

They stood at the edge of the clearing, watching as the men paired off with their blunted swords. They'd been trained well, and all knew their positions.

"So your wife allowed you to escape? I assume she sickens of your overbearing presence?"

Toren shot him a glance, warning him away. But that look never scared Alex quite as much as his brother would have liked. And so he pressed on, smiling.

"Your wife. The same woman, for all eternity." Alex shuddered. "At least one Kerr will have done his duty."

"That's enough, Alex."

"Enough? Never!" He reached behind his brother so quickly Toren didn't have time to react. He wrapped his arm around Toren's neck, squeezing until his brother was finally able to loosen his grip.

Alex relented good-naturedly. "'Tis good to see your stubborn arse again, Toren." Turning to the men, he yelled, "Switch," and they did. Alex watched as they changed sparring partners and took up their swords against new opponents.

"I'd say the same if you'd manage to be serious just once." Toren ruined the effect of the chiding comment by lifting the corners of his mouth just slightly.

"You'll find I can be quite serious when the situation calls for it."

He drew his eyebrows together, mocking his older brother's expression as best he could.

"Tell me."

"Either you or Reid should bring men to the Day of Truce. I need to ensure Juliette's father encounters no further trouble."

Toren's new father-in-law, Stewart Hallington, had been falsely accused of taking bribes to allow Englishmen who'd committed crimes against Scots to walk free. The criminals *should* have been brought to the monthly Day of Truce, where crimes against men from each side of the border were judged and punished. Hallington's sheriff, unbeknownst to the lord, had been taking the bribes. Sent to kill the warden, Toren had instead fallen in love with the man's daughter. Ultimately, he had discovered Hallington's innocence, and by breaking Clan Kerr's tradition of remaining neutral and refusing new allies, he'd managed to rally enough support to convince Douglas, Scotland's Warden, and the king to abandon their original plan. The matter had been settled, but some Scots still wanted the warden's head served to them on a plate. Toren was right to worry.

The situation had put their clan in the unlikely position of having new allies. Though Alex and Reid were glad for the development, their mistrusting chief was not. Much like their father, Toren had spent years cultivating a perfectly unallied, neutral clan who cared only for keeping themselves safe.

Now, they were anything but neutral. With their sister's marriage to Bryce Waryn and Toren's marriage to the daughter of the English Warden, Clan Kerr was as embroiled in border politics as any clan in Scotland.

"And now deSowlis is firmly an ally once again." His brother winced. "We should ensure the recent raid on their land remains nothing more than a nuisance. Word is they lost men, though I've yet to confirm as much."

Toren frowned. "If that's true, we should increase the watch. The raids have become more violent lately. It worries me that these men are so brazenly violating the tr—"

"What is he doing?"

As they talked, Alex's eyes had been drawn to his new squire, who, rather than taking a sword against an opponent, stood to the side, watching the spectacle. Each day the lad made himself available—he ran with the others and climbed as well as most. But it suddenly struck Alex that he'd not seen his squire swing a sword.

"You can't expect him to pair with someone of that size." Toren gestured toward the field. Most of the men were full grown, almost twice the lad's weight and heft.

"I forget the lad is English. Do they stand aside when a battle takes place, perhaps cleaning the mud from their lord's boots as—"

"You'll remember my wife is English."

Alex frowned.

"And your sister is married to an Englishman."

That reminder did not improve his disposition. Alex's dislike for the English was well-established. At one time, all of his siblings had shared that feeling—a relic of having an English mother who'd abandoned them and living on the border where strife was the way of things.

"Alex..."

"Don't worry, brother. I will conduct myself quite courteously with Lady Juliette, you can rest assured."

"Is that why you failed to welcome her to her new home? Did you hope to make her feel unwelcome?"

He had been waiting for his brother to bring that up again.

"I'm more surprised that Reid agreed to go along with such nonsense," Toren continued. "But you no doubt came up with the idea."

"We are allied with them now," Toren said.

It was a fact he could not change. He'd even grudgingly begun to accept that the Waryn men were worthy of his respect. When he brought Catrina back to England to visit, before she and Bryce decided to marry, he'd spoken to both brothers on more than one occasion. "By Christ's—"

"Alex." His brother's tone was sharp.

But he didn't want to have this conversation now. . . and he didn't want to think about how the English had infiltrated his life —like the reedy squire who had been foisted upon him. The lad would learn nothing if he stayed out of the way of danger.

"Begging your pardon, Chief," he said, turning away from his brother. He once again yelled for the men to switch as he pulled his sword from its sheath. "Alfred!"

The boy was obedient enough—he'd give him that. The lad ran toward him.

"Alex, what are you doing?" Toren asked in an undertone.

"Training my new squire," he replied smartly as the lad came to a stop in front of him. "Alfred," he said, looking at the lad, "Why are you not training with the men?"

Alfred hardly looked up. He did indeed carry a sword, albeit a smaller one than even most boys his age handled. But he made no move to wield it.

"Tis a fine looking weapon," he said. "May I?"

The lad stuck his arm out, and Alex exchanged swords with him. While Alfred held his own out in front of him, Alex admired the craftsmanship of the unusual blade.

And the inscription. *Non ducor, duco.*

He handed the sword back to Alfred and took his own once again. "It's been too long, brother."

Toren placed his own sword between them—a silent invitation. It had indeed been too long since he and his brother had met on the practice field. Truth be told, he'd much rather parry with his brother than with the lad.

Alex looked back and forth between Toren and the boy, then told Alfred, "It seems you've one more day's respite."

<hr>

It was only much later, after the training had ended, that Alex realized Toren had deliberately dissuaded him from practicing with Alfred.

He and his brother had always been close, and they'd become inseparable after losing their parents—their father to death and their mother to England.

Which was why Alex knew, without question, that something was amiss.

And he would discover what it was.

4

———

"**A**lfred."

Oh dear.

So far, Alex Kerr had demanded little of her. Much to her relief, he'd kept his word and made no demands for assistance with his person. And despite their close proximity in the west tower, she'd seen him only once on the way to break their fast. The conversation had been brief.

Since she took pains to avoid the other men as much as possible when not training, Clara had thus far raised no suspicions. She'd begun to let down her guard, if only a little, and planned to venture down to the river where they trained the next morn so she could bathe before the household awoke for mass. She'd watched the gatehouse through her narrow bedroom slit at that early hour, and it seemed there was enough activity for her to avoid rousing anyone's suspicion.

But it would seem her streak of good luck had come to an end. Alex had called her out earlier for not training with the others, and Clara was sure she would now be asked to answer for it. She could wield the sword Gilbert had made for her. Crafting a weapon made for her small hands had been an easy task for him, but while Gilbert had wielded a sword passably well, and a dagger even more so, he'd been no trained knight. So he had paid others to train her. She could likely hold her own against the young boys who trained back at the castle, but she didn't dare take up her sword against a grown man, especially not the large, braw men trained by Alex.

She turned and allowed the others to walk ahead of her back to the main keep.

"Why did you not train with the men?" Alex asked her.

She chanced a glance up at him and wished she hadn't. Sweat beaded on his forehead, and the sleeves of his loose tunic were rolled up, revealing thick, muscled forearms beneath.

"Look at me, Alfred."

Oh dear, indeed.

She did. His bright hazel eyes stared back at her. They were lighter than his brother's, more green than brown. His smile was usually easy, from what she could tell, but he was certainly not smiling now.

The man staring down at her was a pure, unbridled warrior exuding strength and power.

"You've not yet bathed."

Though she had cleaned up with the cloth and water basin, it was true that she had not washed the dirt off her face. She couldn't risk it. Nor could she continue to meet his gaze. He unnerved her. Not in the way some men had, as if they posed a threat. But there was an awareness of him, of his handsome looks and constant smile that she could not easily dismiss.

"If you're to continue to train with the men, I'll know why you didn't join them today. And why my brother has taken such an interest in you. And—" he looked beyond her as the last of the men left the area, "—from where you come."

So many questions. But she was prepared with answers.

"In serving as a tournament squire, I fear I've had little time for my own training. I believe your brother took pity on me at

Condren. And as to your last question," she said, drawing on the words she and Gilbert had rehearsed so many times. "My master was killed at the Tournament of the King when I was but ten and six. I've been following the tourney ever since."

"Who was your master? How old are you?"

"His name was Sir Robert Kinney. I am ten and eight."

"Lady Juliette said you were from a prominent family."

Something had raised his suspicions. For days he'd asked her nothing, and now he was asking question after question, so quickly that Clara was glad to have answers.

"Sir Robert claims my parents were both of noble birth. He was a vassal to my father, who lost his lands in a dispute with a neighbor." Which was close enough to the truth.

"He claims?"

"Aye, my lord. I was orphaned as a young child. I knew them not."

And that was where anything approaching the truth ended. A vision of the father she very much remembered, his slightly greying hair and beard, always a touch too long, fluttered through her mind, and the memory nearly made her eyes well with tears. But a male squire simply did not cry, so she willed them back and continued to stare straight ahead.

Directly at Alex Kerr's chest.

He must have taken pity on her then, for rather than asking more questions, the handsome Scots warrior crossed his arms over his chest and continued to peer down at her.

Attempting to divert his attention away from asking further questions, Clara ventured to ask one herself.

"Have I displeased you?"

She looked up.

"Nay, Alfred, you have not. But I find myself with an English squire who is hesitant to take up a sword."

His uncharacteristic scowl indicated he was not being

completely truthful—she'd hardly ever seen him without a smile on his face—and Clara was eager to mend things between them.

"May I ask why your brother did not take me as his own squire?"

It was a question she'd been wanting to ask, and though she was hesitant to speak too much, she also needed Alex to relax his guard around her.

"He has one already," he stated simply. "My own left for the Isle of Man well before Toren travelled to Condren." He shrugged. "And Toren knows I'm always glad to teach a lad who's willing to learn, even if I'm not necessarily in need of a new squire."

It was exactly the opening she needed.

"And I am, my lord. Willing to learn, that is." She said it with sincerity, and though he didn't quite smile, she could tell he at least believed her in this.

"I'm glad to hear it, Alfred."

He nodded and began walking the well-worn path back to the keep.

She followed.

Lord, the man was large.

She did not want to pry, and perhaps it was a mistake to continue a conversation that had surely gone on for long enough, but something he'd said had struck Clara's interest. Or, more precisely, *how* he'd said it.

"You don't like the English."

He looked down at her and winked. "Nay, I do not."

His expression did not match his words.

"I am English," she said, as if he had not already known that fact.

"I'm well aware of it. With luck, you are one of the few who can be trusted."

Clara couldn't tell if he was serious, or if the words had been said in jest.

"And yet you've two English relatives." She clapped her hand over her mouth. She certainly had not meant to say that.

"And an English squire," he added. "Alfred, do not mince words with me. If you truly are to serve me, I'll not have you minding everything that comes from your mouth. Do you understand?"

"Aye, I do."

"So if you're so inclined to call me a Scottish bastard, then do so. You are to be my squire, not my handmaiden."

Good lord, never that! She imagined assisting him in undress—

"But I do insist on one thing," he said, his tone serious.

They had just emerged from the trees, and the magnificent sight of Brockburg Castle loomed high above them.

"Anything, my lord."

He stopped, and she followed his lead. She looked up at him, the sun setting behind him in a magnificent display of orange and blue. Though not quite as magnificent as the sight of this powerful, alluring man towering above her.

"Do not ever lie to me."

***

"Alfred, what do you think?"

Juliette stood in the great hall, looking at the new tapestries that had been hung on the walls.

Two days after Alex's ominous warning, Clara continued to avoid him as much as possible. She was eager to leave before he appeared for supper, but she also wanted to help Juliette, who was determined to transform Brockburg into a more appealing keep. Though well-maintained, it had lacked a woman's touch for many years.

"I think a squire is an unlikely choice to assist with the new decorations in the great hall."

Juliette winked and walked around the wooden trestle tables

to get a closer look at the colorful tapestries. "Why so many beautiful pieces sat in storage for so long, I'll never understand." And then, abruptly changing the topic of conversation, she asked, "How goes your training with Alex?"

Alex.

It seemed the man's name was on everyone's lips. Just that morning she had been stopped in the courtyard by the priest, who'd asked where the chief's second could be found. Alex was everywhere here at Brockburg, even when he was not present. There was simply no way of avoiding the man.

"Fine," she said, moving toward Juliette, drawn to a blue and gold tapestry depicting various oxen and boar gathered about a mighty sword that dominated the center of the scene.

"Interesting," Juliette replied.

At first Clara thought she referred to the scene in front of them, but when she looked at the new lady of Brockburg, Juliette was staring at her and not the tapestry.

"Pardon?"

"You were witness to our courtship," she whispered, evidently referring to herself and Toren at the tournament.

"Aye, or some of it."

"When did you know there was something between us?" Juliette reached up, just barely touching the point of the sword etched into the hanging.

Clara thought back, trying to remember the first time she suspected Toren's feelings. Perhaps it was the time he'd bolted out of the lists to find Juliette after his second match?

Nay. She knew the answer.

"It was when you visited the tent city," she said. "I was about to retire for the evening when I saw you approach."

"My lady." A servant moved toward them, weaving around the tables, her arms filled with another folded tapestry. "Beggin' your pardon, but I was told to give ye this."

Juliette smiled at the woman and held out her arms. "Cleaned already?" She thanked the woman, who beamed at her new lady, her smile growing even wider when she glanced up at the previously bare stone wall.

She had once overheard Toren speak of his home in a way that had made her think something at Brockburg was lacking. No longer. With Lady Juliette, Brockburg would be whole again. The wounds of the past would finally be healed.

Juliette set the wall hanging down on a nearby table and then returned to her. For some reason, Clara knew she was not going to like the remainder of Juliette's speech.

"And you knew because it was hardly proper for a lady to be visiting the tent city at night?"

Oh dear.

"Nay, my lady. I knew because I heard your voice before moving off. And you asked Toren why he'd kissed you. It wasn't the words, but the way you said them."

Even as she spoke, Clara realized she'd walked into a trap. "I really must get to—"

"You are a fine squire," Juliette said before lowering her voice. "But 'tis only a matter of time before Alex realizes the truth, as I did."

"But I simply said training was 'fine.' Nothing more. There is nothing—"

"It was not what you said, my dear Alfred, but *how* you said it. That night, I did not yet know Toren and I were meant to be together. I just knew I felt something for him. And I dared to allow myself to explore it."

She looked up at Clara's hat and then lowered her gaze to the smudges on her face. "I do believe your training is going fine..." She smiled. "As is the man in charge of it, aye?"

Clara scrunched her lips together, attempting a frown. "I've not noticed," she lied.

Juliette turned her attention back to the wall, nodded her

apparent satisfaction with the tapestry's position, and then moved to retrieve the new one from the table.

"Well then," she replied. "I suppose your instincts are better than my own. And of course, you will not care that your master makes his way toward us."

Clara immediately turned about, searching the hall with her eyes. There was no sign of him. Whether it was her baffled expression or simply Juliette's finely honed intuition that made the Lady of Brockburg burst into laughter, she couldn't be sure. But there was no doubt that Clara was indeed in trouble.

5

Clara peered out through the arrow slit in her chamber. The sun had not yet risen. After just over a week at Brockburg, she knew the morning routine well. Mass with Father Simon at sunrise, a quick meal in the hall, which had finally been attended by the lord and lady of Brockburg yesterday, followed by an endless day of training.

Though Clara had watched many training sessions at many different tournaments, she'd never seen such training methods as the ones employed here at Brockburg. There was not a quintain in sight. And she had not seen a single baton. Instead, the men ran and climbed. They crossed rivers and hoisted other men across their backs. Yesterday, when they'd finally taken up swords against each other, it was the first time Clara had felt remotely at home. . . until the realization had struck that she could not match up with any of the men.

Choose your opponent wisely. It was one of the first lessons she'd learned from a skilled knight who had later earned his place as tourney champion. While he'd admitted this was not always possible, an offensive against a smaller man, in her case, would be more advisable than a defensive one against a much larger one.

She opened the door to her bedchamber and treaded lightly down the winding staircase. The path to the gatehouse was short, one of the boons of staying so close to the entrance of the castle rather than at the other end in the main keep. The portcullis was raised, and none of the guards on watch even gave her a glance. She was leaving, after all, not entering. Two additional men stood in the short walkway of the massive stone gate house, which served as both a deterrent to invaders and a home to the men who stayed on watch both day and night. She approached the final exit —a smaller version of the mighty metal gate behind her.

"State your business." Without hardly glancing at her, the lightly armed guard reached for the lever that would allow her exit.

"To bathe in the river," she said. Truth, whenever possible.

He raised it just enough for her to leave and kept it up, presumably for an approaching wagon. The two tired horses looked much like she felt each time Alex made them run up the steep incline that led to the castle.

Aside from the supply wagon, no one used this path in the early morn. She'd watched each day before sunrise from her chamber to ensure it would be safe. Careful of her footing as she approached the wooded area just beyond sight of the castle walls, Clara almost skipped to the river bed.

Finally, to be clean!

She made her way downriver to the spot where Alex had taken them across. The water flowed slow and steady here as opposed to the rush abovestream. Dropping her small sack beside her, Clara glanced around, not expecting to see anything, or anyone, stirring. And she did not.

As she stripped off the dirty, travel-stained clothes from her body piece by piece, Clara tried to decide if she should clean herself or her garments first. Picking up the piece of scented soap the maid had kindly given her that first night, she decided the clothing could wait. She stepped into the water, not caring about its chill, and splashed it on every part of her body. She scrubbed everywhere, finally submerging herself to her waist.

She'd almost forgotten to remove her hat! Clara undid the pins that held the clever fabric in place and, removing it, tossed it ashore. Returning her attention to the task at hand, she shook her head, relishing in the feeling of the tips of her hair brushing against her shoulders.

If only she could stay here all day . . . if only she could stay like *this*. No dirt smudged on her face. No pins holding her hair in place.

Oh, to be free.

To be herself.

Alex shifted his weight, careful not to make a sound.

With every piece of clothing she removed, he became more and more uncomfortable—and not because he was spying on her. The reason for his discomfort turned toward him and looked in his exact direction. But she didn't see him. The sun had not yet risen, and it was only the wayward moonlight that gave him a clear view.

And what a view.

When he'd followed her from the castle, his first thought had been of treachery. Was Alfred meeting with someone? Planning an attack? When he'd realized he—or, more accurately, she—was actually planning to bathe, he'd felt only relief. Toren would have been sorely disappointed if Alfred, of whom he clearly thought highly, had turned traitor.

And then she'd begun to remove her clothing.

First, the shirt and strip of cloth that, unbound, revealed two perfectly shaped breasts tapering to a slim waist. And then the loose breeches she wore in favor of hose. Now he knew why. . .

Dear Lord, do not turn around, woman.

The curve of her delicate buttocks stirred him to arousal. If she turned, Alex would be lost. To his relief—and slight disappointment—she entered the water before giving him an even more scandalous view. Alfred, or whatever her name was, reached up and removed her hat. It was the first thing he'd noticed about her, a cap styled similarly to those usually reserved for servants. It covered more of her head than was typical. And, of course, the smudges of dirt that were ever-present on her face.

Dark hair, either brown or black, he could not tell in the darkness, spilled onto her shoulders and stopped just below them. She did turn then, to toss the hat onto the shore, and Alex got a glimpse of her freshly washed face. Though the features were still imperceptible, he could see enough to chide himself for a fool.

She was not only a female, but a damned beautiful one. Slim enough to pass for a boy, though not so slim that he could not imagine himself running his hands along every one of those lovely curves.

A gentleman would have turned away the moment he realized what was happening.

Clearly, he was not a gentleman, for Alex couldn't look away. Her transformation from a young squire to this curvaceous, sensual woman had so startled him that he did not even consider the matter of why until she turned away. The questions came quickly, one on the heels of the other. Why the ruse? Why would a woman wish to train as a squire?

His breath caught as she once again emerged from the water. She stood before him, utterly naked, unquestioningly female. Still hidden among the bushes, Alex watched as she pulled clothing from her sack and began to dress. He couldn't take his eyes off her.

Should he confront her now? Nay, he would learn what he could from Toren first. If his brother knew the truth, then her purpose for disguising herself as a lad posed no threat to the clan. If that were the case, mayhap he would have a bit of fun with this revelation. Granted, she was an Englishwoman and therefore off-limits to him. Even still, the day promised to be an interesting one.

With a final glance back at his female squire, who was now fully dressed, bent by the river washing clothes, Alex set off to find his brother. By the time he made his way to the main keep, the castle inhabitants were just beginning to stir. Alex sent a maid to fetch Toren, who was none too happy when he entered the great hall.

"Alex Kerr, if Brockburg is not under attack—"

"Walk with me." His tone quieted his brother, who, in a state of half-dress, followed him down a winding staircase to a chamber typically occupied by the steward during daylight hours. But the steward was likely still abed, and though servants had already lit the chamber, it was still mostly dark due to a lack of outside windows.

Alex closed the door behind him and turned to Toren.

"My squire," he said, "is female."

One glance at his brother told him what he needed to know. Goddamn it, Toren already knew. "So that's why you defended her yesterday in training," he said.

"We vowed not to tell anyone. Including you."

"We?"

"Juliette is the one who discovered her secret at Bristol. The girl was terrified of discovery. So much so that she fled after Juliette learned her secret. She only reappeared as we prepared to ride here."

Not only had he known the truth all along, but Toren was wholly unapologetic.

Alex felt his body tensing. He crossed his arms and waited for a real explanation.

"We made a promise, Alex. I don't break my word."

"Admirable."

His brother had nothing further to say, apparently.

"So let me assure you," Alex said. "That is no 'girl' you brought from England. She is very much a woman. What am I to do with an Englishwoman who poses as a lad? Did she tell you why?"

He uncrossed his arms and began to pace the room.

"Alex, you're not marrying the girl. Just training her. She's capable in many ways. I told

you, she served me well in Condren. Let her prove it to you."

He stopped in front of Toren. "Why does she disguise herself so?"

When Toren hesitated, Alex threw up his arms in disgust. "You don't know. Toren, have you gone daft? What if she's a spy—"

"Calm down, brother. The girl is no spy. She's scared. And alone. Juliette and I owe her a debt of gratitude."

He met his brother's eyes and nodded, a sign that he should continue.

"Without her intercession," Toren continued without pausing to let him speak, "I might not have gone after Juliette the night she left Bristol Manor. Alex, I would not abandon the squire, and I ask you not to either."

"Then let her squire for you. Or take a different position, one less. . ."

"Think of Catrina. How would our sister feel if you refused to train the squire because she's a woman?"

An image of their fiery, red-headed sister flitted through his mind. Surely Toren was right; she would scream at him for what he was saying.

"Perhaps she can train, but let her do so with you."

"I already have a squire. Alex. . . please."

He had never denied his brother and chief before, and he would not do so now.

But that didn't mean he had to like it.

Scowling, he sighed as Toren clasped him on the shoulder. "Aye, your new squire is English. . . and a woman. I'm not asking you marry her, Alex, simply train her. Allow her safety, to hone the skills she needs to feel safe. And be done with it." He paused, giving Alex an intent look.

"Trust me, brother. My wife is gentle and pure. You've met Lady Sara at Kenshire and other ladies, good ones, who live just across the border. Just because Mother—"

"Enough." Alex was not so stubborn as his brother, but neither did he feel inclined to relent easily. He would not think of their mother. Not now, not ever. "I'll do it."

"Thank you."

Toren released his grip, and for the first time since their conversation had started, Alex smiled. "But I'm going to have a bit of fun with this. And you'll not interfere."

If his brother looked worried, Alex didn't care. He asked much of him. And if he was going to play nursemaid to an English-woman, he would damn well enjoy it.

6

Clara made it back to the castle without incident. She was even able to slip into the quick morning mass. Brockburg's shape was similar to English hilltop estates, with each building attached to the other, all surrounding a central courtyard; the chapel was attached to the outer building. Although there was likely an entrance which allowed the inhabitants to go directly from the second floor chapel to the great hall, it appeared to be out of use because everyone, with the exception of the priest, headed to the lower floor to access the keep's main entrance. She spotted Lady Juliette, who gazed at her husband with such love and joy, Clara had not wanted to interrupt.

While sitting in the mass with a room full of people, Clara had almost felt like she was a part of something. Now, as everyone eased away and she made her own way to the great hall, she felt very alone again. Such was the life of a runaway and fugitive. It was at times like these, when she felt somewhat safe, that she missed Gilbert's companionship most.

Lost in thought, she followed the crowd past the well at the center of the courtyard and was preparing to enter the keep when she heard her other name posed to her.

"Alfred, can I speak to you?"

It was a voice that she'd quickly come to know. Heart beating, Clara turned to face her new master.

"In private." Alex Kerr motioned for her to step aside.

"My lord."

He looked at her with the most peculiar expression. Dressed for training, as always, he donned nothing more than trewes and a loose linen shirt rolled up to his elbows.

"It occurred to me, Alfred. You've not yet seen all of Brockburg. After the meal, I'll give you a tour of the castle."

Although it was not unusual that he should be smiling, something, perhaps his tone, made her leery. But of course she had no choice but to accept.

"I would be delighted, my lord."

She concentrated on his forearms, not daring to look up. But that plan did not work. He reached down to roll his shirtsleeves even higher.

Oh dear.

"Meet me here when you've finished. I've already broken my fast."

"Already, my lord?"

He lowered his voice to a whisper. "Shhh. Don't tell Father Simon. He'd be vexed I did so before mass. But I found myself unable to sleep this morn."

"Indeed?"

She peered up over her lashes.

"I'm an early riser, as you may have surmised. In fact, I've been known to train in the clearing well before the men at times."

The clearing! Surely he doesn't mean. . . She did look up then. His lips were turned up in a smile so big she could see faint lines appear around his eyes.

"You know, where we train each day?" he pressed.

He was mocking her. Not in a malicious way, but there was no doubt he knew something. Could he have seen her earlier?

Nay. It was not possible. She had been so careful to ensure no one was near. Otherwise, she would never have revealed herself.

"Go, you must be hungry. Meet me here later."

With that, he disappeared into the courtyard.

Clara stared at the woman pulling a bucket up from the well without really seeing her. What was that about? She had a tendency to worry even when it was unnecessary. But the brief conversation left her unsettled.

As quickly as she could manage it, Clara fled to the hall, ate a bowl of porridge sweetened with honey, and returned to the spot where she'd promised to meet Alex. She spotted him a moment later in deep conversation with his younger brother. Whatever he was saying to Alex, it was clear he wasn't happy about it. Finally, Reid shook his head and walked away, ignoring his brother's plea to return.

Alex looked at her and nodded his head in the direction of the gatehouse. She scrambled to follow, his strides longer than her own. Finally, when they reached the closed portcullis, he stopped.

"This gatehouse, the chapel, and the keep are the only three original structures. The others were all made of wood and have since been replaced by the stone you now see. This structure, however, was built with stone during its first construction."

He walked from building to building, giving her the history of each. She tried to concentrate, but found it quite difficult. She'd never become accustomed to his easy smile and effortless charm.

"Can you imagine where this leads?"

He opened one of the interior doors, though not the one leading to the guardsman's chambers. Stepping inside, Clara shivered. Alex grabbed a wall torch to light the way as the stairs ahead afforded no source of light.

Its location near the guardroom and unused smell offered a clue.

"'Tis the dungeon," she said, following him down the steps.

"Aye." At the bottom of the landing, he moved the light to

reveal a single empty cell. When he opened the gate, a creak reverberated against the stone wall. He moved toward the center and motioned for her to follow. She noticed the wooden door in the floor before he pointed to it.

"And this?" he asked.

There could be only one reason for a trapdoor within a dungeon. Barrington had one as well, though it had never been used.

"An oubliette."

He pulled the light up, toward her, and turned to leave.

"You've seen one before."

"Aye, in—" She stopped. It was rare for Clara to slip, although she'd only mentioned her home in conversation once before. Gilbert had quickly helped her to recover, and she'd not made the same mistake since. "In a castle once," she finished, hoping he would not inquire further.

They exited the dungeon none too soon. Clara hated such places. And even though Brockburg's dungeon appeared not to have been used in recent times, she nevertheless was anxious to leave.

Back outside, they toured each floor of the castle. She relaxed a bit as they walked down a narrow passageway adjacent to the great hall. The sound of hammering filled the air, becoming more pronounced as they got closer. She walked ahead, the familiar sound forcing out thoughts of the man who followed her.

The armory.

Typically positioned on a lower floor and rarely this close to the great hall, the armory was one of a castle's most important places. Its armorer, a man skilled enough to heat metal and cut sheets of it into armor *and* to train the apprentices under him for mundane tasks such as repairing horseshoes or dented armor, was a well-regarded and vital member of any keep.

As the armorer came into view, working over a hot sheet metal, Clara stopped, not wanting to disturb him. She watched the master craftsman, an older gentleman, until he finally stopped to look up.

"A coat of plates," she guessed, looking at the cut that had already been made.

The man looked from her to Alex, who stood behind her.

"My new squire," Alex said, introducing her. "Alfred, this is Brockburg's armorer. Allen has served three generations of Clan Kerr—"

"And will finally see a fourth now that your brother's brought home a wife."

"This," Alex said, "is clearly where we come for advice on love and marriage. Although he hasn't quite mastered the art himself, have you, Allen?"

The armorer ignored the barb and went back to work, though his smile told Clara much about his relationship with Alex.

"Come," he said, leaving the room and escorting her back to the courtyard. "Allen has been married four times," he added once they were out of hearing.

"Four?"

"Aye. Two made him a widow and the third. . . Och, that's a scandal best left for another time."

He leaned against the stone wall not far from where they'd begun the tour that morning.

"Tell me, Alfred. Have you ever been involved in a scandal?"

The truth, she heard Gilbert say. *As much truth as possible.*

"Once," she said, trying hard not to look up. "I fell in a lake and had to be rescued."

The lord's daughter had nearly drowned. It had been quite an affair from what she'd been told later. The handmaiden who'd allowed her to slip away and into the lake had never returned to the keep. Clara often wondered where the woman was now.

She was too young to remember the incident, but her father had insisted she learn to swim afterward, despite her lingering fear of the water. She had come to enjoy swimming, even though it was not something most did for pleasure.

"You don't fear the water, then?"

"Nay, I do not. My father made sure of it."

"You must have been quite young?"

"Aye, I was—"

"Since you were orphaned at a young age."

She smartly held her tongue.

"Raised by a vassal to your father, Sir Robert Kinney. I've not heard of the man."

He was suspicious, and rightly so. It was as she'd thought.

"Do you know many knights in England then?"

He shrugged. "Enough."

"Don't let him fool you, lad." Brockburg's priest approached, grinning at them. Thank the heavens. "Alex knows much less than he claims."

Alex smiled at the priest, who looked no more than a few years older than the eldest Kerr brother. Mayhap thirty and five? And yet, he exuded a sense of wisdom beyond his years.

Clara liked him immediately.

"I know you are wanting something, Father," Alex said. "You have that look about you."

"Ahh, do I now? Well, boy, you're right on that account."

Alex rolled his eyes. "I've not been a boy for many years."

"To me, you will be one always."

Clara looked back and forth between the men. She'd heard of Father Simon while at Bristol. Lady Catrina spoke highly of him.

"I've just heard the rumors."

Clara felt an immediate jolt of fear, but the priest wasn't looking at her. His eyes were fixed on Alex. These rumors weren't about her, then.

Alex shook his head. "Reid told me earlier. I care not if—"

"Tell yourself that if you'd like, but don't lie to a man of God."

The men stared at one another, and Clara began to back away.

It was a conversation she should not be a part of. That much was clear.

"Stay with me, Alfred," Alex insisted. He turned to Father Simon. "Father."

Obviously dismissed, the priest walked away with a nod to them both.

Alex tipped his head back and looked up to the sky. For divine intervention? These rumors, whatever they were about, clearly troubled him.

For a moment she thought he was going to tell her what Father Simon had meant, but instead he began walking through the courtyard toward the gatehouse. "Are you ready for today's training?" he asked over his shoulder.

He didn't give her time to answer, so Clara scrambled after him instead. Just as they were passing through the massive arched entranceway, Alex stopped. A merchant, the same one she'd seen approaching the gates earlier, walked alongside a cart filled with spices, judging from the smell that wafted back to them.

"You there," he called, jogging ahead to reach the man, who looked as if he'd been travelling for days. Mayhap more.

Clara couldn't hear when they were saying, and although she did not want to intrude, their raised voices carried back to her, rousing her curiosity. She moved just a bit closer until she could hear their conversation clearly.

"And you are quite sure?"

"Aye, my lord. She was most clear. There was no denying it."

Clara didn't know Alex Kerr well, but he always seemed to be in good humor, smiling or even laughing. But there was no joy in him now. He gripped the hilt of his sword so tightly she could see his knuckles whiten even at this distance. Did this have something to do with the rumors Father Simon had mentioned?

"She did not deny it?"

The ominous tone to his voice seemed to affect the merchant

as well, for the poor man began to have difficulty forming his words.

"No. . . she. . . uh, no. She bragged of it."

After staring at him a moment longer, Alex dismissed the man, who rushed ahead, likely glad to be leaving Brockburg Castle.

Returning to her, he spoke as if not realizing she was a virtual stranger.

"The merchant brings word of my long-lost English mother, who is still very much alive, it seems."

The sheer honesty and openness of the admission slayed her, and for a moment she could think of nothing else. Then the words themselves penetrated her mind. His mother? Clara had assumed both of his parents were dead. She'd never heard any mention, here or at Bristol, of either of them.

Nay, that was not true.

Clara did remember whispers of their father who was killed in battle. At Largs, perhaps? She could not remember.

"Never mind. Come."

As she followed him down the steep path, Clara could see the merchant below them. So he'd brought word of a woman claiming to be Alex's mother. An Englishwoman? Why was she not at Brockburg? Had she left of her own accord?

So many questions that would have to go unanswered. For the time being, Clara needed to concentrate on the training. If yesterday was any indication, it would be a long day indeed.

7

———————

Four days had passed since her tour of the castle. She'd seen little of Alex outside of the long, grueling training sessions. Clara had asked him more than once if he needed special assistance, but she was beginning to think Alex Kerr did not have a squire for a reason. Mayhap he did not want one.

Though he joked and laughed often enough and he was always surrounded by people—men during training, his family members at meals, and comely servants nearly every other time—there was one person he held back from speaking to.

Her.

She caught him looking at her more than once, so he was obviously aware of her presence. But each time she asked if he needed something, he declined her help. The day he'd shown her Brockburg, he'd partnered her with another squire in training, a young boy she'd not seen in the clearing previously, someone with whom she could actually train. And then he had promptly begun to ignore her.

If only she could do the same.

Clara's eyes were always drawn to him. During their training, she sometimes caught him looking at her with interest, but it could only be her imagination. In his eyes, she was Alfred, not Clara. She'd told Juliette as much the evening before. Like she'd done twice already, Juliette had come to visit her in the somewhat lonely tower where she and her charge stayed. Clara was grateful for those brief moments with Lady Juliette when she could actually be herself.

Today had begun like any other day, with Alex ignoring her, so it shocked her when he waved away her companion in the lists and took up his sword against her. Gilbert had made her a blunted sword for training nearly as fine as the one he'd crafted for her to use in truth.

"Let us see what that weapon can do," Alex said.

Though Clara was competent at the other exercises, and she could easily keep up with her new sparring partner, she knew she would need to dodge Alex in order to win. Clara could never overpower such a man. In fact, she'd not seen any present who had successfully done so with the exception of his brothers. Occasionally, the chief or Reid would succeed at besting Alex when they trained with him.

With the sun's bright rays shining behind him, Clara lifted her sword and deflected his blows the best she could.

"You must not always remain on the defensive," he shouted.

It was the only way she knew how to survive. But the maneuvers she'd learned were useless on him, and Clara began to despair until she finally found an opening. He was holding back, deflecting her gently, and in so doing, he was making himself vulnerable on the retreat.

She waited for the right moment, stepped back, and pivoted quickly, striking Alex with her blunted blade. He stared incredulously as her.

"How did you do that?"

She shrugged.

"Being small has its advantages."

"My lord." One of the men approached him, the red gash in his shirt growing.

"Go," Alex said simply, giving him leave to attend to his wound. Though they used blunted swords, accidents were common in training—something they shared with their southern neighbors. Indeed, with the exception of Alex's unusual training methods, many of the customs she'd encountered here were the same.

But that didn't mean she had met anyone quite like Alex before.

"You've been trained well," he said, sheathing his sword.

Clara did the same, smiling at the compliment.

"I've never met a woman who can wield a sword," he added in an undertone.

Her hand froze on the handle of her weapon. She stared at him in shock, wondering if she'd heard correctly.

The sound of clanging metal rang in Clara's ears as she considered how to react. Was he guessing? Had Toren or Juliette told him? Nay, neither of them would have willingly revealed her.

"Come with me," he said. And then to the men, "I leave your fate to Gregory here." He clapped a red-headed man on the back.

"Shall we dine among the trees or retire to the keep for the midday meal?" Gregory bellowed.

The men's smiles indicated it was a rare boon. Indeed, they took a light repast with them most days, so an extended break would likely be welcomed by most of them. But Clara couldn't think beyond what Alex had said.

A woman.

If he had guessed, would the others? She would be forced to leave, for as Gilbert had said often enough, her boys' clothes and new identity were all that shielded her from a prison cell. Or worse.

"Then I say we stay. The men may as well be English, they're so weak," one man called out. Clara winced at the insult. She'd heard it often enough, but it still rankled when everyone laughed in agreement.

To her surprise, Alex's smile faded.

"I've no love for our southern neighbor," he shouted for all to hear. "But the lad here cannot help that his parents were born on the wrong side of Hadrian's wall."

The man who had hurled the insult immediately apologized to her.

"I meant no offense, Alfred."

"'Tis as I would expect," she said, loud enough for only his and Alex's ears.

Alex's mood turned light once again as he said to the others, "I give you leave to dine and meet me afterward to finish training within the castle walls."

A cheer was raised, and before it had faded, Alex tugged on her arm. "Come," he said once again.

He led her toward the river, and suddenly she knew. This was the exact spot where she'd bathed.

"You were there," she choked out.

"Aye lass, I was there."

There was no mistaking his expression as he turned and once again made for the water's edge.

He had seen her. All of her. She should have been embarrassed or panicked. Instead, a rush of pleasure coursed through her as she thought of him watching her that day. As she realized that mayhap he *had* been watching her with interest these past days.

Alex walked toward the water and bent down to it. Turning, he gestured for her to do the same.

Did she have a choice?

He splashed water onto his face, drying it with the edge of his loosely hung tunic.

She swallowed, knowing what he wanted from her. She shook her head.

"You owe me this much," he said. "Deceived by you, my brother, and the new lady of Brockburg." His jaw clenched. "I wish to see your face in truth. And," he added, "you will remove the hat as well."

Clara's heart pounded. The last person to see her without her disguise had been Gilbert.

Even during her meetings with Lady Juliette, she'd remained in the guise of a boy.

But Alex would not be dissuaded. His expression told her as much, and although she was appalled at the thought, terrified of doing the one thing Gilbert had told her never to do, part of her wanted to do it. She wanted him to see her as she really was. She wanted him to know her.

Without another word, Clara bent down next to him and cupped the water as he'd done. It took a bit of scrubbing to remove the dried mud. Once she did, Clara mustered enough courage to look at him.

His expression had not changed.

His. . . maleness was so powerful, every part of his body exuding pure, unbridled strength. But Clara knew, despite the fact that she'd lied to him, Alex Kerr would not harm her.

She reached up and pulled out the slim ivory pins that Gilbert had purchased for her at great expense.

One by one, she took them out from beneath the fabric that had been made just for her. Finally, her fingers trembling, she pulled the hat from her head.

"All of them," he said.

She stood, her legs aching from bending, and Alex did the same.

With every pin she removed, Clara tried not to think of what this would mean. What he would do or say. Where they would go from here. Instead, she focused on the delicious feeling of her hair flowing loose around her shoulders.

She was, once again, a woman.

Shaking her head, Clara took a calming breath and waited for him to speak.

"Remarkable."

Clara shivered despite the warm August day.

"Why? How?" he asked.

She had no answers for those questions. Except for the truth, and that would not do. So she asked her own question instead.

"How did you chance upon me?"

Alex crossed his arms.

"I grew suspicious after the way my brother coddled you during training the other day. After that, I simply waited and watched. I didn't expect for you to reveal so much so soon."

"So Toren didn't tell you?"

"Nay, he did not."

"And you watched me here?" The question was a bold one, but she did not regret asking it.

"I did."

The look in his eyes. . . He looked as if he would devour her, and she would be lying to herself if she pretended not to enjoy it. The sensible thing to do would be to back down. To step away from him, but she found herself saying instead, "So you saw. . ."

"Everything."

This time, she held his gaze. Clara lifted her chin.

"You want to know if I liked what I saw?" he asked.

She gasped. "I said no such—"

"You didn't have to."

His insolence should not have surprised her. Alex Kerr was a man who took what he wanted. One who worked hard but enjoyed life. And right now, he wanted her.

Of that, she had no doubt.

Neither could she deny it was a feeling she shared. It was absurd, really. Her fascination with this Scots warrior was most unwelcome. But he was unlike any man she'd ever met.

He answered the question she'd not asked. "Once the shock wore off, I enjoyed it very much. You are a beautiful woman."

Words she'd never thought to hear. The rush of pleasure at his compliment was shameful.

Why was she not more scared? Gilbert would have told her to run away. Fast. And yet her feet stood rooted to the spot.

"And you are a beautiful man."

Oh dear. Had she really said that aloud?

Oh, that smile. . . Alex's smile was always appealing, but the smile he was giving her now was devastating. *Sensual.* Clara needed to get away.

Before the thought took root, Alex grabbed her hand, mayhap sensing she was prepared to run.

"Stay," he said.

He'd not yet let go. His hand, warm and strong, enveloped her like a protective shield. She would not be the one to pull away.

Neither of them moved.

"Tell me," he said.

Still holding his hand, Clara envisioned herself sharing everything with him. It would be so liberating to share her secret and her burden at last. To truly let someone know her. The temptation nearly compelled her to tell him all, but the memory of that day was so vivid—so utterly awful—it stayed her tongue.

"I cannot."

He did let go of her hand then, and Clara was sorry for it.

"You've told no one, not even my brother, of your reasons."

"Nay. And yet he offered to bring me here—"

"As my squire."

"He said you were always looking for men to train."

"Men, aye. Lasses, nay."

He did not sound angry any longer. But that certainly did not mean he'd keep her secret. Or that she could stay. But Clara was afraid of the answers to the questions she needed to ask, so she remained silent instead.

"It makes no sense."

She simply waited, letting him work the matter through his mind. Letting him speak.

"A woman, such as you, disguising herself as a lad. A squire." His eyes widened. "You assisted Toren in the tournament. He said as much. And you can wield a sword. How did you become strong enough to do such things?"

She shrugged, as if it were no great or uncommon feat.

"God's teeth, woman, give me *something*."

"My name is Clara."

"Clara."

It had felt liberating to share her name with Juliette, but it was different to hear it on Alex's lips. It made her feel like a woman again.

He inclined his head. "Alex, if it pleases you."

It pleased her well enough. That he was giving her leave to call him by his given name meant something, though she wasn't sure what exactly.

"So what am I to do with an Englishwoman who gives me nothing more than her name? Who pretends to be a boy, will not trust me with the truth, and has learned to hide herself so well that none can see the treasure beneath?"

Treasure? Clara lowered her head, as she had become accustomed to doing.

"If you would allow me to remain as Alfred—"

"Tell me why this is so important to you."

If her choice was revealing the truth to him or leaving, she'd be forced to leave. But it had been so wonderful not to run. To sleep in a bed. . . to see the same people each day.

"Look at me, Clara."

She did, and what she saw pained her. Alex Kerr was stood before her, tall and proud. But his expression. . . it was that of a man resolved to stand his ground.

She would have to leave.

Before he could stop her, Clara grabbed the hat and pins at her side, turned around, and ran. She knew he could catch her if he tried, but with any luck, he would not try.

Should she stop to gather her belongings? Nay, she could not risk it. At least she had her sword.

She'd made a mistake coming here. She'd broken Gilbert's rule not to trust anyone. She'd broken it with Toren. And Juliette. And though she hardly knew him, she'd begun to trust Alex as well. Because of it, she now had no supplies. No clothing other than what she wore on her back.

Nothing save her life, which, for now, would have to be enough.

8

———————

The Englishwoman was afraid for her life.

The look on her face directly before she fled told him as much. He cursed himself as a fool for pushing her away. Not that he desired a squire who lied to him. Deceived him. A squire who was, in truth, an Englishwoman.

But the alternative was unacceptable. He knew why Toren had brought her here, and despite his dislike for the English, his need to protect this woman was stronger.

He could have stopped Clara from running, but he'd assumed she would head up the hill to the castle. The truth—that she'd actually run away—only dawned on him when he'd emerged from the trees to find the uphill path quite empty. The guards confirmed his suspicion—she hadn't returned and they'd not seen her—and he immediately headed to the stables.

Bad luck for him, his brother found him there before he could ride off to find her.

"What do you mean, she's gone?" Toren blustered after he explained the situation.

Alex, who'd just mounted his horse, took the reins from the groom and dismissed him.

"Juliette will—"

"Have my head. You've said as much. Now, would you prefer we stand here and argue, or shall I go after her?"

It was bad luck he'd come across his brother on the way to the stables. On foot, she would not be able to go far, so if he took his horse, he'd have a much greater chance of finding her. But he needed to leave *now*.

"By all that's holy, if she's harmed. . ."

Alex loved his brother, but at times like these, he'd prefer a sibling to a father.

"Not now, brother."

He spun his mount away from the stable and toward the gate-house, but Toren stopped him again.

"Alex?"

He quieted his mount with his hand, the horse responding to his soft touch as he'd done for years. "Aye?"

When he looked at Toren, Alex knew immediately what his brother was asking. He'd talked to both of his brothers about the reports regarding their mother. Toren and Reid claimed not to care about what had become of her. Both said they had no mother. That the woman who'd abandoned them the day after their father was buried meant nothing to them.

But Alex wanted to know why she had left. Where she'd been these past years. He wanted to confront her with what she'd done. He'd searched for her for over a year, stopping only when Toren convinced him to leave it alone. And he was tempted to go after her now. . .

"I don't know," he said flatly. He could not deal with the revelations about their mother just yet. One problem at a time.

With that, he took off. Racing through the cobblestone court-yard, his horse's hooves clanking with every step, Alex made his way through both gates and out onto the path that led to the small village below.

Something niggled at his thoughts as he rode toward the

village, and he stopped his mount when the worry finally clicked into place. Clara was intelligent enough to fool all those around her about her identity. She'd obviously fended for herself for some time, which meant she was much too smart to have run on foot. She would have looked for transport.

The merchant.

When Alex found him, he'd likely also find the English lass who posed as a squire.

Using the old Roman road, he followed the wagon's tracks south. It was a rare merchant who moved back and forth along the border. Most stayed in their country of origin. But this particular one chose to make his living in a region many others avoided. Not the kind of person he'd want Clara, or any female, to call a travel companion.

There!

The very wagon he sought had come into view along the next ridge. Alex sped up, kicking dirt and rock behind him as he dipped into the valley and climbed once again. The wagon slowed, and Alex knew he'd been spotted.

He pulled up alongside the merchant and wasted no time.

"Where is he?"

The "he" in question promptly poked his head out of the wagon as the merchant peered around the side.

He could try to convince Clara to come back, but she might not be amicable to the idea. He'd end her escape immediately.

"The boy you harbor is my squire, sworn to the service of Clan Kerr and—"

"He's yours, my lord," the merchant rushed to say. "Take him."

Alex nearly laughed at the expression on Clara's face. She rolled her eyes, clearly exasperated at the man's quick surrender of his new travel companion.

She must have known the futility of attempting to dissuade either man that she should stay. By claiming her as his own, Alex had ensured the merchant would not intervene. Clara jumped from the wagon, offered the merchant her thanks, which sounded more like a curse than anything, and the wagon pulled away.

"Get up," he demanded.

She didn't move.

"Clara, you've nowhere to go. Toren and Juliette would have flayed me alive if I'd allowed you to escape. Do you really think little enough of them to believe otherwise?"

He assumed she felt indebted to his brother and sister-in-law—correctly, it would seem, for she moved toward him without further argument. Reaching down, he lifted her onto the mount behind him.

And immediately regretted it.

Although they were bound, he could still feel her breasts pressed against his back. And it would only get worse.

"Wrap your hands around me."

She did, and Alex nearly groaned. The wee lass felt as if she belonged there.

As they made their back to the keep, Alex waited for her to speak. He was torn between wanting to demand answers and ensuring she felt safe enough not to run again.

"I cannot tell you," she finally whispered.

The panic in her voice prompted him to break his silence.

"I will not demand it."

She said nothing.

They rode in silence, a comfortable, easy silence. He forced his thoughts away from the woman pressed against his back, and they quickly landed on the question of whether his mother had been found at last.

He should not go looking for the woman who'd abandoned them. Neither of his brothers were tempted, and he was the worst kind of fool to even consider it.

But he was considering it nonetheless.

There was also the matter of the Day of Truce. It was fast approaching, and he should attend it. Both his brothers had said there was no need, that they would both be there, but Toren was newly married and Reid was, well, Reid. Strong and capable, he was nevertheless the youngest Kerr brother. And neither Alex nor Toren were willing to see him hurt.

But he had to know. If there was even the slightest chance he could find her, Alex had to look.

"I'm travelling to England."

The decision was made.

"You can continue to train with the men if you'd like," he continued. He'd give her no further reason to flee.

"Where in England?" she asked.

"Northumbria. Northeast, along the coast."

"Why?"

"'Tis the same simple question that caused you to flee, alone, rather than remain at Brockburg."

As he expected, she said nothing about herself or her decision to run. What she did say shocked him.

"I'm coming with you."

It struck him that her tone was that of a highborn lady. His English lass was gently bred. How could he have missed the fact before? The hat was back in place, and she'd restored the artfully placed smudges on her face. But he easily saw past the disguise now that he knew it was one. The high cheekbones and dark, delicate lashes. Her smooth, pink lips that he ached to feel beneath his own.

Aye, she was a woman in every way but her dress.

"Nay, you are not."

"I am much more comfortable on the move. I—"

"Nay," he said firmly. "I travel alone."

His brothers would not like it, but Alex wanted no witnesses to his folly. "It's much too dangerous for you to—"

"I've been travelling without an escort for some time now. At least you will be there. Please let me come."

It was a terrible idea.

Not only was it dangerous, but he *desired* her. Others may think her a lad, a squire, but he knew otherwise. He could not find himself alone with her—

"I watched my father be murdered."

She'd said it so quietly, Alex had to ask her to repeat herself. When she did, he was only left with more questions. But to voice them would silence her, and so he simply nodded for her to go on.

"I cannot close my eyes even now, years later, without seeing the dagger slice through his neck. Since then, I've moved from place to place. Usually following the tourney. Even still, movement makes me feel safe. As grateful as I am for your brother's offer to stay here, I feel. . ."

He waited, but she said no more. No mention of why her father had been murdered or who he had been in life. Alex could guess at some of it. A lord, no doubt. Judging from her accent, though, not a border lord, and she was clearly not from the south.

She'd made no mention of her mother. Or siblings. Alex tried to imagine living through his father's death and mother's abandonment without the support of Toren and Reid and Catrina.

He'd not have managed well.

"Please," she added, her voice soft but urgent.

Why she wanted to come so badly, he could not understand. But neither could he deny her, especially not out of an inability to control his own desire.

He was stronger than that.

They halted just as Brockburg came into view. Alex turned, her grip on his waist loosening.

"You may come," he said, knowing it was a bad idea.

For his efforts, he was granted a brilliant smile. It was the first one she'd given him since he had discovered her secret. Her straight white teeth peeked out from her parted lips. . .

He had made a dangerous mistake.

—

When they began the incline to the castle, Clara tightened her arms around Alex. She felt as if they would topple backward. It reminded her of when she'd once ridden what she had thought to be the highest mountain in all of England. Gilbert had laughed, telling her it was nothing more than a small hill, but she'd been afraid enough to get off her horse and refuse to ride, preferring to walk alongside the beast instead.

"If you keep that up, it will be a long journey indeed."

"Oh! Did I hurt you?" She hadn't realized how hard she was squeezing him.

"That depends, lass, on the kind of hurt you refer to."

Now what in the devil was that supposed to mean?

She loosened her grip slightly as his meaning finally registered. Clara smiled against his back. At least she was not the only one affected. When he had turned to look at her earlier, she'd thought for a moment he was going to kiss her.

"You're a churl to say such things to a lady," she teased.

"A woman or a lady?" They were admitted entry through the gatehouse.

"Does it matter, sir?" He already knew too much. She didn't want to give anything else away.

"While it should not, I confess it does. But as you say, such topics are much too delicate for your innocent *English* ears." He wasn't able to hide the laughter in his voice.

"I doubt that very much. You forget, I've lived as a boy."

Posing as a boy had indeed given her a unique perspective. Men spoke more openly around small, insignificant Alfred than they would around Lady Clara. As such, she'd learned one thing about men over the past few years. Their desire for the fairer sex was insatiable. Married men and the newly betrothed often spoke of liaisons that, by rights, should not have been possible. Their crude talk had given Clara an education Gilbert had never intended her to have. In turn, she'd also learned to speak more openly than she ever would have as a noblewoman.

"Neither does the fact that I am English seem of consequence," she added as an afterthought.

When they stopped, Alex held out his hand to help her dismount. Quickly realizing his mistake—he never would have made such an offer to Alfred, and someone could be watching—he pulled it away. They each dismounted on their own.

"The English ears are more delicate."

"More delicate than. . . ?"

"Their less refined and savage northern neighbors." He made a face so ridiculous that Clara couldn't help but grin.

"You look more like a wild boar than you do a savage Scot."

"And when have you seen a wild boar?"

Alex handed his reins to the groom, and Clara followed him to the main keep. They would likely be visiting with the lord and lady of Brockburg, if she guessed correctly.

"At the Tournament of the King one year, I was hired by an English knight who took part in the earl's hunt. They were seeking deer, but they found and killed a boar instead. It was quite terrifying."

"I'd imagine no more terrifying than making your way through the borderlands without an escort."

He said it so casually, Clara nearly forgot herself and answered truthfully. That she'd lived in terror every day since she'd lost Gilbert. That she'd only felt safe—or somewhat safe—after meeting Toren.

"Just slightly so."

"I can't look at you."

The change in topic took her aback. Entering the large wooden door, Clara hurried to follow Alex up the single flight of stairs leading to the great hall.

"Pardon?"

He stopped and turned. "I can only see the woman now, not the lad. 'Tis not natural to treat you like a squire."

She shrugged. "But 'tis necessary," she insisted.

He turned away, and she followed. Would he continue to ask questions? Could she continue to deny him answers? Likely he would press her. As would Toren and Juliette. This was the reason she had never stayed in one place for this long. The reason she would likely be forced to move on once they were back in England.

"If you say so."

"Oh, thank the heavens!"

The moment they crested the top of the stairs, Juliette rushed toward her, and for a moment Clara thought she would hug her in full view of everyone in the hall. Her friend held back, however, and soon they were surrounded by Toren, Juliette, Reid, and Father Simon. They all spoke so quickly, asking questions one on top of the other. She didn't know where to turn first.

Clara caught Juliette's eye, and the two women headed toward the back of the hall.

"Where did you go?" Juliette whispered.

Clara glanced back at the cluster of men near the stairs. She could hear Alex's voice, likely explaining what had happened. Or some of what had happened.

"He knows," Clara said simply.

Juliette frowned. "Toren told me. But how did he—"

"He followed me out to the river." Clara felt her cheeks grow warm. "I needed to bathe."

"Oh."

She couldn't look into the other woman's eyes. Clara was afraid Juliette would somehow detect her newest secret. Though she should be mortified, Clara was not sorry Alex had discovered the truth. . . nor was she disturbed by *how* he'd discovered it.

"But why did you leave?"

"I was afraid he would continue to ask questions."

She looked back at the others again. Toren shook his head, and when they all turned her way, Clara guessed Alex had told them about their upcoming trip.

"And I'm leaving again," Clara said softly. She rushed to explain when she saw Lady Juliette's stricken expression. "Alex is going to find his mother. He did not wish to take me with him, but he relented."

"But—"

"I feel more comfortable moving around. Please understand, you've been nothing but kind to me here. And I do hope to come back, but. . ."

"But?"

Clara really did want to be as honest as possible.

"I'm just not sure that I can."

She glanced back at Alex again, curious to see how his news had been received.

"Oh my," Juliette exclaimed.

"What is it?"

Juliette raised her brows. "'Tis nothing really. Just. . ." She lowered her voice. "If you ever tire of the ruse and decide to settle down, I would be extremely happy to count you as a member of the family."

Clara's head whipped back to Juliette's face. "A member of. . ." Did she mean? Oh dear, she did. And what made it even worse, the impossible thought had flitted through her mind as well. . . and she *liked* it.

But Juliette did not know what Clara did.

She could never marry, as that would mean revealing herself. Unless she wanted to meet the same fate as her father, that could never, ever happen.

9

Two days after she had left with the merchant, Clara rode out once again, this time with Alex. She knew from Juliette that Toren was worried about Alex, who was missing the Day of Truce, something he never did, to search for his mother. She had bid goodbye to her friend, knowing it was entirely possible she'd not return. Juliette must have sensed as much—she'd implored her to be safe, never once asking about her identity.

Alex, on the other hand, clearly did not intend to keep silent. They'd travelled only a short distance before he began to question her.

"You ride well, yet have no mount of your own?"

Clara adjusted her headpiece and tried to think of an answer that would suit.

"The truth or no answer at all, please."

Confound it, the man was too clever by half.

"I had to sell her," she said. Which was the truth.

Once he realized she'd say no more, Alex fell silent. Clara watched him ride just ahead of her, admiring his form against the lush landscape around them.

They rode at a hard pace, but not so hard she couldn't handle it. Clara had long since learned how to stay in a saddle all day. Long gone were the days when she had ridden for pure pleasure. When they finally did stop to water the horses, they dismounted and settled onto a hard patch of earth just off the path and next to a small stream.

"Between here and Kenshire, there's just one inn. Most nights we'll sleep here." He patted the ground beside him.

"Kenshire?"

She knew they headed south to search for his mother, but he had not told her their destination.

"Aye. We've recently forged an alliance with the Countess of Kenshire, and my mother was spotted near Elkview."

"And you've no word from her before now?"

The easy smile fled from his face. "She's not given any indication she wants to be found. The merchant only said a woman matching her description was overheard speaking of her 'three sons and a daughter in the Scottish borderlands.' Whether or not 'tis she. . . " He shrugged.

"Will you tell me about her?"

Though Clara was curious, she immediately regretted the question, knowing what he'd ask in return.

"Will you tell me who you are?"

They looked at one another, Clara knowing he wished to speak of his mother as much as she wished to reveal her identity. Neither would do so.

Perhaps a less threatening question would break the uneasy tension between them.

"While we were at the Tournament of the North, Toren mentioned to me that you were once a skilled tourney player?"

He hesitated, then said, "Did he mention the injury?"

"Aye." Mayhap 'twas not such a good subject to raise after all. . .

"Then you know I was nearly killed. That wound festered for days."

"There was a man by the name of Lord Blackburn at the tournament who tried his best to defeat your brother by any means necessary. Toren said 'twas much the same with your last match."

She looked away, realized she was staring. It was difficult not to do so. Alex was the kind of man who simply commanded one's attention.

"When you force enemies into combat, some will do whatever is necessary to win."

"But not you."

"Nay." He did not brag but merely spoke the truth. She knew his brother enough to surmise the character of the man who sat across from her. He would not cheat.

"In truth, I'd like to blame your countrymen, but I've seen men from both sides of the border commit the same selfish, dishonorable acts."

"As have I. English. . . Scottish. . . it matters not."

Alex cocked his head to the side. "You've seen much as a squire."

For once, he was not questioning her for information about her past. He seemed curious—no more, no less. "Aye, more than I'd have liked. Some good and some not. But I do believe everyone has the capacity for both inside them."

She'd never voiced that thought aloud, but it had stuck with her throughout the years, and her experiences on and off the field had convinced her it was true.

To her surprise, Alex nodded. "My father once said much the same. He warned against alliances for that reason."

"Which is why Clan Kerr had so few until recently." She knew as much from Toren.

"Aye, and even now we've only joined forces with others by necessity. First to help Catrina marry the man she loved, and then to help Toren settle things with Juliette. Soon, thanks to 'love,' we'll be allied with half of Scotland and England."

She winced inwardly at the way he'd said the word 'love.'

"You say the word as if it were a curse."

"Is it not? The future of our clan is now intertwined with the decisions of others. If they go to battle, we go with them."

"But you serve the king the same way, do you not?"

"By necessity, not choice."

Clara smiled. "Love. Allies. Is there anything you do not despise?"

Alex returned her smile. "Battle. Training. Ale. Women."

She laughed. "'Tis not necessary to continue."

But he did anyway. "And the company of a good man. Or woman."

Somehow she knew he no longer spoke of intimacy with a woman, but the type of companionship they now shared. Indeed, he was an easy man to speak to.

They sat in silence a moment longer, and then Alex abruptly stood and turned toward their mounts. She followed.

It would be a long journey indeed.

***

Alex erected the tent, already regretting his decision to allow Clara along. He'd avoided 'the pass,' a well-worn old Roman road that was fairly flat and well-marked in most places, because border reivers used it regularly to wreak havoc on both sides of the border. The one they took now was slower, the terrain less friendly, and it afforded them less opportunities for proper shelters. It wove through the thick forest, however, which would give them much needed protection. Clara hadn't complained once, not even when he'd told her they would be making camp on the road. She was just as competent as Toren had assured him she'd be.

He didn't regret taking her because she slowed them down. . . he regretted it because she'd just washed her face and discarded her cap, and the woman, not the boy, walked toward him now.

"Would you like me to start the fire or hunt for food?" Clara asked.

It was the least likely question he'd ever been asked by a woman.

"I've enough provisions for two more days. Tomorrow will make for better hunting, and I'd prefer that we stay together."

He'd already gathered materials for a fire while she was washing herself. And though the sun had not yet set, the warm summer day would give way to a cool night, as it did most evenings in this part of the world.

"How long until we reach Kenshire?" she asked.

"It should not take more than a week."

"Here, let me help you."

He had begun to arrange the sticks he'd gathered. Without waiting for an answer, she knelt beside him to help him stack them the right way.

"You've done this before."

She nodded, the waves created by pinning her hair barely touching her shoulders as she moved. Alex could not stop staring at this warrior-woman. He could not imagine a more erotic sight than Clara leaning over the budding fire, her shirt and hose hugging every curve, save the ones that were bound. And her face. . . she had the most perfect, beautiful face of any woman on either side of the border.

"Aye, many times," she said, snapping him to attention. "My master ensured I was well-trained."

He was intensely curious about her past, but experience had taught him that the more questions he asked, the less inclined she was to answer them.

So he waited, and was rewarded.

"He was an armorer."

When the sparks turned to flames, they worked together to ensure those flames became the fire that would warm them this night. Once that task was complete, Alex pulled the dried meat, bread, and cheese from his pouch and handed a portion to Clara.

"Not a knight?"

She tore a piece of bread from the thick loaf. "Nay, not a knight. And I lost him very recently. He died just a fortnight before I met Toren."

"How does an armorer come to be master of a lady?"

He'd pushed too far. She was sitting just a few feet away from him, and she'd looked so relaxed with her legs crossed, one hand in her lap and the other holding the bread. But she'd tensed immediately upon being reminded of her noble birth.

She surprised him by actually answering his question. "More of a companion than a master. Gilbert. His name was Gilbert, and he was one of the finest men I've ever known."

Though she put her head down quickly, it was not quickly enough. He saw her eyes fill with tears. She'd likely never talked about his death to anyone.

"Tell me."

Alex understood the pain of losing a loved one.

She wiped her eyes with the sleeve of her tunic and took a deep breath.

"Gilbert was quite skilled, and because of it, he was able to buy everything we needed. Food. Shelter. Even training for me. At nearly every tournament we attended, a queue would form outside of his makeshift forge. You've seen the sword he crafted for me."

"Indeed, a fine weapon."

He almost asked about the origin of its inscription, but thought better of it.

"It was the second day of the tournament at Dunstable. An English knight whom neither of us recognized sought Gilbert out."

She lowered the chunk of bread into her lap.

"He asked for Gilbert to reforge his sword and poison the tip."

Alex clenched his fists. He knew of the practice and had even seen men killed because of it. Poison was a coward's weapon, but some men would win at any costs. Especially when the stakes were so high. The tournament at Dunstable was infamous for the ruby awarded to its champion.

"Gilbert refused."

"You don't have to—"

"The man returned later that night while Gilbert was still working. He slept little at tournaments. The coin it brought would feed us for months."

Clara closed her eyes and bowed her head. Alex wanted more than anything to go to her. To comfort her. Instead, he sat still and waited.

"He brought companions with him. Gilbert had refused my help that night, insisting that I get some sleep. So I was inside the tent when I heard them."

She looked at him then, her eyes still glistening.

"I could hear only muffled voices, and one man said something about putting the body in the river. By the time I realized what was happening, they were gone."

Alex clenched his fists. It physically pained him to imagine Clara at that moment, alone and terrified, her only companion and friend murdered.

"Gilbert was very smart."

The pride in her voice was evident.

"He'd prepared me well. I carried what I could and left immediately."

"In the night?"

"Aye."

"Where did you go?"

She wiped her eyes once again.

"I didn't travel far that night. At least one of the men who'd killed Gilbert, the knight whom he'd refused, had seen me. I made my way slowly north, closer to. . ."

She stopped talking.

"Places that I knew. Gilbert told me if anything ever happened to him, I should go to. . . " She looked at him and he held her gaze. He was sure she would not reveal the specific location, but she finally said, "Keston House."

Alex looked at her quizzically. "The border tavern whose owners are known to harbor smugglers? You stayed there after Gilbert died?"

Clara nodded. "He said I could tell the innkeepers the truth. And though I remained a lad there, they knew my identity. They insisted I stay with them, in fact, but I couldn't do that."

"Do what?" Now he was confused.

"Place them in danger."

"How would your presence put them in danger?"

Clara pursed her lips so tight, he laughed. Her eyes widened.

"You look as if your meal was soured. You needn't tell me. You should know by now I'll not demand anything of you."

He spoke the truth. She'd been through enough. How she had survived for this long, alone, Alex wasn't sure. But he knew one thing. She would never do so again. Whether she returned to Brockburg as his squire or, if she chose to trust them with her true identity, a permanent guest, Clara was alone no longer.

Englishwoman or nay.

1 0

———————

S he'd said too much.

Something about her companion made her feel safe, and she'd been frighteningly close to telling him everything.

"Alex," she said, purposefully changing the subject. "Where is my tent?"

"Our tent," he answered, "is over there." He nodded toward the single tent he'd pitched.

Our tent.

Nay, it was not possible. She could not, would not, sleep so close to him.

"'Tis not proper—"

He laughed so loudly Clara was sure they'd be discovered because of it.

"We're an unmarried man and a woman travelling alone. Clara, nothing about this journey is proper. Surely you know that."

But she'd never sleep! She'd spend the whole night awake, tormented by the knowledge that he was right next to her. . . and she could not touch him.

"But to sleep together. . ."

"Gilbert taught you well. And I continue to be impressed by your abilities. But. . ."

"But?"

Alex opened his mouth, frowned, and then closed it again. That frown soon turned into a scowl. How strange. He always seemed prepared with an easy retort.

"Alex?"

"Damn it, woman. You'll make me say it. You are. . . a woman."

"And?" She still didn't understand.

"St. Ann, give me guidance." He looked up to the heavens. To pray to St. Ann or to avoid eye contact with *her*?

Finally, his gaze returned to her. "You may be skilled with that weapon." He pointed at her sword. "But you are still a woman. I could not sleep at night knowing you were unprotected."

"Unprotected? Who do you think has been offering me protection since Gilbert was killed? I do not need—-"

"There is only one tent. A fact I cannot change. Besides, it will be warmer that way." He stood. "I'll check on the horses before we retire."

The cloak of night began to fall, and the brilliant orange-streaked sky was slowly being replaced by grey. She added a log to the fire, entered the tent they were to share, and quickly pulled a soft tunic and another pair of boy's leggings out of her bag. She changed quickly into her night clothes and stuffed her other things into the satchel. Clara peered down at the two makeshift beds. Two linen coverings lay atop leaves that Alex had apparently gathered earlier in the evening. He must have stuffed additional material with extra clothing, as there were even two pillows awaiting them.

Though the fire was nearby, a chill quickly began to seep into the tent. Clara crept inside one of the blankets and turned toward the light of the fire, attempting to get comfortable.

"Try to sleep," Alex said, entering the tent from behind her. "We leave at sunrise."

She didn't answer; she simply lay there, imagining how Gilbert would react if he could see her now. Would he be pleased she'd secured protection or troubled by how much she'd revealed?

Clara tried to ignore the movements behind her. Was Alex undressing? She'd already spied him without a shirt, and the mere thought made her eager to turn and look upon him. If she was to sleep at all tonight, Clara needed to stop thinking about Alex's muscular chest.

"Tell me something of you," she said quietly, without turning.

She could feel him lying down behind her. The heat was most welcome, though she'd not admit as much to him.

"Such as?"

"You would not reveal yourself to me before because I wouldn't do the same, but you now know of Gilbert."

He made a sound that could either be frustration or dismissal.

"There's naught to tell."

Clara was sure that was not true. "You are very close to your siblings. You're lucky to have a sister and brothers." If only she'd had someone else to share the burden of her father's loss, someone to comfort her and grieve with her. He was, indeed, quite lucky.

"When our father died. . . at Largs. . . Toren became chief. Our father trained him well, and he does a fine job."

"And Catrina?"

"My sister," he said, a sweet fondness in his voice. "My mother left when she was still young, and I used to fear what the loss of her mother's influence would do, but she's become quite a remarkable woman."

"It must have been awful when she was captured by the Waryns." When the Waryn brothers had retaken Bristol Manor, Bryce Waryn had taken Catrina prisoner. Of course, the tale had ended quite differently from how it had begun, and the two were now happily married.

When Alex didn't answer, Clara turned to face him. "I'm sorry. . . ."

"It was a. . . difficult time," he finally said.

Clara wished she had not turned. Although darkness had fallen in truth, just enough moonlight made its way into the tent for her to see his face clearly. Though she tried to keep her tone even, she was afraid her voice would betray her.

"But she's quite safe now, is she not?"

When he looked at her like that, Clara felt anything but safe. Safe meant distant. Not getting too close. And the heat and hunger in his eyes promised to blast away all of the walls that had kept her safe these last years.

She looked away.

"Why do you turn from me?" he said, his voice husky and so intimately close.

"Because of the way you are looking at me."

"And how am I looking at you?"

She gave her attention fully to the peak of the tent, not daring to turn her head back.

"As if you want to kiss me."

She'd become much too blunt since her time with Gilbert.

So be it.

"I look at you that way because I do wish to kiss you," Alex said.

She forced herself not to move.

"'Twould not be a good idea."

"Aye lass, I agree."

She did look at him then.

He was smiling.

"I am a virgin," she blurted out.

"I know."

"How could you possibly know such a thing? It's not—"

"Because of the way you move away from me, as if you're afraid I will devour you at any moment."

"And will you?"

Her heart thudded as she waited for his answer. And which answer, precisely, did she want him to give?

"Likely, aye. Which is why you should go to sleep."

He closed his eyes, his face so much softer when he did so. In repose, the warrior almost looked like a regular man.

He was anything but.

Clara turned away again, attempting to breathe normally. It was simply impossible. She would never be able to sleep like this.

She was sleeping.

Alex could hear the change in her breathing, and he was glad for it. At least one of them would be well-rested. This trip had surely been a folly. . . it was hard enough to ignore her draw during the day, and now he was just inches away from her. Surely he was strong enough to keep from touching her, but he likely wouldn't get a moment of sleep.

He'd simply been too long without a woman. When they arrived at Kenshire, he'd find a willing maid and sate the lust that had overtaken his good sense.

They just had to make it there. And back.

That is, if she would agree to return with him. The woman was as skittish as a stag who sensed the bow and arrow aimed at his heart. Even so, he was determined to protect her—now and in the future—even more so after hearing part of her story.

She shifted and Alex turned away. Better not to tempt himself unnecessarily. He forced his eyes closed, listening for the unlikely intruder. He knew this area well and had never seen travellers this far off the path. But he lay with one hand on his sword nonetheless.

Alex had just begun to drift off when a sound forced him to sit up, sword in hand. He listened carefully, chastising himself for thinking they were safe here. Nowhere was truly safe along the border. Only when he was fully awake did he realize the sound came from Clara.

She turned her head and moaned. Not the type of low, lustful moan he would have loved to hear from her, but a pained one. He listened, trying to make sense of her words, but when her cries became louder, he shook her shoulder gently.

"Clara," he whispered.

She continued to mumble.

"Clara, wake up."

He spun her toward him, shaking her a bit more forcefully.

Her eyes flew open, and he thought for a moment that she might strike him. But when she realized who he was, where she was, her features softened.

"Alex."

"Aye."

He lay back down and pulled her toward him. Placing her head in the crook of his arm,

he reached down and covered her with the blanket she'd lost in her dream. She wiggled at his side, and Alex tried, unsuccessfully, to ignore the breasts that pressed, unwrapped, against him.

She sighed, murmured something, and promptly fell back to sleep.

The terror on her face in the moments before she'd fully awakened had been very real. A nightmare from the night Gilbert had been taken? From watching her father's murder? Alex closed his eyes and listened to Clara's even breathing.

Surprised he was able to sleep so well on the hard ground with an Englishwoman sleeping in his arms, Alex woke with the bright light of the early morn. He listened for noise outside the tent but heard nothing save the regular breathing of Clara, who was still tucked inside the crook of his arm. He tried to lift her gently, not wanting to wake her just yet, but as soon as he moved, she stirred.

"What... why am I..."

She clearly had no memory of the night before.

"You dreamed. . . called out," he said simply.

She sat, her hair tousled about her shoulders. Unbound and uncovered, she looked nothing like the squire who'd trained with his men at Brockburg.

"Did I say. . . anything?"

Alex crossed his arms behind his head as Clara moved away from him. She tugged on the covering Lady Juliette had begged him to take, one much thicker and warmer than he was accustomed to travelling with, and pulled it around her shoulders. His own tunic was heavy and warm, but Clara's was better suited to a bed than a tent in the middle of the Scottish marches.

"Nothing that could be understood."

She reached behind her head and smoothed out her hair. Alex reached up and pulled aside an errant strand.

"Do you remember the dream?"

He knew by her expression that she did. But she was not going to tell him.

"You said we needed to leave at daybreak."

She scrambled out of the covering and grabbed her satchel. Alex did the same. They walked in silence toward the small stream. Clara moved behind a thicket of bushes, and when she emerged, she was fully dressed as a squire once more. But when she moved to the riverbed to begin her ministrations—the careful masking of her face—Alex held out a hand to stop her.

"Don't."

She looked at him, eyebrows drawn together.

"There's no need to disguise yourself, Clara."

"No need? There is every need. I've been doing so every day for—"

"You do not wish to remain yourself instead?"

She stood, clearly agitated.

"I wish for nothing more, every single day. But 'tis not possible. Gilbert—"

"Is not here," he said gently. "But I am. And I will protect you, Clara. There's no need to disguise yourself for our journey. The path we take is not a common one, and I don't expect to meet anyone along the way, with the exception of at the inn."

"And if we do? And I'm recognized?"

"Recognized by whom? Is your face so well-known?"

"Nay, but—"

"The reivers who roam this land are more interested in looting than—"

"Raping women? Would I not be safer as a boy?"

Had she been raped? "Has someone—"

"Nay, but Gilbert said—"

"Clara, by all that is holy, I won't let anyone close enough to touch you or even dream of touching you."

"And if something happens to you?"

"I would not be so careless with my life. I know this area well and can assure you that nothing will happen to me. I won't allow it."

She began to soften.

"You won't allow it?"

Even though her lips were turned up in the slightest grin, Alex remained serious. "I will not."

Clara looked down at her satchel and then back up at him.

"You are not marring Gilbert's memory by disobeying his orders. He was your protector, but you have a new one now. Nothing will happen to you."

Whether it was the conviction in his voice or her desire to let Alfred rest for the moment, Alex wasn't sure, but he was grateful when she slung the satchel over her shoulder without opening it.

"Alfred can make an appearance at The Anvil Inn," he said.

"Aye, he must. But in the meantime, I will very much enjoy being Clara."

"You are free to unwrap yourself as well."

She glanced down at her flattened chest and looked back at him with a smile.

"Perhaps I shall."

He nearly said, 'Please do,' but somehow restrained himself.

She turned, presumably toward the bushes, when he reached out and grabbed her hand. Mayhap he was not so adept at restraining himself after all. He needed to touch her, if only for a moment.

"You have that look again."

He was sure he did.

"Which one precisely?" he managed to ask. He tugged her closer, imagining her lips on his own.

"The one that makes me think you're going to kiss me."

She was standing so close he could smell the mint she must have chewed moments before.

"I could have kissed you last eve but did not. What makes you think I'll do so now?"

His warrior-woman swallowed. She was nervous.

"You're holding my hand. And are standing too close to be proper." Her voice wavered.

"Nothing about our arrangement out here is proper. I thought we'd established that already."

He let go of her hand and used it to cover her cheek. "'Tis much too smooth and pretty to cover with mud."

His thumb ran a trail from her cheek to her lips. She parted them, and he traced her lower lip before moving his hand back toward her cheek.

"I wanted to do this as you slept."

Alex allowed his hand to roam freely, sliding it behind her neck.

"But you did not."

"Nay, lass, I did not."

When she licked her lips, he could no longer resist temptation.

"I couldn't have asked for your permission then."

"Neither have you asked for it now."

He pulled her head toward his.

"You could stop me at any moment."

Their faces were so close, Alex could feel her breath against his face. His heart raced like that of an untried lad.

"Why would I do that?"

He groaned at her words and pulled her toward him in truth. At the first touch of their lips, Alex immediately had to get closer. He brought his other hand up and pulled her head toward him. He vaguely felt her arms wrap around his back.

She was hesitant, as if she'd never been kissed. He pressed his lips to hers, opening them slightly to show her what to do, when a loud splash startled them both. He pulled away and looked around.

Nothing.

He ran closer to the bank of the river, still nothing.

"Likely an animal, but I need to be sure. Stay here."

He looked for tracks and, finding none, returned a moment later.

"We'd best be off," he said.

He wanted to resume where they'd left off, but he didn't dare. When she'd blurted out that she was a virgin, he'd believed her. But if he hadn't, the evidence was in the way she'd held herself against him. She was as pure a maiden as he'd ever kissed. And English. And determined to keep her identity secret. None of which boded well for a happy ending between them.

Whatever had made that sound had saved him from himself.

What in the name of the king of England was that?

He'd kissed her. From the moment they'd met, Clara had imagined what it would be like to be kissed by such a man, and yet she'd felt completely unprepared. Even so, she had never once thought of stopping him. She'd wanted it as badly as he had.

They rode hard all day and stopped only twice to feed themselves and the horses. As promised, they met no one along the road. And, so far, the weather cooperated. While the mornings were cool and grey, the day grew warmer as it went on, the sun peeking through just enough to be comfortable but not hot. Clara wished she could borrow some of that warmth at night.

Last night, it would appear, she'd borrowed Alex's heat. Though it mortified her that he'd heard her cry out in her sleep, the rest of her slumber that night had been smooth and peaceful and free of dreams.

"There's a loch just up ahead. The last one before we reach the border," Alex called back to her.

She spurred her mount forward. "We'll stop here for the night?"

The sky had already begun to darken, and Clara had just been about to ask when they'd stop.

"Aye," he said, circling the area around the edge of a most interesting loch. A small, rock-faced hill stood in the center of it, the water surrounding it in a ring.

"What is it?" she called, taking Alex's lead and dismounting.

"Volcanic rock," he said. "Ancient cairns stand over there." He pointed. "'Tis said this is a sacred spot."

"Can you swim there?"

"Aye, though you'd likely freeze for your efforts."

She walked to the water's edge and dipped her hand into the water. Indeed, it was quite cold. "Surrounded by trees and the rock's shadow, the water has little chance to warm."

Clara stood at the water's edge, watching as the last rays of sun lit the top of the grassy hill and surrounding rock at the center of the lake. She'd never seen anything quite like it.

By the time she refreshed herself and returned to the small clearing behind them, Alex had already erected their tent. They traded places, and she started the fire while he ventured up near the water. Not long after the fire grew from just a few embers, he returned with two fish.

"Trout," he said.

"How did you catch them so quickly?"

His devilish smile told her his retort would be bold.

"I've many skills, fair maid. Would you like to see some others?"

She smiled. "You tease."

"Never," he said, making quick work of removing the bones and cooking the fish.

They ate in companionable silence, Clara content to enjoy the last remaining vestiges of an unusually warm Scottish day.

"I've never felt so safe," she blurted out, because it was true.

"Never?"

"Not since Gilbert and I left home."

He took a bite of the freshly caught fish. "You mean Sir Robert Kinney?"

Of course, he thought the men were one and the same and that Sir Robert was not real. "Nay, Sir Robert was a vassal to my father. But he did not raise me, as you know."

"Nor were you orphaned as a young child."

"Nay, but I was orphaned nonetheless." And since he'd already worked out most of the facts, she explained, "My mother died before I knew her. My father, nearly six years ago. 'Twas why Gilbert and I were forced to flee."

"I'm sorry, lass."

He stood, and for a moment Clara thought he may try to comfort her. Would he kiss her again?

"Ale?"

He handed her a flagon and sat back down. Foolish girl. He was simply sharing his drink. Mayhap he'd thought better of the kissing. After all, they'd just last night agreed it was a bad idea.

"You're lucky to have known your mother," she said.

Alex made a sound suspiciously similar to an epithet not suitable for her ears.

"Tell me of her."

"She was lovely," he said.

That was not at all what she'd expected. Everything she'd heard about the woman who'd left her children was rather unpleasant.

"You've met my sister?"

"Aye, briefly. At Bristol."

"My mother had the same shade of red hair. But the similarities between the two women stop there."

He looked up into the sky as if he might be struck down at any moment for his words. "She was very. . . English. She complained of the cold. Mother grew up in a small village southwest of London, and apparently disliked Scotland from the moment she arrived."

"How did she meet your father?"

Alex sighed. "A tale for another time. Suffice to say, when he was killed at Largs, she left almost immediately."

Clara simply could not imagine a woman leaving her children, especially at such a difficult time for the entire family. "And said nothing in parting?"

He shook his head. "Nay. One day we had a mother, the next, we did not. She could have died for all we have heard of her since. . . until now. To my siblings, she is already dead."

The pain in his voice was evident. Clearly his mother's desertion affected him still.

"But not you," she finished in a whisper.

He frowned. "I'd come to accept that I would never see her again. And I may not. But if I could just. . ."

He stopped.

"What is it?"

He looked as if he'd not continue. He stood and began to clear the area where they ate. Then he abruptly stopped and blurted out, "I would just ask her why."

He picked up a nearby log, tossed it into the fire, and walked away.

How difficult it must have been for them to lose their mother that way. Clara prepared for bed, unable to stop asking Alex's question. Why had she done it? If she'd hated Scotland so much that she felt compelled to leave, could she not have at least said goodbye? Or taken them with her to England? Something. Anything other than abandoning her children.

Clara didn't know the woman, but she disliked her nonetheless.

Much the same as the evening before, Clara prepared for another night's sleep on the hard ground of the small tent. This time, she lay awake for what seemed like hours, waiting for Alex to join her. She knew he would not have gone far, so intent was he on 'protecting' her. Part of her despised that she needed his protection at all. Another part quite liked it.

She felt herself getting sleepy when a hand shook her shoulder.

"Clara, wake up."

Wake up? She hadn't even slept.

"Clara."

She shook her head as if to clear it. "Was I sleeping?"

Alex pulled her toward him, and she accepted his silent invitation. Nestling into the crook of his arm, she closed her eyes.

"Dreaming, more like."

She tucked her chin into her chest for warmth.

"This is quite comfortable."

Alex chuckled behind her. "You should try it in a bed."

She strained her neck to look up at him.

"Sleeping?"

This night was much darker than the last, so she could hardly see his face. But his eyes. . . those she could see.

"Of sorts."

His voice had changed, and suddenly Clara was neither tired nor comfortable. Instead, she could feel his body next to hers. His arm under her head and his leg pressed up against hers, both nearly as hard as the ground they slept on.

"I'd gladly do so if the opportunity presented itself." She shifted backward to get a better look at his face.

"And what exactly would you do so gladly?"

Clara wasn't sure what they spoke of anymore. She only knew she wanted Alex Kerr to kiss her—almost badly enough for her to tell him so.

"Sleep." She remembered now. "On a bed."

The hand that rested on her arm moved lower, sweeping across her back toward her buttocks. And that was precisely where it stayed.

"But you don't even appear tired."

Tired! How could she be tired with him looking at her like that? With his hand, oh dear.

"I'm not." She could no longer act the coy maid.

"Good."

He moved so quickly, Clara had the briefest of moments to realize she now lay underneath him, but was not being crushed in any way, before she felt his lips on hers. This time, it was no light touch. His tongue forced her mouth open, and once she realized what he wanted her to do, Clara touched her tongue to his.

She was lost.

Utterly and completely lost.

His mouth swept across hers, his tongue instructing her. She moaned and shifted under him, not because she was uncomfortable precisely, but because she wanted him to move closer.

Clara reached her arms up and pulled him down to her.

He made a sound that prompted her to pull away. "Have I hurt you?"

"Not precisely."

Poised over her, his outline looming above her, Alex stared down at her.

"This is a poor idea, lass."

"Aye," she agreed.

"As you say, you're a virgin still."

"I am," she admitted.

"And I don't even know your surname."

"That I can't tell you. But—" she smiled, not ready for him to stop, "—I will share anything else, if it pleases you."

"*You* please me," he said before he lowering his head once again. The touch of his lips on hers, the sensual way his tongue moved. . . This was what all of those ribald jests and crude remarks were about. This feeling, it was. . .

Indescribable.

"Ah, lass, don't move."

She hadn't realized she'd moved at all, but when he rolled onto his side, moving away from her, Clara felt the loss immediately.

"What have I done?"

"Clara. . ."

He pulled her toward his body once again, the warmth immediately welcome.

"You've done nothing at all."

"Then why did you stop?"

He reached around her and lifted her chin to him until she was looking directly into his eyes, the only thing she could see clearly in the dark.

"If I did not stop, the sun may not have risen on a Scots' second son and an English maid but on a scoundrel and the woman he forced from grace."

Forced from grace? How could he force something she'd freely give?

Would she? To a man she hardly knew? Over the past several years, Clara had given more thought to safety than she had to pleasure or marriage. Neither had seemed like a possibility for her. Once, the loss of her virginity would have meant something; indeed, when she had stood to inherit Barrington Castle, it would have meant a great deal.

But now?

"Get some rest," he said.

Was he attempting to convince himself or her? Clara lowered her head back down and tried not to think of the man whose arms were wrapped around her. She closed her eyes and, much later, finally allowed sleep to claim her.

This was perhaps the most foolhardy, misguided thing he'd ever done.

If he found his mother, Alex could add this misadventure to

the litany of things she'd done to torment him. Alex lay awake late into the night, contemplating whether or not they could reach The Anvil Inn the following day. He wanted to allow Clara to sleep in a proper bed, and he frankly wasn't sure of how much more of this sweet torment he could take.

Though clearly untried, her lips, so soft and gentle against his own, called to him, a siren's song like nothing he'd ever experienced before. No woman had ever made him feel like *this*. He pictured her body beneath him, completely unclad, the way she'd been at the lake the day he'd discovered her secret. He could clearly see each curve in his mind.

He tried to remind himself of his goals—find his mother. Return to ensure all had gone well with the Day of Truce. And yet, his last thought before sleep finally took him were of Clara and the soft sounds of pleasure she'd made before he pulled away from her.

Alex awoke painfully hard and aware of every movement Clara made against him. Though he tried not to wake her, she stirred the moment he shifted out from under her, sighing softly, sensually. He was not going to make it to Kenshire at this rate.

"'Tis morn already?" she asked.

"Aye," he said, standing. He had to put some distance between them. Alex stood, wanting to take the covering with him. It was as cold as an autumn morn. He'd just as well lay back down with Clara in his arms. . .

Nay, not that.

"Wait!" She cried out as his hand touched the side of the tent.

He turned. The wide opening of her boy's shirt had become untied, revealing part of one shoulder. That long stretch of smooth, creamy skin demanded his attention.

Until he saw her expression.

"What's wrong?"

"I slept!"

She stared at him, her eyebrows lifted and her eyes wide.

"Aye lass, 'tis a common thing for a person to do at night."

"But my dream. . ."

He shook his head, indicating that he didn't understand.

"Did I call out while I slept?"

"Nay, you did not."

She shook her head, as if to dismiss their conversation, so he turned once again to leave. Some instinct stopped him and he turned back to face her.

"How long have you had that dream, Clara?"

Her head was bowed over her lap, and he found himself walking toward her rather than away. Bending down, he lifted her chin. Tears escaped from under her closed eyelids.

It seemed he'd get his wish. Alex sat beside her and covered them both. He held her to him, comforting her as best he could. She cried openly against him, her shoulders shaking.

"Shhhh. . ."

She sniffled and wiped her eyes with the edge of her sleeve. He moved away for long enough to reach into his satchel and retrieve a dry cloth, but as soon as he handed it to her, he pulled her against him once more.

"He. . . he. . ."

She continued to cry while attempting to speak. The pain in her voice pierced Alex through.

"He did it on purpose," she managed. "For me to see."

Alex remained quiet as her sobs subsided.

"I could not see his face. The men. . . they came prepared for battle. I should have listened to my father. I should not have come back."

So, this was what she watched each night; she was forced to relive her father's death.

"How could I leave him? He was all I had. If only I had been trained. If I'd been armed. . ."

"You'd likely be dead too."

Her head was cradled against his chest, and her tears continued to make quick work of wetting his tunic.

"I ran back from the secret passageway. They were everywhere by then. They'd breached the walls, and as soon as I pushed open the door in the floor and climbed up through it, I knew I'd made a mistake. But I was never afraid."

Alex lifted her shirt over her bare shoulder and rubbed it, listening.

"I would have been," she amended. "But there was no time. The man who walked up behind my father saw me. His face was helmed, but I always imagined his sneer behind it. He lifted the knife and plunged it into my father's neck beneath his helm before I could even call out. He slumped to the ground."

She turned, her face streaked with tears, and looked at him.

"'Twas the last I ever saw of him."

She blinked and returned to her previous position on his chest. Which was just as well. The pain in her eyes was something no words, no gesture of comfort, could ever take away. He felt helpless and inadequate in the face of it.

"How did you get out?"

Clara's father had been killed in the hall of the castle where she'd lived. Her description of the secret passageway confirmed something he'd suspected. She was an English noblewoman. One who was lucky to be alive.

"I could hear his voice, yelling at me to get to safety. Then the man. . . he saw me. Sometimes, in the dream, my father is still alive—lying on the ground, telling me to get out." She swallowed. "That night. . . whether the man who saw me was killed or simply never bothered to chase me, I do not know."

She'd stopped crying. Taking a deep breath, she finished her story. "He was so angry that I'd gone back. I remember him emerging from the trees and pulling on my hand. . . Much of the rest is a blur."

"And then started your life as a lad."

She moved away from him as if she'd only then realized the intimacy of their position.

"Nay. The idea came to Gilbert later, when he realized that while peasant's clothes could hide my identity, they did not keep me from another kind of danger."

"Another kind of danger?" The words had hardly left his mouth before he already understood.

"Men are not quite as discreet in their attentions to a woman in my new station."

He could imagine as much. Anger at the unknown, faceless men welled inside him.

"Gilbert joked that 'twas as much for his safety as mine."

"When I asked you to remain as a woman, you feared being recognized."

Clara jumped up so fast, Alex didn't have time to grab her. She fled from the tent, and he did not attempt to stop her.

She'd clearly not expected to reveal so much. But though he knew part of her story, he still had so many questions. Why had they been attacked? Why did she still hide her identity? Could she not attempt to reclaim her rightful inheritance? Who was Clara, the most enticing, innocently fierce lass he'd ever met?

Clara's scream pierced his soul. In one fluid movement, Alex grabbed his sword and pulled back the tent flap.

An overpowering rage coursed through his body at the sight before him.

He would kill them both.

One man held his hand over Clara's mouth while the other reached for her. Reivers by the looks of them. English or Scottish, he couldn't tell. Nor did it matter. Both would die.

"Hold or she's—"

Alex would do no such thing. Not giving either man time to recover from the shock of seeing him emerge from the tent, he moved on them so fast that his thoughts never caught up to his actions. He removed the most imminent threat first, the dagger wielded by the man who held Clara. Kicking it from the man's hand, Alex ran his sword through the blackguard so quickly that his only reaction was to fall backward on the cold ground where he would remain.

The second reiver was already upon him, but Alex had watched his movements from the corner of his eye and easily ducked the thrust of his lance. Alex spun to the left, away from Clara, and held up his sword in defense. Now fully prepared for a fight, the reiver came toward him once again. As he'd done to the man's companion, Alex quickly found the exposed area beneath his leather jerkin. With one thrust of his sword, the man fell backward. But unlike his companion, this one did not die immediately.

"We just wanted a turn with the wee lass," he foolishly croaked up at them.

Scottish. For today, at least. Though some reivers were honorable, others simply lived to prey on the instability of the border, making a living from others' hard work. Scottish one day. . . English the next. . . whenever it suited them.

These were the second sort of men.

Alex saw the movement, as did Clara apparently. When the reiver grabbed the lance at his side, Clara's sword arm darted toward the same spot Alex had already injured him.

"This lass," she said, "is neither wee nor Scottish. Know 'twas an Englishwoman who ended your life."

Alex watched as the man's eyes widened just before the emptiness set in. Clara turned toward the river.

Alex walked up to both men to ensure they were, in fact, dead.

He stood there for a moment longer and finally made his way toward Clara.

Though the sun had risen, the sky stubbornly refused to lighten. Rain threatened, making the prospect of that day's ride a wet one.

He found her bent at the riverbed, cleaning her sword.

"I'm sorry—" he began.

She turned, her face expressionless.

"'Tis my fault." She turned her attention back to her task.

He disagreed. "I never heard them coming." It was inexcusable that he'd allowed this situation to unfold, and it might have ended in both of their deaths. He had been so intent on her story, he'd allowed himself to forget that they were vulnerable.

Toren would never have made such a mistake.

"I should not have discarded Alfred so easily."

Alex knelt down beside her. Clara's hands were shaking as she wiped her weapon clean. Where had she gotten the linen cloth?

"Have you killed a man before?"

She'd obviously been trained to do so. But training and killing were very different.

"Nay," she said flatly. She finished her task and looked at him. "How did you move so quickly?"

He shrugged. "Apparently my feet are quicker than my ears are keen to sound."

That, at least, brought a smile to her face.

"Your tongue is as quick as your feet," she said. "I didn't mean. . . that is. . . your wit. . ."

"I understand, lass." He stood when she did. "Are you all right then?"

It was no small matter to end a man's life. Even if it was justly deserved.

"Aye. I mean, I think so. He was wrong to have attacked me. . . and then to say such a thing. . . I just. . . 'tis not fair."

"'Tis the way of the world."

He had heard the same complaint from his sister, who'd struggled with the harmful misconception that women were somehow inferior to men.

He, of course, knew better. It was a wonder any man with a daughter could not see the world as he and his brothers did.

"I will be Alfred once again."

"Clara, no, I—"

"Nay, Alex. I will not be dissuaded."

And so his companion for the rest of the day was not the comely maid he'd come to enjoy looking at, but the squire who'd come to Brockburg to serve him. Seeing her with her hair piled into that plain hat, the familiar smudges of dirt on her face. . .

He should never have allowed such a thing to happen.

They pushed past both meals, stopping only for their base comforts. Both mounts were trained for hard conditions, and despite the hilly, often difficult path, they arrived at The Anvil Inn just past sunset.

Only one inn along the border could be considered safe for Scottish and English alike; alas, that inn was The Boar's Head. Owned by a man whose wife had been killed by Scottish reivers, and now run by the man's two sons, The Anvil Inn was large and fairly clean, which meant they'd likely have a warm bed—possibly two—waiting. The temperature had dropped markedly, which made the prospect even more appealing.

"'Tis not a place fit for a lady," he said, apologizing as the inn came into view. It was surrounded by a stone wall and two other structures. . . a stable and another small building Alex knew to be for storage. A few years earlier, the only other inn for miles was robbed and razed by a Scottish border clan intent on staking a claim to the area. Since then, no others dared to try to establish themselves here.

As they dismounted from their horses, the brothers who ran the inn, Bo and Berit, came out to greet them. The brothers bore a close resemblance; brown hair covered their heads and faces in waves. Indeed, if anyone reminded Alex of England's Norse invaders, it was their descendants, Bo and Berit.

"Twice in one year! Look Bo, Kerr has come back with a big strong lad to serve him."

"You may be twice his size, Berit," Alex said gamely, "but Alfred could outwit you without saying a word."

A groom poked his head out from the stables, and Berit nodded to him, indicating he should see to their horses. Scurrying to carry out his order, the boy took their mounts, leaving Alex and Clara—*Alfred*—alone with the brothers.

"Greetings, men. You've met my new squire, Alfred. Many thanks for the warm welcome." Alex turned toward Clara with a grin. "A personal greeting from Bo and Berit. They must have known you were English at first sight."

"English?" Bo turned toward her. "Leave this bastard and work for a real man," he blustered. "I'll offer ya—"

"The squire's not for hire, you overgrown ox," Alex said.

"Better an overgrown ox than the worst sort of man, despite your humor."

At Clara's confused glance, Alex clarified. "Scottish. You see, Bo and Berit haven't yet reconciled that we're not very different here along the border, with the exception that they fight for the wrong side."

"Fight?" exclaimed Berit. "Not for this king."

That he was so willing to speak words that could see him hanged for treason was yet another reason they needed to be on their guard this eve. Bo and Berit cared for one thing, their inn. They were raucous, teasing men, and while they could not be trusted, they would offer them clean beds thanks to Bo's wife, who managed the household tasks.

"Admirable," Alex said, catching Clara's horrified glance. "Poor Alfred will think you brutes the most inhospitable of hosts if you don't invite us inside."

Berit's laugh was cut off when Bo clasped Alex on the back, prompting their entire party to move toward the inn. "Do join us for the evening meal, sire," he said, mocking a proper English noble.

"'Tis your own countrymen, not mine, who are so intent on propriety."

They moved under the wooden sign bearing an etched image of an anvil, the sound of raucous laughter reaching them already.

"'Tis said the Scottish nobles are just as—"

"Be careful, Bo. Alex Kerr is the brother of a chief," Berit said with laughter in his voice. "Which makes you the second most important person in the clan, does it not?"

"Not quite," Alex shot back. "How nice to see you're running a clean establishment these days."

The moment the door opened, Alex moved to block Clara's view. But it was too late. Her gasp drew attention from both brothers, and Alex could have kicked himself for not being more explicit in his warnings. Scantily-clad serving woman competed for the attentions of patrons with coin to spare.

"My squire will take dinner in his room if you can show him there." He tried to guide the group through the door and to the left where a wall separated a corridor and the common room. "Good night, Alfred," he said.

"He's not that young, is he?" Berit said. "How old are you, boy?"

Alex silently prayed Clara would lie.

"Ten and six," she said. He could kiss her.

"Too young for proper entertainment?" the innkeeper scoffed, looking toward the scantily-clad serving wench closest to them. He wrapped his bulky arm around Alfred and pulled him toward the hall.

Why had he thought this a good idea? He'd knowingly brought Clara to an inn infamous for activities beyond eating, sleeping, and drinking. He'd put her in the company of Bo and Berit. All for a warm bed?

And a night away from you.

Alex wasn't sure where she'd be in more danger.

And so they were escorted into the chaotic heart of The Anvil Inn. A large fire roared in the corner, and Bo's wife smacked a servant on the head, presumably for tossing a log into it before it was needed. Music played, though not likely the kind Clara had once listened to in her own hall, wherever that may be. This flutist played a fast tune, one that prompted dancing, and not a very proper kind. Its fast pace acted as encouragement to the patrons, who'd likely sampled the ale for many hours, and more skin was exposed than was appropriate in a public space.

But it was only when one of the women, likely hired by Berit, stood on one of the trestle tables and flipped her skirts up, giving everyone a clear view of her attributes, that Alex took action. He was getting her out of here.

"Nay!" She threw back the hand he'd wrapped about her arm. "I can handle this," she whispered frantically.

The hell she could.

He gently pushed her toward the corridor that led to the rooms upstairs.

"Alex, I said nay." He wasn't sure if her words or the tone stilled his hands. But when he looked into her eyes, he immediately took his hands off her. For her own reasons, Clara wanted to stay.

By all that was holy, this damned woman was stubborn.

Fine.

They would both stay.

Bo and Berit moved off, taking a bag of grain from the store room just off the great room into the kitchens.

Alex and Clara sat, and when a serving wench slapped two tankards of ale in front of them without asking what either wanted to drink, Alex knew it would be a long night.

"And two meat pies?" he asked.

In response to the sharp look he was given, he rewarded the servant with a smile that he knew would have them treated well for the night.

Unfortunately, the suggestion would also get him a willing maid in his bed if he wasn't careful.

"Anything for you, mi'lord."

She walked toward him and promptly sat on his lap. He didn't chance a look at Clara.

"I thought ye wanted a meal is all." She wrapped her arms about his neck and leaned closer. "But if yer needing something more, I'm happy to oblige, mi'lord." As if to secure her position, she reached between his legs before he knew what she was about. "If 'tis always so hard, then mayhap you'll stay for more than just one night to entertain me."

Releasing him, she stood, presumably to get their repast.

He forced himself not to look at Clara. It wouldn't do if anyone saw him looking at her with more interest than a master would spare his squire, but despite her disguise, he no longer saw a lad when he looked at her. Only a breathtaking woman.

The servant returned with their meal.

"And how 'bout yer little squire. Have ye ever even kissed a girl, lad?"

She leaned down, as if intent on giving Clara a demonstration, and Alex forced a hand between them.

"I don't share."

It was the first thing he could think to say. But besides earning him a befuddled glance from Clara, the comment served its purpose.

"Later, mi'lord." She walked away with a wink.

"Alex—"

"Alfred—"

They turned toward each other.

"We can't stay here," he said.

"I love this place!" she said.

They'd spoken at the same time, and it took him a moment to understand her words.

"Are you mad? Bo and Berit have more women working here now than ever. It's less an inn than it was the last time I passed through. We're eating our meal and—"

"And mayhap you'll allow me some decisions? Or as your squire, am I not—"

"You are most certainly not my squire."

He ignored everything around them. The music, the lewd behavior. The two English knights who had been staring at him since they'd arrived. Instead, he looked at his companion sitting across from him at the table made for two. It was unique—Alex had seen only a few such tables before—it afforded a unique intimacy that was not typical of a common dining hall.

"If not your squire, then what am I?" Clara asked in an undertone.

He leaned down to whisper, "A woman who torments me day

and night. One whose surname I don't know. . . one who knew how to kill a man and who trusts no one."

"More ale?" The serving wench, who appeared from nowhere, leaned closer to Alex than was necessary. Then, before he could stop her, she reached down and ran her hand along his chest and shoulder.

"So hard," she said, giggling.

If he'd worried how Clara would react, he needn't have. She laughed boldly, and he wanted to grab her in full view of everyone and kiss her.

She understood. Her experiences in the tournaments had taught her about a man's world. She knew that he'd elicited the woman's attentions earlier to distract her. She knew, somehow, he did not want the serving wench.

But did Clara know he wanted her?

She took a bite of her meat pie as a new song, more suggestive than the last, began. An English knight made his way past them with a woman on each arm, headed in the direction of the private rooms.

"Are they— "

"Aye."

"With two women?"

"Aye, lass, with two."

He took a bite of the spiced meat, its thick gravy as good as Bernard's back home.

"Alex? Alex, you have to look at me."

He turned toward her.

"Gladly." The meal was quite good. The view, much better.

"I want to know. . . the man with those women. I've seen much of the same, not *seen* precisely, but when that happens. . ."

"What in the Lord's name are you talking about, Cl— Alfred?"

He looked around. No one appeared to be listening.

"Two women. And one man."

He nearly choked on his ale. "You cannot be asking me—"

"I suppose I can imagine, but with my limited—"

"And where, exactly, have you seen such a thing before?"

He had previously liked this Gilbert, but now he wasn't so sure.

"You know, near the tents mostly."

Tournament wenches. Of course.

He took a deep breath. "What would you like to know?"

Her eyes, always so expressive, widened. Alex found himself fixing his gaze on them so as to avoid looking at the absurdity that was the rest of her disguise.

"Do they? That is—"

He really should not discuss this with her. But then, Alex had never been known for either decorum or a wasted opportunity. This would be enjoyable.

"It depends, lass, on what he desires. Some men prefer to have themselves pleasured all over." She still didn't understand. "One woman may. . . make love. . . to him while the other simply teases him from behind. Others may simply sit back and watch as the women—"

"No!" she burst out, her eyes even wider. After a moment, she added, "And?"

"And that is all you will learn from me."

At least, for now. He took a swig of ale.

"Alex, please. Treat me as if I'm. . . Alfred."

He would surely be struck down for continuing this conversation. And yet, he found himself saying, "Come closer."

She leaned in toward him.

"A man gets great pleasure from a woman when she. . . well, when she puts her mouth on that most intimate part of him."

"You mean. . . Pleasure from—"

"You do realize how highly inappropriate this conversation is?"

"More so than me travelling unescorted, sleeping by your side, and allowing you liberties that no man has ever taken?"

He only registered the last part. 'No man has ever taken.'

And, if he had his way, no other man ever would.

She had asked; he would answer.

"When a woman touches that part of a man, it feels, well, good. Very good. Depending on her skill—"

"And she obtains this skill—"

"How did you learn precisely where to strike your sword into a man?" He asked, lifting a brow. Her eyes sparkled. "Aye, Alfred. Practice. But if she uses her mouth instead to please him in that way—"

"Her mouth?"

He chuckled, watching her attempt to understand.

"Aye, and he can do the same for her."

She looked up at him, peered off in the direction where the three lovers had disappeared, and looked back, eyes narrowed.

"He can touch his mouth—"

"To her very core." He lowered his voice so no one else could possibly hear him. "He could use it to show her what's to come, even use his tongue to mimic the more intense feelings of his—"

"Alex."

"Aye, lass?"

"I've had. . . feelings there, more than once. And I do right now. What does that mean?"

His Englishwoman could slay a man and wipe his blood from her sword, but she could not identify the source, or the cause, of her own desire.

He waved to the servant for more ale. This time, when she attempted to sit on his lap, Alex avoided the overture.

"Nay, not tonight. But—" he knew they'd not get very good service if he dismissed her altogether, "—extra coin is yours if you can arrange two rooms together."

She looked at him oddly, glanced at Clara, and likely came to the wrong conclusion. So be it. He needed Clara next to him, for her own safety—and his sanity.

"Drink." He handed Clara a mug of ale.

"So. What exactly does that feeling mean?"

Alex had never, ever, had such a conversation with a woman before.

"It means. . . your body is saying it wants to be touched. *There.*"

"Touched?"

It was all he could take. Alex stood from the table.

"Come."

He didn't wait to see if she followed. Alex found the serving wench, spoke with her for a moment, gave her the necessary coin, and walked out the front door into the night. He'd brought Clara here so she could sleep in a proper bed, but there weren't two rooms near each other, and The Anvil Inn was rougher than he remembered it. He could not comfortably leave her, but he had another plan. . . Bo and Berit were nowhere to be seen as they had left the main part of the inn, which was just as well.

He walked into the stable, paid the remaining stable hands enough coin to ensure their privacy, and climbed the ladder, listening for Clara's movements behind him.

"What are we doing here, Alex?" she asked, sounding completely baffled. "I thought the purpose of stopping at The Anvil Inn was a warm bed? Why are we—"

"Aye, 'tis the only private place we can stay together. I'm finding it quite difficult to explain what you're asking of me."

Clara gestured to their surroundings. "This will help because—"

"I can't tell you what that feeling means, Clara. But I can show you."

13

"**S**how me?"

Clara's heart thudded faster in her chest, and she inhaled deeply, taking in the familiar scent, a mixture of horse and hay. It was not unpleasant. She'd slept many nights in stables like this one, though the accommodations were vastly different than the soft feather mattress of her childhood.

"That feeling, lass, is desire."

"Oh." It came out as a strangled sound.

He walked toward her, straw crunching under his feet. "'Tis the same feeling I get every time I look at you. When you lie in my arms at night, the feeling is so strong I can hardly sleep."

He nodded to her hat. "Take that off."

A little thrill shot through her, but she said, "If I'm not your squire, then I don't believe you've the right to order me as such."

"You are—"

"What exactly?" It was the question she'd asked him earlier—the one he hadn't answered. Because there was no answer. If she was not his squire. . . if she did not train with his men. . . she was no one to him. The incident back at camp proved that her disguise was still necessary.

"Clara, I said I'd answer your questions, which I cannot do with that ridiculous disguise in place."

"But 'tis not safe here to—"

"We are alone and will remain so for the evening. None will be arriving at the inn this late, and I've ensured we will not be disturbed."

"How could you ensure such a thing?"

"I paid for it. Now will you please. . ."

"Hush," she said impatiently. She was curious. And there was no denying that she did want this.

Clara removed the hat and pins, shook out her hair, and bent down to the satchel Alex had carelessly discarded. She wiped her face as best she could without water and turned toward him once again.

"You've got smudges," he said, taking the cloth from her hand, "here." He wiped her cheek. "And here." He did the same to her forehead.

Clara stood still, mesmerized by his gentle yet precise touch. While she watched, Alex finished his ministrations and then tossed the cloth aside.

"You see," he took a step toward her, his head nearly touching the rafters of the loft that would be their home for the night. "When you look upon someone you desire. . ." He came closer still and lifted her squire's tunic above her head. "Your body tells you in many ways."

Tossing it aside, he touched the binding.

"When I first saw this—" he touched the cloth with his hand, "—I could not clearly see what was hidden beneath it. But my body already knew what it took my mind a moment to understand." His second hand moved to help the first, unwrapping the tightly wound fabric from her body. She could see his expression thanks to a small window opening in the stables beneath them that let in the moonlight. She reached up to hold onto his shoulders, afraid she might fall.

"I desired you immediately, though not as I do now. I did not know you well enough to admire you then. And I was angry at your deception."

Her breasts were finally fully uncovered. She moved her hands to conceal them, but he wouldn't allow her to do so.

"But those feelings you mentioned were there, anyway. Just as they are right now."

He cupped her breasts in both hands, and Clara thought for sure she might die. It was as if he'd branded her. She closed her eyes, luxuriating in his touch.

"Desire," he said, his voice so low she could hardly hear him. And then his hands moved, his thumbs brushing across the tip of each breast. "'Tis a powerful emotion. One that makes people do unusual things."

She opened her eyes. "Such as?"

He took a step toward her. "This."

His mouth came down on hers in a rush of heat and warmth. Of pleasure. His tongue dove into her mouth and he hauled her up against him. This kiss was unlike the others. It was hard and fast, demanding. She gave what he asked for, tentatively touching her own mouth to his and then becoming bolder as the sounds he made encouraged her.

He broke away, moved her hair to one side, and began to kiss her neck. His tongue flicked against her skin, behind her ear and then lower.

"I want you, Clara, as I've wanted no other."

"Want?" she managed to say.

He took her head between his hand and ran his thumb along her lower lip. He looked down, groaned, and took a deep breath.

"I want to make love to you. I want what I can't have." He licked his lips and left behind a trail of wetness she longed to trace with her own tongue.

"Give me your hand."

She didn't even think twice. Clara raised her hand between

them. He took it, turned it over, facing her palm downward, and said, "Do you promise not to be shocked?"

"Aye."

He guided her hand down their bodies until it rested. . . there! Even beneath the fabric of his tunic and breeks, she could feel it. Quite easily. It was hard, very much so.

"Desire," he repeated. "The evidence is there."

She'd heard talk, of course. Had been forced to look away many times, for the men who'd hired her to squire for them in tournaments had often changed in front of her. But she'd henceforth managed to avoid this part of a man. Now, she did not want to avoid it. Rather, she wanted to know more.

"'Tis hard," she said simply.

Her hand pressed on her own accord, and the sound Alex made deep in his throat forced her eyes to his.

"It hurts?" she asked.

"Not precisely." He moved her hand away. "Let me show you."

He reached down between them and cupped her in the same spot. None had ever touched her there before, and at first it felt curious and strange. Leaving his hand in place, Alex kissed her again. This time, his touch was gentle. He teased her lips with his tongue all while continuing to press against her.

When she began to press her hips toward his hand, he abruptly pulled away.

"Does it hurt?"

"Not. . . exactly," she said. And then she understood. "You felt the same way when I touched you?"

"I did, lass."

"And when I sleep next to you?"

"Aye, then too."

"Because you desire me?"

"Very much."

Clara smiled up at him. "It seems I desire you as well."

"Aye, it does," he said, smiling back.

"So what happens next?" She tried to make her voice sound as if she was unaffected—when in truth she was anything but.

"That, my fair English lass, is the question I've been asking myself since the moment you demanded to come with me."

He was hard, throbbing, and very ready. He could reach out and take her, show Clara the joys of lovemaking. Alex had never wanted anything more in his life. Almost every instinct urged him to touch her bare skin once again, run his hands along her breasts, tease those taut peaks, and take them into his mouth.

But he could not. Would not.

"I wish that we could continue our lesson, but I'll not take the virginity of a maid. A woman whose name I do not even know."

"I do not understand how that matters," she said, leaning into him.

Ah God, this was going to kill him.

"It matters a great deal."

Clara reached down, grabbed her shirt, and pulled it over her head. "Not to me," she said.

She turned from him then and found the blanket in the corner of the loft. After arranging it on the ground, she promptly curled up on it, pulled the second one over her, and ignored him.

That she'd known the blanket was there, ready for the next guest to make use of it, proved she had taken refuge in more than one stable in her life. Disappointment coursed through him, but he did not go to her. No matter how much he wanted her, this was for the best.

As a second son, he was free to marry whomever he liked. But though he might desire her, though he certainly admired her, he could not take Clara to wife. It would break him if another woman he loved ran from him, and Clara had proven on more than one occasion that she had an inclination to do just that. She'd run from Toren at Bristol. She'd run from him after he'd discovered her secret. Nay, he would not be taking this woman as his bride so she could leave at the first sign of trouble. Which meant he would not be taking her innocence, either.

Alex climbed down the stairs, found their steeds, and pulled a bedroll from the saddlebag. Returning to the loft, he unfurled the bedroll well away from Clara and prepared for sleep.

He had finally convinced his body it was sleep, not pleasure, that it needed when the familiar sound of Clara's nightmares began. Nay, he would not go to her.

Then she made another sound that confirmed she was, indeed, scared.

Muttering under his breath, he picked up his bedroll and moved it next to her. When he awoke the next morning, she lay in his arms, as relaxed and peaceful as a newborn babe. Of course, she was no babe and his thoughts for her were anything but motherly.

So it went for every remaining night of their journey. They slept in the open most nights except the evening before they were to reach Kenshire. That night they slept at another inn, though this time in a proper bed.

Ever since the night at The Anvil Inn, he'd kept his hands off Clara's soft, creamy skin. . . with one important exception. He slept with his arms around her each night, even in the second inn. He'd fallen asleep on the floor that night, but he'd moved to the lumpy bed in response to her familiar cries. With hardly enough room for them both, he'd scooped her into his arms, and she'd promptly fallen asleep.

They never talked about their late-night arrangement or anything of consequence. Alex knew her favorite foods, the pastimes she'd enjoyed prior to becoming Alfred. He knew more about her, but there was an undeniable distance between them.

In truth, it was the longest, most torturous journey Alex had ever taken—the push-pull he felt toward Clara would be the ruin of him. At least they'd met with no further trouble along their path. Only a group of pilgrims and a sole English knight.

Arriving at the village of Kenshire, Alex and Clara wove their way through a crowd of peasants, merchants, and tradesmen until they came to a clearing that offered a most spectacular view. Though he'd been here once before, the sight before him affected him now just as deeply as it had then.

"'Tis so beautiful," Clara said, riding next to him.

"Kenshire was once the seat of the king of Northumbria," he said, repeating what his sister had told him on his first journey from Brockburg to Kenshire.

"I've been told about the trouble after the countess's father died without a male heir, but I'm afraid I don't know much else about Kenshire. Rumor tends to travel—"

She stopped abruptly, as if worried she'd reveal too much. He didn't press her.

They wound their way through dusty but well-kept roads—a chapel on their left, a tavern on their right. It was a well-ordered village, much larger than Brockburg's, and only after they passed the last of the buildings did the splendor of Kenshire Castle truly reveal itself.

Set upon a rock outcropping with the North Sea as one of its borders, the large stone castle had so many towers and buildings it rivaled Edinburgh Castle, though it was a wee bit smaller.

Curious glances followed them up the path to the guardhouse.

"—and Catrina told me there is quite a tale," she finished.

"I'll gladly tell Clara, but not Alfred."

Alex wasn't sure what had made him say that. The tentative truce between them relied on his relationship with *Alfred*. But he wanted to know the woman, not the boy she'd posed as for the last six years.

"We shall see."

And although it was said innocently enough, the slight huskiness to her voice forced Alex to shift in his saddle. It was not a promise that held any more possibilities than a simple conversation, but. . .

They dismounted when the guard called down to them. After a brief exchange of words, the portcullis was lifted and they were admitted into the outer ward. Kenshire Castle boasted more paths and corridors than any castle where Alex had previously stayed. He prepared to be lost once again.

"Good day, my lord. And greetings to you—"

"Alfred," Clara said.

"We've met before." The steward bowed to Alex. "Under much more. . . "

"Tense circumstances," Alex finished.

"My lord and lady are taking the midday meal and would be honored if you would join them. Are you hungry, or would you prefer a brief respite first? Oh, and I am the steward here," he said to Clara. "Peter."

"A meal would be most welcome," she said.

This was another thing he loved about Clara. She ate nearly as much as he did. Though she was not thick around the waist, neither did he feel the outline of her bones, something he'd experienced with a few other lasses, who, in his opinion, were simply too thin. Clara's body, what he'd seen and felt of it, was made perfectly.

They followed Peter through a second gate and the inner ward. Unlike Brockburg, where the buildings were close together, Kenshire was spread out. The small party finally arrived at the main keep, and once they'd relinquished their reins to a stable boy, Peter waved his hands.

"I give you Kenshire Castle." Clearly he was quite proud of it. And well he should be.

They looked up, the four turrets of the keep towering above

them and appearing to skim the clouds. But before they could enter through the doors Peter had just swung open, a woman appeared at the entrance.

"Alex Kerr," the countess of Kenshire said, her voice firm and strong. "Why does your squire dress as a boy?"

14

$\mathcal{C}$lara simply stared.

She was quite spectacular in every way. Lady Catrina was certainly lovely, but there was something about the countess that stunned her into silence—and not just her words.

Lady Sara was dressed in purple velvet with a simple string of beads hanging from her waist, and her long sleeves draped low and waved on their own accord when she moved her arms. She stood tall and proud, as if Kenshire was hers, which of course it was. The massive double doors that led to the great hall should have made her appear small, but this confident slip of a woman filled them easily.

And now, with a few simple words, Clara's secret was out in the open.

"I'm not sure—" Alex began.

"I'll forgive that you've spent the past several nights attempting to keep yourself alive on the road. I'll even look past the fact that you're a Scot."

Clara's eyes widened until it registered that the countess was teasing Alex.

"But if you think to lie to me before enjoying the hospitality of

Kenshire for whatever purpose you've come here to serve, then leave the girl and return to Brockburg. If you do so, and stop at Bristol on the way, please tell Catrina I offer greetings and good wishes, of course. I do adore your sister."

Despite the fact that she just had revealed her secret, Clara immediately wanted to *be* this woman. She wanted to shed her boy's clothes, her past, her present, and become. . . well, not the Countess of Kenshire, precisely, but as brash and fearless as the woman who wore that title. Despite the fact that she just outed her.

"I'd not presume to do so, my lady."

Peter cleared his throat. "Shall we continue the conversation in the hall? Our guests are much in need of sustenance, I suspect."

Lady Sara turned from them, which was when Clara realized. . . she was pregnant. She was not so far along that it was easy to tell from the front. But from the side, there was no doubt the countess would become a mother.

Although it was easily the grandest great hall Clara had ever seen, it nonetheless possessed a warmth that Brockburg lacked. Every wall was covered with colorful tapestries, the ceiling was spectacular in its height, and wooden beams crossed from one end of the hall to the other. What surprised her most was the number of people present. The trestle tables were filled with retainers, knights, and visiting nobles—or so she assumed.

As they walked toward the raised dais, Lady Sara reached out to touch her arm.

"Will you come with me?"

Clara looked immediately to Alex, not realizing she'd done so until Lady Sara glanced his way as well. Clearly agitated, he watched them closely.

"I will not hurt you, nor will I ask anything of you. I merely wish to speak with you." Alex moved to follow them. "Alone," she added pointedly.

Clara nodded her head in assent.

The lady of Kenshire led her toward an anteroom tucked at the front of the hall. A bench sat at the base of a rare stained glass window looking out into the courtyard.

"My lady's maid, Faye, chastises me for wearing breeches," Lady Sara said. "At least, a woman's version of them."

Clara looked down at her own attire. "You were in hiding as well?"

Her laugh was not the dainty laugh of a great countess but the hearty one of a woman who cared little about social graces. Clara already liked her. "There were days when I would have very much liked to be in hiding, but nay, I was not."

Lady Sara pulled the long sleeve of her gown onto her lap and folded her hands. "Just this past year, this—" she swept her hands to indicate everything around her, "—was in jeopardy. My father had died, and his only male relative attempted to claim Kenshire for his own."

Clara could tell by the quiet, serious tone of Lady Sara's voice that she was sharing something important. But why? Why would she reveal herself to a stranger?

"But before his death, my father sent two reivers here to protect my inheritance." She sighed. "And me."

"Reivers?"

"Aye. And I was none too pleased. But it happened that one was a good friend of my father's. The other?" The smile that reached her eyes told Clara all she needed to know. "Is now my husband."

Clara knew from Alex that Sir Geoffrey Waryn, brother to Sir Bryce Waryn, was the countess's husband. Although he certainly had not told her the man had once been a reiver. Though she was still curious about the countess's decision to reveal herself in such a way, she was too polite to pose the question. If the countess was attempting to elicit a confidence in return, she would be disappointed.

"And your relative?" Clara pressed.

Lady Sara sighed. "Was killed because of his attempt to end my life."

Clara gasped. "He tried to kill you?"

"Tried and failed, thanks to Geoffrey."

And now he was as powerful as any of the border lords.

"Come, you must be hungry." Lady Sara stood, leaving Clara quite confused. Had she brought her to this room merely to tell her this tale?

"But, my lady—"

"Sara," Clara corrected, silently grateful for the kind gesture of familiarity. "Sara. Why do you tell me this? You—"

"Want to know why you're dressed as such? Aye, but if you wanted me to know, you'd not be hiding your identity."

She began to walk toward the hall.

"But then why—"

Sara turned back to her. "Yes?"

"Why would you tell me, a stranger, that story? 'Tis a fascinating one, but..."

Sara peered beyond the wall where they stood and out into the hall before glancing back at her. "Because any woman who dresses as a boy does so for either one of two reasons. Out of the desire to show those around her that she will not follow the rules, consequences be damned, or because she is afraid to reveal herself. I believe such is the case with you..."

"Clara," she said, filling in Sara's pause. Never had she given her real name so freely and so quickly to anyone.

"I believe you are hiding for important reasons, but in time, perhaps those reasons will change."

With a swoosh of her skirts across the clean rushes, Lady Sara once again turned and walked toward the hall.

Still attempting to sort out the curious conversation, Clara stepped back into the hall and locked eyes with Alex, who had just lifted a spoon to his lips.

Relief filled his eyes, followed fast by desire. These past few days, Clara had found herself thinking of the moments they'd shared again and again. Of how he'd touched her breasts and kissed her and caressed her. . . It seemed she could think of little else with the exception of the tenderness he displayed each night, taking her into his arms to comfort her whenever her mind replayed the horror of her father's murder.

And then she caught Sara's eyes.

She knew.

The woman was so perceptive, it was a wonder she hadn't already guessed her identity. The longer she stayed with Alex, the more and more mistakes she seemed to make. She might as well simply reveal herself to everyone this moment.

Clara had a decision to make while she was here, and though she wanted to put it off and pretend all was well, the memory of her conversation with Sara made her stomach clench in dismay.

Her vigilance was slipping, and what scared her most was that she didn't seem to care.

Clara ate quickly, avoided Alex as best she could, and asked to be shown to her quarters. She was surprised when Sara escorted her personally to a well-appointed room in the East Tower, which afforded views of the shore and North Sea below. She was kindly given a water basin and soap made from wood ash and olive oil, scented with lavender. She recognized it at once, for it was the same sort she'd used in her life as Clara.

The bed, so much more comfortable than anything she'd been used to recently, beckoned to her, so she decided to take a short rest. Only she fell asleep. Peacefully.

When a knock startled Clara from her sleep, it took her a moment to realize she'd fallen asleep for the majority of the afternoon.

"Clara?"

She jolted from the bed, unused to hearing her name on anyone's lips. With the exception of Alex.

"I'm sorry to wake you," Sara said, entering the room. "Alex told us of your long journey. But dinner will be served soon."

Sara closed the door behind her as Clara sat up easily, propped up on a multitude of pillows. Some were soft and practical, others ornate and meant for decoration.

"I would like to take dinner in here if it pleases you."

"Of course." She smiled. "I will attend to you myself in the meantime."

"My lady, no!"

Sara's eyes widened.

"That is to say, you've no need to do such a thing. I—"

"Will be forced to remain as a lad. Nay, I will see to your meal, and you'll not be disturbed by anyone."

She was allowing Clara the freedom to be herself. Gratitude nearly choked her.

"I've just one question," the countess of Kenshire asked on her way to the door. "Alex does know your true identity, I presume?"

My true identity? Nay, never that.

"He knows I am not a lad," she said, evading a direct answer.

Sara turned and left. Why was she being so kind? It was this unbidden but entirely welcome kindness, from both Lady Catrina and Lady Sara, that made Clara feel even worse about her deception. But what choice did she have? Either reveal herself and put her life in danger, or run. Again. But she was so weary of running. Always being scared and unsure of the dangers ahead. Unsure of how to reconcile the girl she'd once been and the lad she'd become.

Clara paced the chamber, picking up the candlestick and looking for a flint with which to light it. It was not quite dark yet, and the windows afforded enough light for the moment thanks to the orange sunset streaking across the sky and the fire that had already been lit when she'd entered the chamber.

She struck the steel, produced the needed spark, and was about to light the candle when a knock on the door startled her.

Sara.

She lit the candle, placed it in the holder, and replaced the flint where she'd found it. When the door creaked open, she moved toward it.

"Thank you for bringing me—"

It was not Sara, but Alex.

"Lady Sara said you're taking dinner in here tonight?"

He stepped inside, carrying a tray of food and drink. She stepped around him to close the door quickly before anyone saw him.

"You should not be here."

Which did not mean she didn't *want* him there. He smelled of oak and leaves. His hair was damp and his shirtsleeves rolled to his elbows.

"I am not here, fair lady. 'Tis a spirit you see in front of you, one who will take this tray back down to the hall if you wish it."

She'd never heard a more absurd jest. He was no spirit, but pure flesh and blood man.

"I am a bit hungry." She'd hardly eaten earlier, worried, as always, that others were watching her and would guess her secret.

"Lady Sara sends roasted duck and her finest wine for you to enjoy."

For *you* to enjoy. It was just as well. It was hardly proper for him to be here. Even less so for them to eat together.

"And the most enjoyable company in all of Kenshire to share it with," he added with a small grin.

He was staying! But he should not. "Do you think 'tis wise?"

For an answer, he placed the tray on a table large enough to hold it and moved to the candle she'd lit earlier. He picked it up.

"It was not wise for either of us to come to England. And certainly not for you to have accompanied me. But that has not seemed to stop our course as yet."

Alex used the candle to light the others. Clara was glad she'd taken off the hat and washed her face earlier. And even more grateful to Sara for providing her with this opportunity to be herself—with Alex.

"May I?"

He pulled out the chair, its gold-trimmed maroon velvet cushions the height of luxury. Indeed, everything about Kenshire was at once richly appointed and comfortable. Approachable.

Like its countess.

Clara vowed to leave her worries behind for the night and enjoy Alex's company somewhere other than on horseback or in a stable.

She sat, her boy's clothes allowing for an easy transition.

Alex sat across from her, split the food between them, and poured wine for them both.

"I'm glad you declined an invitation to dinner."

"Why?" She didn't mean to blurt out the question, but there was no denying she was eager for his answer.

"We need to talk."

Aye, they did.

"About what happened. . . "

Her cheeks grew warm. Without her hat and smudges, she felt exposed. And Alex was looking at her *that way*, as if she were one of the courses placed in front of him.

She blurted. "You were right—"

"I was an idiot—"

They spoke at the same time.

Her grin was immediate. "Please, do continue. I find your opening much more intriguing."

Clara popped a morsel of cumin-spiced duck into her mouth. She was hungry indeed, and the fare was so much finer than the meals they'd shared on the road.

"You're so kind," he said, obviously meaning just the opposite.

"I was an idiot not to have explained my thinking that night. Clara. . ."

Her smile faltered when his voice turned serious.

"I will not be coy with you. I told you that I want you, and I do. I think of that morning at the loch. Of the nights you've slept in my arms. Our conversation at the inn and that night, in the stable. . ."

He took a sip of wine, peering at her from above the rim of his goblet.

"I meant what I said, however. That I don't know anything about you other than—"

"You know my name."

"Your given name."

"And that I have nightmares each night."

"But I don't fully understand what haunts you."

"You know I served as a hired squire and that—"

"Clara." He placed the goblet back on the table. "I know nothing other than the carefully selected bits you've chosen to reveal to me. I don't know where you were born. Or why you are posing as a boy. I don't know why you're terrified to reveal yourself or what your intentions are after we leave Kenshire."

"My intentions?"

"You aren't coming back to Brockburg, are you?"

To hear it said aloud. . .

Clara sighed. "You don't know that."

"I know you're considering it. Each time I mention returning, you hardly speak."

"What does it matter, Alex?" He hadn't answered before, and she could see he was not inclined to do so now.

"What if I was born a servant, raised in a noble household, learning enough to emulate my superior's mannerisms. What then? Would you feel free to be with me? For one night? For a fortnight? Until you tired of me?"

She could tell she was angering him, but Clara did not care.

"Or what if I am the illegitimate child of the king? A lost princess? Then you will be forced by some honorbound—"

"Clara, that's enough."

"Nay, Alex. You're asking me to share more of myself than I am able. And with someone who does so little sharing himself."

"I've held back nothing from you," he said.

"Except for the real reason we're on this journey."

He ground his teeth, his jaw moving back and forth as his eyes narrowed.

"You already know I am looking for my mother."

"Why?"

He was not the only one who could ask difficult questions.

"What do you hope to learn by finding her?" she pressed.

Clara knew she pushed too far, but she had begun to care for this man. And even though she was angry at him. . . though she couldn't exactly say why. . . she wished to save him from being hurt.

"What do you hope to gain from this journey?"

"I already told you. I want to know why she left us. "

"And then what?"

She could tell it wasn't a question he was prepared for. "What if she tells you something you don't wish to hear?"

He grabbed his cup and drank deeply. "I expect as much."

That's when she realized. Alex hated his mother. He was not merely curious about why she'd left. Nor was he simply upset that she had abandoned them. It was an unsettling emotion from a man who appeared to hate no one, save his enemies. From a man who always smiled. His face bore out the intensity of his feelings, and Clara wanted to put her arms around him.

Instead, she waited.

And decided to trust him, as she hoped he would trust her, while she did so.

"I was born a baron's daughter."

He looked up.

"Gilbert was our armorer. I was forced to leave, and he saved my life."

"He must have been very special to your family."

If she kept taking, Clara would tell him everything. He already knew too much, and if she wasn't careful, she'd put him in danger too.

"Aye, he served my family loyally for many years."

The finality in her voice quieted them both. The playful mood forgotten, she retreated to more somber thoughts.

"I do hope you find her," she said quietly.

Alex shrugged, but the seemingly flippant gesture was undermined by the thickness in his voice. "Sometimes," he said, picking up his cup, "I pray that I do not. What will I do next? Continue to live with the knowledge that I am a man whose mother does not love him. What else could I do?"

Clara wished she knew. She wished she had answers for them both.

---

15

*A*lex rode down the path from the castle entrance before the household began to awaken. He'd made a hasty retreat from Clara's chamber the night before, soon after their discussion of his mother. When he'd told her he would be leaving for a few days, she'd hardly flinched. Because she didn't plan on staying? He'd nearly changed his mind in the morning—he'd nearly gone to her. How could he leave not knowing if she'd be there when he returned?

But as she'd asked him twice now, what did it matter?

"You're a fool."

He glared at his companion, Sir Geoffrey Waryn, who rode beside him. His *unwanted* companion. But when the reformed reiver had learned Alex planned on visiting the small village of Elkview, just outside Kenshire's vast border to the south, Sir Geoffrey had insisted on accompanying him. In fact, Gerald, the castle constable, had actually argued for him to bring additional men.

"I travel alone," he'd told them both.

"The hell you do," Geoffrey had countered, the constable nodding in agreement. "Troubles in the middle marches have spread here to the east. The English Warden may have been absolved of guilt, but the effects of that scandal continue to destabilize the tenuous peace here. That your brother allowed you to travel here with only a squire, and a female one at that, is remarkable."

So he knew. Of course Lady Sara had told him the truth. "Toren is very much aware of the 'troubles' and does not presume to tell me where to go or with whom."

They came to a well-worn path, the sun just beginning to rise, and Geoffrey took the lead.

"Alex," he started again, this time in a lower, more serious voice. "I'm here to help. Your brother has made peace with mine, and our families are inextricably entwined. We can continue to rue the sins of the past or move beyond them as allies."

"We've already made our peace," Alex said, referring to his last visit to Kenshire, when Geoffrey's brother had apologized for his role in Catrina's capture. "Indeed, your family has lost more than most." If a man whose inheritance, home, and parents had been taken from him on the same day could forgive those responsible, the least he could do was accept the gesture graciously. Though the Scottish king had demanded that Toren take Bristol Manor, they certainly bore their measure of guilt. He smiled. "But if I'm forced to do so every time we meet, I fear this will be the last time I travel to Kenshire."

Geoffrey's eyes narrowed. He pointed to a heavily wooded path, and Alex followed. They rode in silence for some time, Alex surveying their surroundings with interest. Though he'd been to Kenshire before, he had never travelled this far south toward its borders and the eastern coastline. At one point along a rare patch of flat terrain, he spied the North Sea.

"How far south are Kenshire's borders?" he asked.

"Far enough that we'll need to move faster to be there by nightfall."

Later, when the sun rose high into the sky, he and Geoffrey

finally stopped. They allowed their horses a rest and ate a quick repast Kenshire's cook had prepared. Though he hadn't met the woman, he'd heard enough about her to know she commanded the kitchen as competently as Lady Sara presided over Kenshire.

"So how do you come to travel with a woman disguised as a squire?"

Alex nearly spat out the ale he'd just drunk. "How does a reiver come to marry a countess?"

Geoffrey's brows raised. "Fair enough. On his deathbed, her father requested my uncle's protection from a distant relative, Sir Randolf Fitzwarren. As it turned out, the request was with good cause. The bastard attempted to slice Sara's throat."

"So you sent him to his maker for his efforts?" Alex had heard most of this tale, albeit not from Geoffrey's lips.

"Aye." He grinned. "But I nearly lost her in my thirst for revenge—"

"Against my brother."

They looked at each other, not as enemies, but with a somberness that could come only from the losses both men had faced in their families' five-year feud.

"Your entire clan, to be precise."

"I don't blame you." None would. Even Toren, who'd tried to kill Geoffrey's brother, Bryce, for taking their sister captive, had reluctantly agreed he would have done the same. "We agreed no more apologies, but I owe one despite it. Your parents—"

"Loved the borderlands."

Alex sensed his companion didn't want to discuss the loss, so he did not push him.

"As dangerous as it had become, it was the only home they'd ever known," Geoffrey said. "The game played by our kings is a dangerous one, and I fear peace will be hard-fought for years to come," Geoffrey said, taking a bite of bread.

"Even so, I am deeply sorry." Geoffrey's father had been a casualty of battle, and even though his mother had nearly decapitated one of their clansmen, she should not have been killed in that raid.

Geoffrey clearly wanted to change the topic. "I know *where* we look for your mother, but not why."

"I'm told my good looks were inherited from her, and I can hardly remember if it's true." Though he smiled, it was forced, and Geoffrey was not fooled.

"Obviously it is not. You're as ugly as your brothers."

If he or his brothers had ever been accused of anything, it was for being unnaturally large and fair featured. So Geoffrey's retort only made him laugh.

Geoffrey tried again. "You're sure the merchant mentioned Elkview specifically?"

"He said she was in the village on market day and purchased a sampling of his wares. When he mentioned travelling across the border, she bragged of having three sons and a daughter in the Scottish borderlands."

"Yet she didn't give her name."

"Nay, and the merchant, new to Elkview, never asked. He said she was richly appointed, a noblewoman. And that her hair was red-brown, which is the same color of—"

"Catrina's," Geoffrey finished.

Though Geoffrey received the news as skeptically as Toren and Reid had, Alex knew it was her. He couldn't explain how, but he just *knew*. He'd seen Clara's face when they'd spoken of his mother. . . he knew that she pitied him. But there was no reason for it. His mother was dead to him. She meant nothing. He just needed to understand what had happened.

"And the squire?"

"Is there anything else you need to know? You failed to also ask when I last relieved myself," Alex said, attempting to lighten the mood.

"No need to ask," the Englishman replied. "I saw you do so myself not long after we stopped."

He laughed heartily. "If you're not careful, reiver, I may not rue the day we were bound by our siblings' marriage."

"I was not a reiver by choice," Geoffrey pointed out. He was still smiling, but his words were serious.

"My brothers and I didn't want Bristol. We felt we had no choice."

"The whims of gods and kings. We all do what we must to survive, and I regret nothing."

That took him by surprise. "Nothing?"

Geoffrey took another swig of ale and stood. "None of the choices I've made, at least. Sara and I attempt to distance ourselves from it all as much as possible. She offered the majority of Caiser's southern holdings back to the crown as an appeasement for breaking her betrothal, but we have Kenshire, and it is enough."

Alex stood and walked toward their horses. "It seems every man I know has grown soft with love for a woman." Geoffrey's emotions were evident when he talked about Lady Sara.

"Not everyone," Geoffrey commented, looking pointedly at him.

Alex wasn't so sure.

Alex was gone, and unless she wanted to don her pins and hat and search for a way to disguise her face, Clara was a virtual prisoner in her bedchamber. She woke to a tray of food by her bedside, which she imagined the countess had likely left for her while she slept.

"May I come in?"

Without Alex by her side, Clara had awoken not once but twice in the night. When she finally rose from bed, she was embarrassed by the lateness of the hour. It was unlike her.

"Of course," she answered the beautiful woman peering through a crack in the door.

Dressed in a simple, bright yellow gown embroidered with tiny navy blue flowers along the cuffs of the sleeves, Sara exuded confidence and glowed with the joy of impending motherhood.

Sara's hand slipped to her stomach. She must have seen Clara's eyes move there.

"I fear I can't stop touching it," she said. "The babe will come this winter, and 'tis none too soon. I can't wait to meet her. Or him."

Her smile was infectious.

Sitting up in the bed, Clara gestured to the untouched food. "You've been so kind," she started.

Sara sat in the chair next to her, the same one Alex had occupied the evening before.

"Catrina wrote to me," she said. "Before I knew you were coming."

So that explained it.

"She told me you had gone missing, and that her brother was upset. She also told me that Lady Juliette had discovered your secret and was quite concerned for your welfare."

"Which is how you already knew when I arrived."

"I like to believe I would have discovered it on my own," she shrugged. "But, aye, I already knew."

"Lady Catrina and Lady Juliette are both very kind."

She nodded. "I haven't yet had the good fortune to meet Toren's new wife, but Catrina is dear to me. You must be hungry, the hour grows quite late."

Clara felt her cheeks grow warm.

"I am normally an early riser and cannot remember—"

"Eat," Sara said, picking up a small knife. "There's no need for apologies."

Clara peered out the window slit, surprised to see how high

the sun had risen. She returned to the table and sat across from Sara.

"This is a beautiful chamber. I've yet to see much of Kenshire but—"

"Let me show it to you!"

Clara looked at her hat.

"Nay, not as Alfred. As yourself."

Her shoulders slumped. "I couldn't possibly—"

"You could. No one will question it."

Clara looked up.

"If not as yourself, then at least as my guest."

"I could not possibly—"

"Clara," Sara's tone was soft but firm. "None will know your identity. I myself don't know why you're dressed as a lad. But I do know that if I had to don that hideous. . ."

Her voice trailed off.

"I'm so sorry."

"Nay," Clara interrupted. "It is I who am sorry. Arriving here, forcing you to serve me just so that I may remain in hiding." She owed Sara for her kindness. "You don't believe anyone will suspect?"

Sara's face brightened. "Geoffrey's sister will return any moment from an extended stay with my dear friend Gillian. We will celebrate her return, and I'll say you've come home with her. Leave the details to me."

Though it sounded divine, Clara was terrified of the prospect of showing herself to anyone, save Alex.

He was different.

But clearly Lady Sara would not betray her. How could she? None knew that she was the daughter of the disgraced lord of Barrington, whose only crime had been choosing the losing side in the bloody baron's war.

Non ducor, duco.

Her father followed their family motto in earnest and had been killed for it.

A thought occurred to her. "Even if I wanted to—"

Sara bounded up from her chair, moved to the trunk at the foot of the canopied bed, and tossed open the lid.

"Here," she smiled, pointing to its contents.

Clara pushed her chair back and walked toward the trunk. She noticed the elaborate carvings first, the heavy lock that was more ornamental than practical, and finally. . .

She gasped. "How did you know—"

"Well, you can't very well present yourself as Lady Clara in *that*," she said.

Lady Clara. It had been so long since she'd heard the title. "That I can never be again," she said, wishing it were otherwise.

Peering at the folded gowns beneath her, Clara could not resist reaching inside to touch the fabric of the deep maroon one on top. Velvet.

"Well, Lady Alfred just won't do."

She pulled her hand away, laughing at the notion.

"Susanna," she said.

According to her father, it had been her mother's idea to name her after St. Clare of Assisi. Every year on the twelfth of August, she and her father had shared a special meal to honor St. Clare's feast day. St. Clare had actually died on the eleventh day of August, only that day had already been declared for Saint Susanna.

Sara watched her, waiting.

"Lady Susanna," she said. She ignored Sara's smile, which looked more sad than triumphant.

"'Twould be an honor to wear your gown and—"

"Not mine," she said, closing the lid. "Emma's. This is Geoffrey's sister's bedchamber, and she is almost exactly the same size as you."

Clara couldn't help but be bolstered by Sara's building excitement.

"You're sure she will not mind? And, of course, I will move now that she is returning."

Sara linked arms with her and guided her back to the table.

"She will be delighted. And will never consent to see you moved. Though I'll need to tell her, of course, if that is acceptable to you."

So many people knowing her secret. But how could she say no?

"As long as you're sure—"

"Sit," Sara demanded, immediately taking over. "Break your fast, and pardon my departure. I've much to prepare."

Sara began to mutter to herself on her way out the door. "Will speak to Cook, and just a few musicians. . ."

Sara closed the door behind her.

Gowns? Musicians? What had she just gotten herself into?

16

Clara stood next to Sara's lady's maid, Faye, just around the corner from Kenshire's great hall. Though the kind woman had been extremely helpful, it worried her that yet another person knew her secret. Not for the first time, she wondered if she'd made the right decision.

"Will ye come down to greet Lady Emma, or are we to stand here instead?" Faye asked.

"Stand here," she ventured, though the look on the maid's face told her that was not the correct answer.

"Lady Susanna," she said in the same motherly tone she'd used all afternoon. "You've nothin' to be afraid of. You can trust my lady with your life."

That, Clara worried, was exactly what she was doing.

"Come." Faye walked ahead of her, and Clara allowed herself to be escorted to the hall dressed in one of Emma's simple day gowns.

Even though Clara had been raised a noblewoman and had frequented plenty of such halls, this one was special.

Spectacularly appointed with a ceiling that seemed to never end and more tapestries than she'd ever seen in one place,

Kenshire's hall had to be the most elegant one in all of England. She spotted Sara with a stunning woman by her side. Could this be Emma?

"There you are! Are you quite all right, Susanna?"

The black-haired beauty walked briskly toward her, grabbed both of her hands as if they were long-time acquaintances, and stared at her with a pair of piercing, light blue eyes. Clara didn't know what to say.

"'Twas the ride, was it not? I remember the first time I travelled any distance on horseback. I was exhausted as well."

So she was to play the weary companion to this raven-haired woman? Clara looked from Lady Emma to the other expectant faces. A small crowd had gathered, and Clara fought back the temptation to run back to her bedchamber.

Except, it was not hers. It belonged to the woman who was holding her hands and awaiting an answer.

"I'm feeling much better," she managed.

Emma's broad smile was rivaled only by Sara's.

"Wonderful," the countess said, clasping her hands together. "Faye, can you please advise Cook we will take a late dinner? I've much to discuss with these two."

The handmaiden nodded, though not as deeply as one would expect. The familiarity between the countess of Kenshire and her servants was another unique aspect of her household. Picking up her gown from both sides, Sara nodded to a corridor. Clara assumed they would speak there, in relative privacy, but Sara kept walking, the twists and turns convincing Clara that she would never be able to make it back on her own. After a time, they climbed a set of stairs and emerged outside. The gate in front of them was locked, but Sara pulled out a key.

"The sea gate," she said. Unlocking it, she gestured for them to follow.

The scene that greeted her was even more resplendent than the castle's interior.

The North Sea stretched beyond them. As they made their way through a path in the tall grass surrounding them, Emma caught up to them from behind, her laughter breaking the silence.

"I could see Peter looking at Susanna. He was definitely suspicious," she said to Sara, who led the way.

"Aye, and your poor companions. Thankfully they had not been travelling for long—"

"Those poor guards. To be sent back to Gillian without even entering the castle." Emma laughed again, then turned to Clara to explain. "Sara didn't want them to reveal they'd accompanied just one lady to Kenshire. So she sent them off with a sack of food from Cook and extra coin for their troubles."

Clara had to admit the countess was quite clever.

Once they were a distance from the castle, Sara turned and pointed behind them, away from the water. "The view of the sea is my second favorite," she said.

Clara turned and gasped. From here, the entirety of Kenshire was visible. It spread like the wings of a bird in both directions from the main keep. Brockburg had looked impressive perched on its hill and seemingly stretching up into the clouds, but compared to Kenshire, it was nothing more than a single Pele tower.

"'Tis beautiful," she said honestly. The sun had not seen fit to show itself that day, and the clouds hovered over the castle, making it appear almost magical.

"Thank you," Sara said, accepting the compliment easily.

"Here." She pointed to an outcropping of rocks, many of which were flat as if they were made for sitting.

"I don't believe we've properly met," Emma said to Clara. "I am Emma Waryn."

"And much too impatient to wait for a proper introduction," Sara finished.

"And I am Clara. . ." She stopped. It seemed rude not to give the woman who'd just covered for her a full name.

"And Alfred," Sara interrupted.

Clara quietly exhaled.

"A lad. A visiting noblewoman. You are many things, Lady Clara—"

"Just Clara."

"But a lady nonetheless."

Emma and Sara both watched her, and she decided she could at least acknowledge that simple truth. "Aye, once I was a lady."

"Once," Emma repeated. "And while you're at Kenshire, you're a lady indeed. In fact, 'tis said we are dear friends already after travelling together!"

Clara smiled. "Then 'tis good to meet you, dear friend."

"Emma," Sara interrupted. "You mentioned news from Gillian?"

"Only that she wishes she could have come to visit."

Clara could tell Emma wanted to say more, but likely she did not wish to do so in her presence. Suddenly, she felt like an outsider. But of course, she was an outsider. She'd been an outsider ever since she'd left home.

"So tell me the plan," Emma said.

There was a plan?

"Geoffrey and Alex are expected back tomorrow," Sara started.

Clara's heart skipped a beat at the mention of Alex's name.

"Since Clara, pardon, Lady Susanna has not had the opportunity to enjoy herself in some time, I've planned a small. . . gathering."

"Oh dear," Emma's facial expression told Clara all she needed to know.

"'Tis just a welcome home for you both. Some musicians and a special meal."

Emma turned to Clara. "Sara refuses to do anything half-measure," she said. "Extra musicians and a special meal likely means something akin to a banquet—"

"Nay," Sara interrupted. "Nothing of the sort."

Clara should be alarmed at such news. . .

Emma rubbed her hands together.

"Can you blame me if I missed my sister-in-law? Now that I am unable to travel—"

"Poor Sara is bound to the most lovely castle in all of Northumbria with a most attentive husband. I do feel so badly for you."

The banter between the two ladies reminded Clara of sisters. If she ever had a sister-in law. . . she stopped herself. Such thoughts were useless. She would never be aught but alone.

"Just remember, it's Susanna, not Clara."

"And if Alex found his mother? You're sure they will return on the morrow?" Clara asked.

"Geoffrey said..." Sara paused and tilted her head to the side. "I suppose you're right. I believe he assumed their search would not be fruitful. I should speak to Cook to make her aware of the possibility they'll be late." She stood, and Clara and Emma followed suit.

"She will not be pleased," Sara muttered.

Emma turned back to grimace at Clara. Her face scrunched up in a way that forced a laugh from her, even though her thoughts had drifted to Alex. She wondered if he was okay. Had he found his mother? What would she say to him? Would anything make it better?

Emma turned toward the castle and rushed to follow Sara. Clara scurried to catch up with them both, her mood not quite as light as theirs. Though it felt wonderful not to don that hideous disguise, as Sara had called it, her concern for Alex and apprehension about the growing number of people who knew of her ruse overshadowed the excitement she'd initially felt.

She would try to dismiss the sense of apprehension that was settling over her. But as she watched Kenshire loom larger and larger the closer they came to the castle, Clara felt more and more trapped and more than a bit concerned for what the days ahead would bring.

———

Alex handed his reins to the groom and followed Geoffrey from the stable into Kenshire's bustling courtyard. The hour grew late and the castle inhabitants were likely preparing for the evening meal. Servants chased wayward children as knights entered the armory after a day of training. Tomorrow, he would join them. Now, more than ever, he needed a good fight.

"We'll find her," Geoffrey said beside him.

His unlikely ally slapped him on the back. "If she's anywhere near Elkview, word will reach us," he said as they made their way toward the entrance of the main keep.

After arriving at the village of Elkview, the two men had spoken to as many people as they could. Geoffrey had even gained entrance to the castle. The lord had recently passed away, and though its lady had been unavailable, the marshal who'd greeted them in her stead had assured them every effort would be made to assist in their search.

Oddly, they had not been invited to stay the evening, which was just as well. They'd already agreed to stay at a nearby inn so they could learn more and speak to a different sort of crowd. Unfortunately, however, they had come away with little information. Rising early, they'd ridden hard all day to get back to Kenshire. Alex was anxious to make use of the castle's proximity to the sea to wash off the dirt accumulated on his travels.

The only thing he looked forward to more was assuring himself that Clara was well.

"My lords," the grey-bearded steward rushed toward them. "My lady has been eagerly awaiting your return."

For the briefest of moments, Alex thought he meant Clara. But of course, that was not possible. To the rest of the world she was Alfred, not a lady.

Geoffrey stopped abruptly.

"What," he said to Peter, "is she planning?"

Alex wasn't sure what was happening, but those simple words elicited a guilty, wide-eyed look from the stern but affable steward.

"I am not sure what you—"

"Peter?"

A rooster chose that moment to escape from its master. All three men turned to the errant creature. By the time Alex looked back up, Peter was walking briskly away from them.

"Any guesses," Alex asked as they made their way through the courtyard.

"None," Geoffrey responded. "But I suspect we'll soon find out what is afoot."

When they finally entered the keep, Alex's laughter turned more than a few servants' heads.

"A banquet!" He couldn't help teasing the man who had, however unlikely, become something of a friend. "And you've only been gone for one night."

Flowers filled every crevice, and servants moved from the trestle tables to the cupboards at the sides of the hall and back again, their arms laden with drinking vessels.

"What the devil—"

"There you are!"

Lady Sara rushed toward them.

"Did Peter not tell you?"

"Tell us?" Geoffrey asked.

"Oh dear. Excuse my poor manners." She turned to Alex. "Did you find your mother?"

He shrugged. "Not yet."

She frowned and then turned to Geoffrey. Without warning,

she threw her arms around her husband, who embraced her in a display of public affection rivaling only Toren and Lady Juliette.

Alex shifted his weight and looked around the hall. Clara was nowhere to be seen. He did not want to interrupt their reunion, but he needed to know she was safe.

Sara unwrapped her arms around her husband, who seemed unwilling to let go.

"I fear your man is ill," she said, turning toward him.

"Ill?" His heart thudded in his chest. Clara was sick? Was it serious?

Sara pushed away from Geoffrey and leaned toward him. "She is not really," she whispered. "But please just trust me."

Not ill? "She's still here?"

"Of course." Then, more loudly to them both, "I have wonderful news."

Geoffrey pressed his lips into a fine line.

"Emma has returned with her dear friend Lady Susanna!"

Emma? Was that Geoffrey's. . .

"Lady Susanna?" Geoffrey asked.

"Oh husband," Sara shook her head and linked her arm to his. "You remember Lady Susanna." She leaned in and whispered something to him.

"Of course," he said, adding, "I look forward to seeing her again."

Nearby servants stared, and Alex didn't blame them. The entire conversation had baffled him. And he really only wanted to know about Clara.

"Lady Sara," he began.

But she cut him off. "You both must wash for dinner, and quickly. As you can see, I've planned a bit of a welcome for Emma, and I feared you would miss it. But you said one night, so I assumed. . ."

Lady Sara kept talking, but he only half listened. He wanted to see Clara. Her rooms were just above stairs, while his chamber was in a different tower entirely. He debated on whether or not to go to her now or—

"My lord," Sara turned back to him. "I'll have someone come to assist you."

He shot an envious look at the lord and lady. Clara was in *their* tower. But how could he go to her now without raising suspicions?

He couldn't.

"There is no need," he finally replied. "I thought to wash in the—"

"I've already had a bath prepared," she finished.

A bath. Alex smiled. "Your husband said you're always in need of new retainers," he quipped.

Lady Sara looked from him to Geoffrey, no doubt shocked at the change in their mutual demeanor. For him to even jest about becoming a retainer to Kenshire. . .

"The legendary Alex Kerr fighting for the English," Geoffrey's smile had started to come more frequently and easily over the two-day trip, and Alex was glad for it.

"Your sister would be pleased," Sara said, and Alex knew she was right. When Bryce and Toren had fought, it had nearly killed her. To have their two families find peace after so long. . .

They came to the place where the two parties parted and he wanted to ask again about Clara, who might or might not be ill. But it seemed best to wait for whatever scheme Sara had fashioned to unfold.

Alex would have to settle for seeing her at the meal.

"Are you in need of an escort?" Sara asked.

"No need," Alex said, trying to remember which passageway led to his rooms. He took a sharp right until he heard male laughter behind him.

Geoffrey.

So he'd made a wrong turn.

He turned and walked down an adjacent corridor, Geoffrey's

laughter echoing behind him. Catrina would, indeed, be grateful at the strides they'd made in mending their differences.

After a few additional wrong turns, he finally arrived at his destination. Opening the oak door to his chamber, he spied a large tub filled with water that, surprisingly, was still hot. Much preferable to the frigid saltwater of the North Sea.

As Alex discarded his dusty breeks, he wondered if his sister and brothers were right. Perhaps their mother was best left in the past, much like their feud with the Waryns. What good would it do to confront her? To ask her why she'd left? The fact remained that she had. . . She was already dead to them, as Reid had said over and over. It was a fool's quest to attempt to locate a woman who didn't want to be found. . .

He stepped into the tub, feeling more at peace than he had since leaving Brockburg. *It doesn't matter.* He repeated the phrase over and over and almost believed it by the time he finished scrubbing himself dry.

Besides, he had more pressing matters to attend to, namely Clara. What precisely was he to do with a squire he didn't want and a companion he wanted entirely too much? If she could trust him with the rest of her story, perhaps he could help her.

And then what?

At least he'd have the opportunity to speak to her tonight. Or, more precisely, "him," as she'd unfortunately be presenting herself as Alfred this eve at the impromptu celebration. One he needed to hurry to attend.

17

"I can't do this," Clara muttered to no one, pacing back and forth. Faye had just left after being summoned by Lady Sara. She didn't deserve their kindness. Clara was becoming more and more of a burden, and now, when they should be celebrating Emma's return, they were instead preoccupied with her preparations.

She'd endured more primping than she had the day her father had welcomed her first potential suitor. She had been young at the time, but her father must have known the years ahead would bring turmoil. He had pushed her to accept, something Clara could not bring herself to do. Her father would never have forced her, however, and the match hadn't gone through. Looking back, it was one mistake she regretted. Not for herself, but for Gilbert, who might still be alive if he hadn't been forced to become her protector.

Gilbert, who would have been appalled that she was putting herself in such danger.

A knock at the door startled her.

"My lady?" The young handmaiden who'd been assisting her

stepped into the room. "The others are already assembled in the hall."

She should be down there already. It was rude of her to delay.

"You look lovely," the girl said in a voice that was barely a whisper. She wanted to tell the girl such a thing didn't matter. But it would have been a lie. Despite herself, despite the fact that Clara was about to present herself—with no disguise—to a hall filled with people, she did care what she looked like.

She cared because of Alex.

When Sara and Emma had descended on her earlier to help her choose a gown—a beautiful deep blue confection with extremely low-hanging sleeves—they'd been all excitement. They'd squealed in delight upon seeing her freshly styled hair. Faye had captured the front tendrils in a braid that extended from both sides and met in the back. The majority of her hair hung unbound, now just a bit longer than her shoulders. She could almost believe their exclamations of delight at how beautiful she looked.

Clara had forgotten her predicament for a time, allowing herself to become engrossed in the process of becoming a lady once more. But doubts began to resurface now that she was left alone with her thoughts. What if someone recognized her? Sara had declared it impossible, that the celebration would be limited to their regular household, all those who lived and worked at Kenshire.

But that didn't stop her from fretting.

"Shall I tell her you're coming?"

Clara had forgotten the girl's presence.

"Aye," she said, following her out of the chamber and down the long passageway that led to the lower floor. Clara made her way toward the balcony that overlooked the hall, wanting to see Alex before he spied her first. Unfortunately, a guard, the man ever present at the top of the stairs, stepped in her path.

"My lady," he said, holding out his arm.

Normally she was perfectly capable of descending the stairs on her own. This evening, she wasn't so sure. A harp played a soft melody below, and the clangs of metal, preparations for the first course, could be heard as they approached the winding staircase that led directly to the hall's east entrance. As they stood at the top, she could see below for the briefest of moments before they began to walk down the stairs.

With her free hand, Clara clutched her dress, pulling it upward in an attempt to avoid spilling headfirst into one of the wall torches that lit their way. As they wound their way down, Clara caught brief glimpses of color and lights. Candles and people.

She couldn't look.

Finally, they were at the bottom.

It took just the briefest of glances to find him.

Alex, along with his host, was staring at her. In fact, everyone seemed to be doing so. Clara wanted nothing more than to turn and run back up the stairs. She was so used to looking down to avoid suspicion—and attention—that she found herself doing so now.

The knight beside her released her arm. She murmured her thanks as Emma came running up beside her.

"Lady Susanna, where have you been? We were worried you may have taken ill."

If that was a question about her well-being, Clara's answer came easily enough. "I just may yet," she said. Emma laughed, but Clara was not jesting.

She allowed Emma to lead her around the trestle tables toward the back of the hall. She stared at the raised platform, looking at the shining silver goblets and candles that seemed to be everywhere. She focused her gaze there. . . anywhere but on—

"Lady Susanna?"

Him.

She and Emma stopped as the others moved around them, making their way to the dais.

She turned, and Emma let her arm drop. Geoffrey's sister winked as she joined the others, abandoning her with Alex.

Was he angry? Confused?

He looked neither. Alex's perpetual grin was back, a welcoming smile that made everyone around him feel compelled to speak. To bare their soul as she had done. The smell of sandalwood competed with his own unique scent. Her fingers ached with the need to touch him.

"I don't believe we've had the pleasure, but it appears there is no one to introduce us."

He was enjoying this. Clara was not. Anxiety crept up her spine.

"Your reputation proceeds you, my lord," she said for the benefit of the servant threading

his way around them.

Alex bowed. "Alex Kerr of Brockburg," he said, taking her hand.

His eyes glinted as he lowered his head and touched his lips to her flesh. A flood of warmth flowed from her hand to the rest of her body. His lips stayed there just a moment longer than was proper.

"And I—"

"Are the most beautiful woman on either side of the border," he finished.

He let go of her hand, and Clara was saved from giving him yet another false name. It wasn't the first time he had complimented her. But it was the first time she felt confident enough in herself as a woman to believe him. His eyes never left her face, and his expression. . . it was if he saw her for the first time. And in some ways, perhaps he did.

"You are most gracious, my lord."

He took her arm in the crook of his own, and they made their way to their seats. Her gentle Scottish warrior. After so many years of posing as someone else, it felt so natural, so right, to look the part of a lady and to be escorted to the dinner by Alex Kerr. Lord help her, she could get used to such a feeling.

"Lady Emma," he said, bowing once again as he released her arm and pulled out the

empty seat next to the youngest Waryn.

His own seat was on the other side of Geoffrey's. She watched him make his way there, her eyes taking in his fine figure in his evening clothes. He was dressed more formally than normal, the surcoat he wore stopping short of his waist, shorter than most men's. His white undershirt deliciously complimented his tanned skin. Emma leaned in toward her.

"Why didn't you tell me?" she accused, the mischievous sparkle in her eyes putting Clara immediately on the defensive.

"I'm not sure what you mean."

She nodded to the cupbearer, who filled her cup with a deep red wine.

"He's a fine man," Emma whispered. "For a Kerr," she added.

"Your brother is married to a Kerr," she reminded her, stealing a glance at Alex, who appeared to be in deep conversation with Geoffrey. But just as she was about to look away, he caught her eye.

And winked!

The Scotsman was incorrigible. Every person in the hall would know of their 'affinity' by the end of the evening.

"You've met Lady Catrina," Emma said eagerly.

"Aye, your brother is quite lucky."

"They are both lucky," she responded, glancing at Sara, who smiled and nodded in agreement.

"I understand you have another brother?"

"Neill is my twin," Emma said, a wistfulness in her voice.

"You miss him."

Clara took a sip of wine. Delicious. Though she'd forgotten how cumbersome the draped sleeves could be.

"Very much," she said. "When we lived with my aunt and uncle, after. . . well, after we lost Bristol, we were inseparable. I love all of my brothers, but Neill. . .

"Where is he now?" Clara thought she'd heard something about him being fostered.

"At Langford Castle."

"Langford," Clara repeated. "I've not heard of it."

"It was once a Caiser holding, but it was given to a man by the name of Sir Adam Dayne many years ago. He was fostered by my grandfather. 'Tis an interesting tale—"

Emma was cut off by the appearance of the first course.

The first of many.

"I've not eaten so much in one sitting," Clara said much later, after the food had finally stopped coming. With every passing moment, she relaxed just a bit more. Emma was an easy companion, and their 'forced' friendship felt like it was fast becoming a real one. As Sara had said, the visitors at the banquet were limited to two wealthy merchants passing through Kenshire to the border. The others were all Kenshire knights, retainers, and servants. It *should* be safe.

"'Tis nice to see you smile," Emma commented.

Clara immediately looked at Alex.

"He does appear in good humor most often. I'm not surprised he and Bryce did not get along very well."

Clara thought it might have more to do with their shared history than their dispositions, though she did agree Sir Bryce appeared somewhat surly. But she kept that thought to herself.

"I'm sorry his quest was not successful," Clara said of Alex's search for his mother.

"We shall see."

Clara looked at Emma. "What do you mean?"

"Geoffrey believes there's hope yet they may find her."

Clara tore her eyes from Alex when Sara caught her staring. He was just so easy to look at, so appealing to the eye.

She sat back, the effects of too much wine beginning to take effect. It had been some time since she'd allowed herself more than one goblet at a sitting.

She allowed the conversation to flow around her and tried not to look at him too much. Clara smoothed the front of her gown under the table, the soft velvet under her fingers reminding her of happier times. Reminding her of home.

"I've never seen you so happy."

She whipped her head around. How had Alex come to be behind her?

"May I speak with your friend, Lady Emma?"

She appeared to consider it.

"Mayhap, sir. Are your intentions honorable?" she teased.

Clara giggled.

"Perhaps. And if they are not?" he teased in return.

"Then you most certainly may not speak to Lady Susanna," she said.

Clara turned to watch the exchange in full.

"Well, then you give me no choice. You have my word, Lady Emma."

Emma was not to be put off so easily. "You forget, Scotsman, I was raised with three brothers. I will have your word your intentions are honorable. Or your word they are not?"

This time Alex laughed aloud and Clara joined him.

"Very well. You have my word my intention is simply to speak with your friend."

Apparently satisfied, Emma moved her chair away so that Clara could stand.

Since their hosts had already left the dais and were currently dancing to the harpist's soft melody, she and Alex were free to move about the hall as well.

"Where are we going?" she asked.

In answer, he led her around the corner at the far end of the hall. A cushioned seat sat in the middle of a circular cutout in the wall, softly lit by a torch. Alex waited for her to sit, then sat opposite her.

"Lady Susanna."

"'Twas Sara and Emma's idea."

"I'm surprised you went along with it."

"Not as surprised as I am."

"But I'm glad you agreed." He sighed, his eyes intent on hers. "Tell me all, Clara. Let me help you."

She didn't know what to say.

"Do you think I'd ever harm you?"

"Nay, of course not," she said, and knew it to be true. "But Gilbert. . ."

"Is no longer here to protect you. But I am."

"For how long?" she asked.

"For as long as you need me."

Clara leaned forward, wanting very much to reach out to him.

Alex seemed to understand and took her hand.

"I cannot put you in danger—"

"Clara," he said and then lowered his voice. Though their conversation was private, neither could see around the corner. "I am in danger, you are in danger—every single person who travels or lives along the border is constantly in danger. But no more so than a woman travelling in disguise from tournament to tournament. You are competent, capable, and stronger than any woman I know. But someday the wrong person will learn your secret, someone stronger than you. You needn't be alone any longer."

She wanted to tell him. To trust him.

"Not here," she said. "'Tis too exposed."

"I will come to you tonight."

Her heart leapt, but she couldn't tell whether it was alarm at the thought of revealing her secret to him or excitement at the thought of being alone with Alex once more.

"Tell me of your journey," she said.

He sighed and sat back, crossing his legs in front of him.

"She was nowhere to be found. Either the merchant was mistaken or Elkview is not

where she calls home."

"So what will you do?"

He grinned, but Clara had learned to distinguish Alex's genuine smiles from the ones he presented to the world to convince them he was truly happy.

"Geoffrey believes we should stay here for at least a few days. That someone will respond to our inquiries. But I'm not as sure." He looked at her. "What do you think, lass?"

"Do you still want to find her?"

He looked thoughtful. "I don't know," he finally said, and Clara knew it was the most honest answer he could give her.

"You've said Toren and Reid have everything under control at Brockburg."

"If Reid starts a war in my stead at the Day of Truce, we'll get word of it soon enough," he joked.

"Then mayhap you should stay."

He lowered his chin, staring at her with intent eyes. "*We* should stay."

She didn't answer immediately.

"Clara?"

"Aye," she agreed. For now. Maybe she would have to leave him, but she wasn't ready yet.

"Then it's settled." He stood and took her hand, leading her back to the hall, but not before he leaned in close and whispered, "Tonight."

When he squeezed her hand, Clara squeezed back.

Gilbert, I hope you can forgive me.

Alex led Clara back to the hall. Or Lady Susanna.

Whomever she was this eve, she certainly was not Alfred.

The moment Clara descended the stairs, Alex had known he was in trouble.

It had almost felt as if he was seeing her for the first time. Clara was more herself tonight. He could see it in every movement. Even her speech, which was nearly always guarded, seemed less stilted. The gown, her hair. . . they certainly drew the eye, but it was the ease with which she'd walked into the room that had grabbed his attention. And her voice which had so easily become one of a highborn lady.

He'd watched her throughout the evening, talking happily with Emma and Sara, and it was more evident than ever that Clara had been nobly born. Though she'd been remarkably adaptive out of necessity, she was meant for gowns and good graces, not smudges of dirt and a constant feeling of apprehension.

And he was determined to give her what she deserved. Permanently.

He could hear his brother laughing at him now. Alex was not too stubborn to admit Toren had been right. It mattered little that she was English. Or that they would have plenty of difficulties to work through together.

"Here," Geoffrey handed him a mug of ale.

They stood to the side, watching as the ladies circled one another in dance, the wives of Kenshire's retainers joining them. It seemed they'd scared the males back to their seats, or perhaps the others were as content as he and his host to simply watch the festivities.

"Gillian's friend seems quite nice."

Nice. He would use many words to describe Clara, and though 'nice' was certainly one of them, so many others sprang to mind.

"She appears to be getting along well with your sister," he said.

"It appears so," Geoffrey commented as the two women in question locked arms and laughed as if they had not a care in the world. She deserved this. Alex was glad the women had talked her into the ruse, even if it only lasted for a few days.

"I was so consumed with the search for my mother, I don't believe I've offered my congratulations," Alex said, nodding to Lady Sara.

Geoffrey beamed. "If it weren't for the dangers, I would be even more overjoyed."

They continued to watch the women, each buried in his own thoughts, until Geoffrey broke the silence.

"Does she know?"

Alex could pretend not to understand. But the effort would be futile.

"I believe so," he said. As if she divined they were speaking about her, Clara glanced over at him. "But she doesn't trust me completely."

"Then earn her trust." Geoffrey said it as if it were the easiest thing in the world to do. "But know your intentions if you don't care to hurt her."

Alex looked at his host.

"I fell in love with Sara well before I was prepared to do so. And nearly lost her because of it."

"What happened?" he asked, genuinely curious.

"I finally decided to value myself as much as I did her," he said as Sara approached them.

"Dance with me," Sara said to her husband.

Their conversation forgotten, Geoffrey handed Alex his mug and scooped Sara up into his arms. "Gladly," he replied, carrying his wife from the hall amidst cheers and the banging of mugs.

Alex couldn't help but smile. He wasn't sure if she'd referred to *that* kind of dance.

He leaned against the cold stone wall, two mugs in hand, content to watch the scene from afar. Once the cheers died down after the lord and lady of Kenshire made their unconventional exit from the hall, the trestle tables were moved to the sides of the room to make way for more dancers.

Alex barely registered the goings-on, his mind fixed on Clara.

How had his feelings for her grown so strong in such a short period of time?

More importantly, what the hell was he going to do about it? What kind of life could he offer her living as a second son at Brockburg? Assuredly, it would be better than travelling from place to place as a squire, but he wanted more for her than that. He wanted to give her the life she deserved.

He would *not* claim Dunmure Tower. He wished to have nothing to do with the place.

And then she looked at him. He noticed the stolen glance because he'd not taken his eyes from her all eve. Who was his former squire? What secrets did she hide?

He would finally find out... tonight.

1 8

Though Emma's chamber was just one floor above the great hall, Clara couldn't hear any of the festivities below. The main keep had been constructed for defense, and the walls were thick. Though modifications had clearly been made over the years, the original intent of the winding stairs which she had just climbed were to prevent attackers from ascending to the second floor. The thick oak door she closed behind her was both ornate and purposeful, its iron lock meant as a last defense—which, according to Sara, had never been tested.

But tonight she left the door unlocked.

She sat on the edge of the bed, grateful for the fire that crackled in the stone hearth in the corner of the room. She had begged Emma to reclaim her bedchamber, but neither she nor Sara would hear of it. They'd insisted there were plenty of empty chambers for Emma. Though the lord and lady had retired earlier, she'd left Emma in the hall. Her new friend had insisted she would not retire until the musicians stopped playing.

"If there's music," she'd said, "there's dancing. Sleep can wait."

Clara had never met someone so full of life as the youngest Waryn, and she liked her immensely. But Alex's departure from the hall had pulled her attention away from her conversation with her companion.

"You're not thinking of going after him, are you?"

Emma's tone had been merely curious, not accusatory.

"Heavens, no!"

It wasn't quite a lie, for *he* would be coming to *her*.

"Oh Susanna," Emma said, tsking softly. "Don't deny that your head has been turned in Alex Kerr's direction every time you thought no one noticed."

"Was I so obvious?"

Emma stood on her tiptoes, stuck her neck in the air, and peered at the place where Alex had last stood in such an exaggerated fashion that Clara couldn't help but burst into laughter.

"I did no such thing."

In answer, Emma pretended to peer around an invisible barrier, first to the right and then to the left. "Pardon me while I stare at that tapestry," she said.

Clara placed her hands firmly on her hips. "But 'tis such a fine-looking tapestry," she said.

The remembered laughter echoed in Clara's ears now as she sat in silence, waiting.

She had Sara and Emma to thank for this night. And Alex as well, for it was he who had first encouraged her to discard her disguise. And even if this escape only lasted a few days, Clara would be able to hold onto these memories the next time she pinned her hair up and—

A quick knock and the door swung open.

Alex wore only his breeks and a linen shirt with its sleeves rolled up. He closed the door and moved toward her with long, purposeful strides. Without a word, Alex reached out to grab her hands, pulling her from the bed.

"I—"

He lowered his mouth to hers, covering her lips with his own. His tongue quickly followed, and Clara's thoughts lost any semblance of coherence. She wrapped her arms around his waist and he pulled her closer, his hands settling gently on either side of her head.

When he pulled his head back, Clara felt the loss immediately.

"You are so beautiful."

She looked down at her gown. "Aye, Emma choose it—"

"Not the gown, you."

His hands continued to hold her as she drew her brows together. "But—"

"This was the first time I've seen you like this."

He dropped his hands and backed away from her.

He gestured toward the gown. "Tis lovely. But your smile. Your laughter. 'Twas as if I saw *you*, Clara, for the first time."

He blinked. "Though I still don't know who you are."

She took a deep breath, confident in her decision but nonetheless frightened to say the

words.

The overly large Scot, who was in charge of a small army, who fought like the devil himself, sat down on the edge of the bed and pulled her down next to him so gently Clara thought her heart might break. He cradled her hand and looked into her eyes, beseeching her to open herself to him.

Gilbert had told her to keep this secret above all else. But he'd also told her to trust her instincts, and she would follow the latter piece of advice now.

"My name is Clara Wheaton, daughter of the late Edward Wheaton, Lord Barrington, a once-favored baron and second of that name."

"Barrington. . ." he repeated.

"'Tis a small castle with no village to speak of. The closest establishment is three days' ride from the northern border of our land. And even that is isolated, for Keston House is known for—"

"Smuggling."

"Aye."

"Your father was a border lord."

"He was. And unfortunately. . ."

She couldn't do it.

"Tell me," Alex said, his voice barely a whisper.

"A supporter of de Montfort," she blurted.

She watched his face, which stayed remarkably neutral despite the implications of such an admission. de Montfort had led a revolt against the King of England. And her father had supported such a folly.

"My father fought for his king," she tried to explain, "and was injured, nearly fatally so, for his efforts. But after he lost my mother—" Clara was grateful for the gentle squeeze of his hand, "—those who knew him said he changed. The father I knew grew angrier, more bitter with every passing year. To me, he was the gentlest and kindest man alive. But he also sheltered me more than necessary to my way of thinking. In his final years, he became nearly crazed with fear that something would happen to me, and though he wanted no part in the First Barons' War, by twelve hundred and sixty-nine, he was firmly in de Montfort's camp."

She closed her eyes, remembering the man she had loved above all others. It still hurt that someone she so respected and loved had allowed fear to override his good sense. "He was nearly killed at the Siege of Kenilworth," she said, almost as an afterthought. Of course, it was not. That siege was the end of the baron's revolt against the king as well as her life as Clara Wheaton.

"They came for him," Alex guessed.

"Aye, and for Barrington Castle. The king's armies were relentless in their pursuit of the traitors. My father returned to me safely just in time to be murdered by the king's henchmen."

He squeezed her hand once again. "I'm sorry, Clara."

Now that she started, she just couldn't seem to stop.

"I watched it happen, saw the blade slide into his neck.

Watched him crumple to the ground." She'd told him this part before, but the words wouldn't stop gushing out of her. Tears threatened to spill onto her cheeks. "I didn't scream. I didn't try to stop it. I stood there watching, immobile."

"You could not have—"

"When Gilbert grabbed me, I thought he was an attacker. I turned and hit him with such force, his shoulder hurt for days. Or so he said."

Her cheeks tingled, the scene so clear in her mind it was as if she were experiencing it anew. "My father, the proud man who kept me safe all my life, who survived the bloodiest of battles only to die in his own hall, a traitor to the crown."

She let the tears flow. Alex pulled her close as she kept talking. Mumbling really. "As I said, I see it every night. Most nights. Not with you, though. But last night."

"Shhh, lass." He held her so tightly against him that Clara could feel the knot in his tunic pressing against her cheek.

"Sometimes, I'm running across the hall. Other times, I simply stand there, as it truly happened. Still others, we're on a battle-field. . . not that I've been on a battlefield before. . . but 'tis what I imagine one would look like. Every time, the man stands beside my father, his face hidden. And Father never looks. He never turns his head, no matter how loudly I scream for him to do so. It ends the same way every time."

She couldn't continue.

"No one should be forced to witness such a thing."

The sounds Clara made were hardly recognizable as her own. But she didn't care.

He pulled her hair away from her face, rubbing her cheeks with the back of his hand.

"I'm so sorry," he repeated over and over.

Eventually her sobs became sighs. She would finish the story. The whole story.

"Gilbert pulled me away from there, and we used the secret passageway to escape."

"You had no time to leave before they came?"

She shook her head. "It was as if they'd followed my father, and the others who'd escaped, directly from the siege." She rushed to continue, "Our people were lucky. Barrington was seized, and my father killed, but most of our household was spared. Some of the 'traitors' lost everything. Everyone. The price for revolt was more than being stripped of titles and land. Some lost their entire families and all of their supporters to death or imprisonment."

"And the ruse?"

"You've heard of Margoth?"

"Was she the woman responsible for Simon de Montfort's loss at Kenilworth?"

"Aye. Rumor was that she disguised herself as a man and warned Prince Edward of the earl's unguarded state. 'Twas his foolishness, and her cunning, that led to the end of his misguided campaign."

"The earl should consider himself lucky to be dead, for it sounds as if you would do the job yourself if given half a chance."

Clara sat up and looked at Alex's poor shirt, which she'd just soaked with her tears.

"My father came to believe in him, but to me, he and his followers were responsible for the loss of my father. So now you know."

"And when Barrington's armorer decided you were no longer safe as a woman, Alfred was born," he said. "And you believe, so many years later, that if your identity were discovered—"

"I would be imprisoned. Or killed."

Alex took both of her hands in his. "But Clara, the Dictum of Kenilworth—"

"Protects those who were not among the earl's most fervent supporters."

"And your father was one of those men?"

She nodded her head. "He gave everything to a cause he believed in. And he paid the ultimate price."

Alex sighed. "I don't know your English politics well enough—"

"But I do." She needed him to understand.

"If you were to live in Scotland—"

"You know the borderlands are unique and nearly indistinguishable. Perhaps farther north. . ."

Panic welled in her.

"Alex, you must never tell anyone. My father was considered a traitor. If his daughter were found alive—"

"I will not—" his voice held the conviction she needed to hear, "—tell anyone without your permission. Ever."

"And I will not give it. Ever."

He leaned toward her then and kissed her, gently this time. His lips, so soft and warm, were a welcome respite from having to relive the worst moment of her life.

But he did not press her. Instead, he pulled away and stood.

"Alex, what are you doing?"

"Undressing," he said casually, as if it were the most natural thing in the world.

Indeed, he took off his boots and trewes, everything but his shirt, before she could form a single coherent thought.

"Stand up, let me help you."

"Alex, I—" She stood, confused.

He untied the laces at the back of her gown quickly, efficiently. Otherwise, he didn't move to touch her. When she was free of the heavy gown, she stepped out of it, and he pointed to her leather shoes. She took them off, leaving her completely bare but for the silken chemise Emma had lent her.

But he wasn't even looking at her. Alex had already climbed into the bed.

"What are you—"

"I will not touch you tonight. Not in that way."

"Then why—"

"Your nightmares," he said simply, and finally Clara understood. He was going to sleep here to save her from the dreams.

"Alex, I don't believe this is quite proper."

He laughed, a deep, sexy sound that made her wish he had not promised he wouldn't touch her.

"I believe you're right," he said, mimicking her more proper tone. "I will be gone before anyone wakes."

"But someone will see you!"

"Clara. . ."

He was asking that she trust him. And she did. Clara moved to the other side of the bed and lay next to him.

Alex pulled her close, the feel of his hard, muscular chest under her cheek more familiar than it should be.

He kissed the top of her head, and Clara smiled against him. She'd told him everything, and he'd not recoiled in horror. He had not run from the chamber to tell everyone or looked at her as if she were a lunatic. Or a traitor.

She allowed the temporary contentment to flow through her as she listened to the crackle of the fire intermingled with the sound of Alex's steady heartbeat. And drifted off to a blessedly peaceful sleep.

By all that was holy, Alex would not get a moment's sleep this night. No matter how hard he tried, he could not calm his body— as if he were some randy lad and not a disciplined man perfectly capable of sleeping with a desirable woman draped across him.

Though she was not just any desirable woman. . . that was the problem. She was Clara. Or rather, Lady Clara, daughter of a baron who'd consorted with the man who had almost defeated and bested the English king. If not for the circumstances at Eversham, which had put the earl in such a precarious position, many believed he would have eventually gained enough support to succeed.

Instead, Simon de Montfort's body had been mutilated and scattered across England. But did Clara still have a reason to be afraid? Though she would likely never reclaim what should have been her inheritance, Alex wasn't convinced the king would be looking for every child, sibling, or relative of de Montfort's supporters. But he could easily understand the reason for her continued deception.

English bastards.

If only she'd gotten a good look at the man who'd murdered her father in front of her. Alex would have gladly hunted the man to the ends of this godforsaken country and slit his throat.

Clara, already sleeping, turned from him, but he didn't have time to mourn the loss of his sweet Englishwoman. From the opposite direction, Clara sought the warmth of his body from behind. She wiggled as close to his side as possible, her bottom pressing up against him.

He groaned.

"Alex," she mumbled, not as deeply asleep as he had assumed.

"Mmm," he murmured.

"Are you okay?" She yawned, and he held back his answer. He'd nearly done something extremely foolish that night at the inn, when he'd instructed her on the 'pains' he was currently experiencing. And if he answered that question, he'd place them in the same compromising position.

As if sharing a bed with an unmarried maid, the one he desired above all others, were not compromising enough. But after hearing the rest of her story, he'd decided this was the one thing he could do for her, the one way he could show his unflinching support. If his presence could at least save her from her nightmares and give her a full night's rest, then by God, he would sleep here every night.

"Alex?"

She turned, moving the feather-stuffed pillow under her head, and faced him. He could see her from the corner of his eye. And she was decidedly awake.

"Go to sleep, Clara." If his voice was harsh, it was with good reason.

"I'm not tired."

The way she said it...

He could not look at her.

"You were sleeping just moments ago." He turned his back to her and prayed she would not pursue this.

"You said you desired me."

"Please, Clara, don't."

"And that you'd not take the virginity of a maid. A woman whose name you did not know."

His cock responded to the implication of her words. But he did not turn to face her. If he did, he would be lost.

"Now you know my name."

He would not do this. Could not do it. He needed to be blunt. Without turning, he finally responded. "You said it should not matter."

She was quiet for a moment. "I was angry you had rejected me."

"Rejected?"

He did turn then, and Lord, he wished he had not. She'd taken out the braids. When had she done that? Her hair splayed across the white pillow, the fire casting a soft glow from behind. She looked like an angel. One he refused to allow to fall from grace.

"I did not, would not, reject you, Clara. Not then, not ever. But I will also not allow myself the pleasure of a woman who doesn't belong to me."

"I am not an ox, Alex. I belong to no one."

He wasn't doing a good job of explaining. "If I took you in my arms, pulled you toward me, took your mouth, your body, your maidenhood. What then? Would we marry? Return to Brockburg to live with Toren and Juliette?"

"I will never be able to marry." She said it with such bleak conviction, he believed her.

"You don't know that," he said.

"Did you not hear what I told you earlier? I am the daughter of a traitor, hunted down by a man who will soon be the King of England. I've already lost my father and Gilbert. Do you think I have any desire to see another man killed protecting me?"

Clara still didn't move. Though her words were impassioned, her expression remained neutral. She truly believed that anyone who tried to protect her was in mortal danger.

"Do you believe either of those men would not give their lives twice over to save you again? That I would not do the same? Would it be necessary to do so living in Scotland?

This time, her expression did change. "What are you saying?" she whispered.

"I'm saying, Clara of Barrington, that some things are more important to a man than his life."

And damn if he didn't mean it.

He couldn't stay here. He had thought he could protect her and act honorably, but he could not. If he stayed a moment longer, Alex would pull her against him and bury himself so deeply inside her neither of them would ever question his intentions again.

Without another word, he turned from her, got out of the bed, and dressed. He forced himself not to look back at her as he made his way to the door. His hand hesitated for just a moment, but good sense prevailed.

Alex walked out as quietly as he had entered.

"I saw the way you and Alex Kerr looked at each other last eve. So no, I don't believe you," Emma said to Clara, who followed her down the sea path to the water's edge.

When Alex had not made an appearance in the hall to break his fast, she'd been both relieved and annoyed. The elation she'd felt the evening before had completely faded.

Lady Susanna was a lie. She could never safely be herself, and Alex could never be hers.

"There is nothing between us," she said for the tenth time that morning. But when Emma spun around and caught her smiling—she couldn't help but react to the absurdity of her own comment—Clara was caught.

"So there may be something, but—"

"May be, might be, *is*," Emma replied.

After breaking their fast, Emma had taken Clara around Kenshire. They'd missed the midday meal because of it, but Emma hadn't seemed concerned. They'd visited the kitchen upon their return, and Clara had discovered why. Cook, a plump, stern-looking woman, had given Emma a basket of bread and cheese with a mild admonishment. "Miss another meal, mi'lady, and don't expect your pears at dinner."

Though Cook was outspoken for a servant, Clara could see she enjoyed a close relationship with Lady Emma. The relationship between the family and their servants reminded her very much of Barrington. Like Gilbert, many of their servants and retainers had been more like family to them. It had made losing her home that much harder.

They sat on the same rocks as before. It was nice to rest for a moment.

Emma opened the basket and tore off a piece of bread, handing it to her with a chunk of cheese. They ate in companionable silence, and Clara tried to enjoy the unusually sunny day. It was easy to understand why this was Sara's favorite spot in all of Kenshire.

"Tell me," Emma said, packing up the remainder of their light repast.

Both dressed simply in front-laced sideless surcoats, hers borrowed, of course. The white of their under tunics peeked out, making them appear almost twins in dress although they were very different in other ways. Clara found herself wishing she could remain friends with both Emma and Lady Sara. If only there was a way she could stop hiding. . .

"There's naught to tell," she lied.

Emma rolled her eyes. "Have you been intimate with him?"

Clara gasped.

"I leave protocol to other ladies. Well, not Sara. And definitely not my new sister-in-law. That woman curses as badly, nay, worse, than any man. Actually—"

"Okay, okay."

"I do suppose we hardly know each other. But—"

"We have," she admitted.

Emma's eyes widened. "Have you—"

"Nay!"

After Alex's hasty departure last night, she'd been left much too angry to sleep. How could he simply walk away without a word in parting? Later, after she'd calmed down a bit, confusion had replaced anger. He desired her. Wanted to protect her. Said that he'd give his own life to keep her safe, and she believed him.

And yet he still wouldn't make love to her.

Strangely, her assertion that she would never marry had seemed to upset him. But he had always seemed the sort of man to evade marriage—didn't he feel the same way? Or had he changed his mind? It mattered not. Even if he would sacrifice himself for her, she could not allow it—but she still did not want to die an old maid, unfamiliar with the ways of love.

"You're thinking of it."

"I've thought of little else," she admitted.

"I don't understand," Emma said. "What is preventing it? He clearly desires you."

"It's complicated."

"Actually, it's quite simple." The two women sprang to their feet upon hearing the deep voice.

Alex! How long had he been standing there?

"Alex, what are you—"

Emma stood, grabbed Cook's basket, and started to walk away.

"Nay, Lady Emma, you don't have to leave," Clara insisted.

Emma scrunched her lips to the side as if in thought. "Mayhap you're right. I could stay. In fact, this should be interesting."

She promptly sat back down.

Alex, who had clearly come directly from training, his tunic tinged with dirt and even a smattering of blood, turned to her.

"While I would enjoy nothing more than to provide you with an afternoon of entertainment, I do believe your initial instincts were correct, Lady Emma. Mayhap you should leave."

Her new friend stood once again and marched right up to Alex. She stood so close Clara thought for a moment she might hit him.

"And you are sorely mistaken if you think to find another woman such as this one."

With that, Emma Waryn winked at her and promptly walked back to the castle.

Clara stared after her for a moment, unsure of how to feel. Then she met Alex's eyes, and both of them burst into spontaneous laughter.

"She thinks highly of me," Alex said, teasing.

"I tend to agree with her," Clara said.

As Alex made his way toward her, Clara shifted on the flat rock.

"Even after last eve?" he asked.

He reached out a hand.

She took it.

"Despite my better judgment, aye."

He didn't let go of her hand when she stood. Instead, he wound his fingers through hers. They fit nicely between her own, and the contact sent a wave of warmth through her.

Alex led her away from the castle and toward the shore.

"Wait," he said, coming to a sudden stop. He removed his leather boots and looked at her, nodding. She took the hint and removed her own as well. They tossed them aside, and he took her hand again as if it were the most natural thing in the world.

Though the sun had not yet set, it would do so before long. "This is my favorite time of day," she said.

"Why?"

They continued walking, the sand now wet beneath their feet as they moved closer and closer to the water's edge.

"My father worried about everything. Reivers, enemies, even allies. The more paranoid he became, the less inclined he was to allow me to accompany him on his travels. To compensate, he built an elaborate bench and even fashioned a pile of rocks that funneled water from a nearby stream through the garden. I could sit there, just before dusk, and listen to the sound of flowing water for hours."

Hand in hand, they stood listening to the gentle lapping of the waves as they came ashore.

"Did you fall back asleep last eve?"

She almost lied, knowing the truth would upset him, but decided against it.

"Nay."

"I'm sorry, Clara. I was a fool to promise to stay and then break that promise by leaving."

"You *are* a fool," she said, "but for other reasons."

He turned her toward him. "That may be so," he said. "But I only spoke the truth."

She wasn't sure they were talking about the same thing.

"I don't know what you want, Clara."

His laughing eyes were strangely dark, uncharacteristically serious.

"You," she said. "I want you, Alex."

The look he gave her was clear. This was why he'd come.

He was finally going to give her what she asked for.

She could sense the change in his mood. Her mouth, moist and ready for him, opened just slightly. He leaned toward her, his mouth moving over hers in a kiss meant to claim. Their tongues dueled in the way he'd taught her, and the groan she heard was her own.

They pressed together so tightly she could feel the evidence of his need against her. Tearing himself away, he discarded his tunic, leaving her with a view even more spectacular than the one to her right. She wanted to touch every inch of him, and she did. Clara caressed and grasped him, his muscles tensing under her fingers, as he moved his mouth from her lips to her neck. She leaned her head back to give him better access, and he took it.

His other hand moved to her bodice. She hadn't noticed him untying the laces when his bare hand moved over her breast. He squeezed gently, in rhythm with his mouth, and she unabashedly pressed herself toward him, the feeling between her legs building.

"Just the surcoat," he muttered. She didn't know what he meant.

He abruptly changed course and, before she understood his intent, Alex pushed both fabrics aside to allow for better access. He cupped her breast in his hand and lowered his mouth to it.

"Alex!"

His tongue circled her nipple, hard beneath his deliberate ministrations. He teased and tortured her until she called his name again. He took her nipple into his mouth and nipped it, holding it lightly between his teeth. She sucked in a breath and forgot to let it back out.

"I..." She didn't know how to describe what she was feeling.

He lifted his mouth and looked directly at her, his eyes hungry.

"I know," he said.

What did he know?

He reached down and pulled up her surcoat, under tunic, and shift in one easy motion.

"I'm going to remedy that."

"What—"

She never finished the thought. Alex moved his hand toward her as if the layers of clothing didn't exist. He was going to touch her. There!

"Alex, I'm not sure—"

"I am, lass. And there's only one way to fix it."

With that, he placed his hand over the most intimate part of her. This time he didn't merely press a palm against her—he actually pushed his finger inside. For a moment, she was frozen with shock, but then he began to move, pressing his hand against her as he thrust his finger in and out, and pleasure coursed through her.

He watched her face and she stared right back. He swallowed, lifting his chin just slightly as his hand began to move faster still.

She couldn't hold his gaze. Clara closed her eyes and tilted her head back.

"Please." She wanted more.

He gave it to her.

Her breaths were coming quicker and quicker, and a shudder escaped from her shoulders and made its way down to where his hand wrought the most exquisite feelings she'd ever experienced in her life.

As the pleasure coursing through her continued to build, she tried to get even closer. She pressed into him, a moan escaping. She didn't care. She just wanted. . .

That!

When the shudder came this time, it started from the inside and worked its way across her entire body. She cried out, holding on to him for fear of crumpling to the sand below. She pulsed around him, and Alex refused to let her go. His hand stayed where it was until she opened her eyes.

His smile started small and then grew into the most devilishly handsome grin.

"Was I right?"

He pulled his hand away, and she immediately mourned its loss. Her skirts fell back around her, and Alex pulled the laces of her surcoat back together.

"You self-assured—"

"Passionate."

"That's not what I was going to say."

Still grinning, he tied her stays as expertly as if he'd done it more than once before.

"Sensual," he ventured.

She shook her head.

"Nay, that's not quite right either."

Finishing, he stood back and crossed his arms.

"Accomplished. I believe what you meant to say is accomplished."

She shook her head, unable to stop smiling.

And then he began to unlace the top of his trewes.

"What are you doing?"

His hands froze. "If your female sensibilities will be offended, now is the time to look away."

She didn't want to turn, but it felt like the right thing to do. So she did. And when she heard the splash a few moments later, she promptly turned back.

"Oh!"

He was walking into the water, and Clara had a very clear view of his backside. The man was utterly perfect. His back, his legs and. . . she didn't want to stop staring at his buttocks.

Oblivious to her gaze, he continued to move into the water until he was waist deep, at which point he promptly disappeared below the surface. A wave crashed, and for a moment panic welled inside her. But Alex re-emerged a moment later, shaking his head and turning toward her with the most devilishly handsome smile she'd ever seen.

And then he began to walk toward her. In a moment he would.

. .

She spun around, trying to ignore the laughter that reached her ears. Was he dressing behind her?

"You're free to look, my shy English maid."

She didn't trust him totally, not in this, so she waited just a moment longer. "That's mostly correct," she said.

His damp, bare arms wrapped around her from the back.

"You were shy when we first met," he said, squeezing her gently.

"Not precisely," she said. "But I did learn that avoiding eye contact kept me out of trouble."

"Ahh," he said. "Part of the ruse." His hand moved to the front of her dress and ran from her waist up toward her breasts. "The Clara who cried out earlier is the real English maid. Is Alfred the demure one?"

"Cried out," she mocked, attempting to keep a straight face.

He dipped his hand below the ties so it rested just short of the peak she knew was hard once again. "Aye," he murmured, sweeping her hair to the side and kissing her neck from behind. "Your release," he clarified. "The result of desire. 'Tis quite an enjoyable state, is it not?"

The feeling between her legs was undeniable even as she tried to humble him. "I think you overestimate your abilities."

His fingers slipped lower and caressed her nipple as if to prove her wrong. His mouth seared a path toward her ear, his tongue flicking against the skin that felt as if it were on fire.

"I've underestimated many things."

The pressure of his fingers increased as his other hand mimicked the first.

"You, for starters."

She leaned her head to the side again, wanting him to kiss her neck. The pressure between her legs built even though he wasn't touching her there. It threatened to overflow.

"But if there's one area I'm quite confident in. . ."

He moved up against her, the length of his body now fully pressed behind her.

"It's this one."

He was relentless.

The triple assault was just too much. The building sensation shattered, and she throbbed all over, crying out unabashedly. His hands stopped their ministrations and spun her around. His kisses only extended the incredible feeling that she didn't want to end.

Finally, he pulled away, and she was able to catch her breath.

Sort of.

"How did you know—"

He placed a finger on her lips. "You don't want the answer to that."

Yet she already had it. Lots and lots of practice. She tried to push the thought aside of the careless, rowdy men at the inn. Thoughts of Alex in such situations were not ones she cared to entertain.

He moved away then to pick up the tunic that lay crumpled on the sand. "Go back, and I'll follow." He shook it as bits of sand fell to the ground.

Her gaze fell to the ridges on his stomach and then a bit lower. She swallowed, knowing he'd been fully unclothed just a few moments earlier.

"You were bleeding," she said, remembering the blood she'd seen earlier.

He shrugged. "Not my blood," he said, appearing unconcerned. She'd seen him fight and pitied his opponent.

She looked up at the castle and knew they would be missed soon. But she couldn't bring herself to leave just yet.

"You haven't told me why you came here." And then it hit her. He hadn't come to find her after all.

"To—"

She stopped him, already knowing the answer. "Wash away the dirt and blood from training." How utterly humiliating. Clara had assumed he'd sought her out, but that was simply what she'd wanted to think.

"I will go first so as not to arouse suspicion." Of course, Emma already knew they were together out here. Alone.

Clara turned and fled, her feet not moving fast enough for her. Fool!

Why hadn't he corrected her?

After taking out his frustrations on a number of English knights eager to best the Scotsman, Alex had finally given in to the need that had been demanding his attention all day. He'd wanted to see her. To touch her. To be with her. He'd finally walked away from yet another sword fight—he'd have to find Geoffrey for a real challenge—and inquired about the whereabouts of Clara, or rather Lady Susanna.

Something about her had made him forget his original intention—to apologize—and though he *had* apologized, he'd done much more than that. But Alex hadn't been able to resist touching her. He wanted to be inside her, imagined it so often he could almost believe it had already happened. But seeing the pleasure on her face as she melted against him had been as sweet as any release of his own. Of course, he couldn't very well walk to the castle in this state, smiling at the memory of how her cheeks had pinkened when he disrobed in front of her.

Shy maid, indeed.

So why had he allowed her to think washing was his only intention? The hurt in her eyes had been evident. Mayhap he'd done it simply to put some distance between them. Taking pleasures where they could was one thing. Taking her maidenhead was an entirely different matter.

And yet. . . he could not bear for her to think the worst. Alex swore as he began to follow Clara back to the keep, his every thought fixed on his English maid.

"There you are."

The steward seemed to be everywhere at Kenshire. Alex had no sooner made his way through the gate, skirting the keep's main entrance, than Peter found him in an open passageway.

"You've a rare ability to sneak up on a man," he said, surprised not to have seen or heard the steward coming.

"If I wasn't able to do so, I'd not be much of a steward to the lord and lady of Kenshire."

"Is there word from Elkview?"

At this point, Alex didn't know what his preferred answer would be.

"Nay, but there is a man inside meeting with Geoffrey now. He sent me to find you."

"Me?" Unless it pertained to his mother, Alex couldn't imagine what Geoffrey would need from him.

"Aye, they are currently occupying my office. If you'll follow me?"

He did so with interest. Leading him into the great hall and then across it and down a short corridor, Peter opened the door to a room with no windows or openings to the outside world. Every surface stacked with old books and parchment, it seemed a fitting room for the steward. Its smell was not unpleasant, though it was a tad dusty.

Geoffrey and his companion, who'd been sitting around a small round table to one side of Peter's desk, both stood to greet him.

Peter introduced him.

"May I present Alex Kerr of Brockburg to Lord Easton."

"Sit," Geoffrey requested, indicating the two empty chairs at the table. Alex and the steward took the empty chairs, and Geoffrey and his guest returned to their seats.

The English lord was young, perhaps the same age as Geoffrey. No one had mentioned his visit. Had he been expected?

"Lord Easton was travelling up the coast and had not planned on stopping here."

"I've recently returned from the crusade," the man explained. "I bring news for you. While passing through Elkview, I heard of your inquiries."

Alex sat up in his chair. Finally, he knew what this was about.

"I know your mother," the man continued.

His chest felt as if Lord Easton had taken a war hammer and slammed him with it. His mother. He didn't even like hearing the title on another's lips. She wasn't his mother. She was merely the woman who had given birth to him.

"Where is she?"

Somehow, he still wanted to know. Alex must enjoy being punished.

"You were in her hall."

"In her—"

"Elkview Castle. 'Twas hers after the death of her husband. The new lord, his son, has yet to take up residence there. But I made the connection as soon as I heard of your visit."

"How?"

Geoffrey and Peter remained silent.

"I was acquainted with her husband."

Her husband. So his mother had re-married an English lord. Did she have any children by him? That would mean—

"I didn't speak to her, but I owe a debt to Lady Sara and hope the information is valuable to you."

Alex looked to each man in the room, who were all looking at him. Were they waiting for him to react?

"She was there yesterday?" Had she avoided him on purpose?

"I don't know."

The lord sat back and crossed his arms.

He wanted to ask more questions, but Lord Easton appeared to have said his piece. Which was just as well. He'd get the answers himself.

"Thank you for bringing me this information," Alex said.

"You'll stay the night, of course," Geoffrey asked.

Lord Easton stood and the others followed. "I would like to speak to your wife briefly, but then I must be on my way."

Good.

He had worried about how Clara would react to the stranger. Would she retreat to being Alfred if this man stayed?

They followed Peter out and toward the great hall. Alex cursed when he heard the whispers coming toward them. He knew one of those voices all too well.

Emma and Clara were walking so fast that they passed them without even noticing the man's presence. Lord Easton had evidently seen them pass by, however, for his gaze followed them down the now-empty corridor.

Alex's fists balled at his sides.

"Come, I will bring you to Lady Sara," Peter said, guiding Lord Easton away.

As soon as they were alone, Geoffrey frowned at him. "Are you surprised by his news?"

It was anger he felt, not surprise. Anger at himself for his reaction to Lord Easton.

"You don't like the man?"

"I don't know him."

Geoffrey clasped him on the back. "I don't blame you," he said.

He looked at the reiver, who smiled broadly.

"In fact, I think I'll find Sara for myself. Easton's reputation precedes him, and I can't say I'm sorry to see him leave. Not," he added, "that I don't trust my wife. But why tempt the fates with such a man?"

Alex knew what he meant. He wasn't too proud to admit that Lord Easton was a very good-looking young lord. Geoffrey walked away, but Alex stood rooted to the same spot, shaking his head. He should have cared more about the news Lord Easton had brought than the natural, quick glance he'd given two beautiful young women.

Jealousy. An emotion he had thus far avoided.

Until Clara.

2 0

What had she been thinking?

Clara had pretended not to notice the men after passing the steward's room. Emma, who had truly not noticed them, continued on toward her bedchamber, where they planned to choose their gowns for the evening meal. But Clara had not survived, alone, since Gilbert's death by being unaware.

She hadn't seen much, but the newcomer had noticed them. By his dress, she could tell he was a nobleman. Clara scurried to catch up with Emma, but the incident had left her rattled.

"What's wrong?"

But Clara kept silent until they reached Emma's chamber, her own temporary lodgings, and entered the room.

Sitting on the edge of the bed, Clara heaved out a sigh. "Why am I marauding through the castle, undisguised, just waiting for someone to appear who can identify me?"

Her words were too revealing, but she no longer cared if Emma knew the truth.

"There was a man down there when we walked by. A stranger. A lord by the look of him."

Clara took a deep breath, folding her hands on her lap to steady them. "My father was a supporter of de Montfort. After Kenilworth, the king's men killed him in our own hall, seized our home, and forced me to flee," she blurted out. It was somehow easier to say now that she'd already told Alex.

She looked up. Emma's eyes were wide, full of pity. . . and understanding.

"I am the daughter of Edward Wheaton, and Barrington Castle was once my home and birthright. My father's dear friend Gilbert, an armorer, helped me escape. He warned me of the risk of imprisonment or death if I were ever discovered."

She pointed to the clothes and cap sitting atop the trunk at the foot of the bed. How she hated both of them. "As much as I despise that disguise, it's kept me alive for the past six years. And now I'm risking everything."

Emma sat next to her. "There's been peace between the earl's supporters and the king. Is the situation still so dire?"

It was the same question Alex had asked. "Can I take that chance?"

Neither woman spoke.

Finally, Emma placed her hand atop Clara's hand, which had finally stopped shaking.

"Are you sure the threat is the only reason you've stayed in the disguise?" Emma rushed to continue. "You've been posing as a boy for so long, you've not had the chance to be Lady Clara. It must be scary to do so."

Scary? Nonsense. Though she didn't want to say so aloud. Emma was just trying to help.

"I should not have told you. My father was killed. Gilbert was killed. I'm putting everyone in—"

"The king's men killed your armorer?"

"Nay, he refused to help a knight cheat at a tournament. . ."

She stopped, unable to recount yet another tragedy.

Emma squeezed her hand. "You don't have to tell me. Though I'm glad you trust me enough to have shared your story."

"I may have put you in danger."

Emma looked unconcerned. "You did not. The only danger we're in at the moment is being late to supper. Since Cook mentioned my pears, I'm expecting a special treat. Come, let's find you a gown."

She stood and began to look through the trunk that seemed to overflow with more clothing than before. Someone, either Emma or the lady's maid, had added more gowns to the wardrobe for her benefit. After seeing the stranger, Clara wondered if Lady Susanna should leave Kenshire. But none seemed to remember Alex had arrived with a squire, so wouldn't Alfred's sudden reappearance seem odd? And she knew Sara and Emma would be disappointed.

And she would be disappointed too.

A few more days.

After that, she'd have plenty of time to don her disguise. In the meantime, she allowed Emma, and later Faye, to assist her in preparing for the evening. She wore a crimson velvet gown and a low-hanging gold-jeweled belt. Just before she left the chamber, Emma returned with a gold circlet and helped her place it on her head. A single ruby hung from the center. When she protested that she could not possibly borrow such a valuable item, Emma pushed her hand away.

"It's perfect," she said, standing back to look at Clara.

The gown was a heavy one, and Clara had to use both hands to lift the folds as they walked. Kenshire's hall glowed with so many candles one could hardly tell it was nighttime. It must have cost a fortune.

Still reeling from the fact that she had blurted out her real name and history to Emma, Clara tried to appear casual as she glanced around the hall.

No Alex.

Geoffrey and Sara entered the hall, hand in hand, and she and Emma followed them to the dais. She tried to tell herself she wasn't disappointed by Alex's absence. And she refused to ask for him. Instead, she made polite conversation with Emma, trying—and failing—to overhear Geoffrey's conversation, especially when she heard him say Alex's name.

But he was seated too far from her.

"He hasn't been seen all evening," Emma whispered.

There was no pretending she didn't know what her friend was talking about.

"That's nice," she said instead. Emma chuckled.

Her companion's eyes brightened when the final dish was served.

"I knew it," Emma exclaimed.

The pears were cooked in wine and spiced with cinnamon, and after one bite, Clara had to agree they were quite tasty.

She tried to concentrate on the delicacy, her companion, and her final days of freedom, but a certain roguishly handsome warrior intruded on her thoughts...

And then he entered the hall.

Their eyes locked. Clara slowly finished her bite of pear. He moved toward them, freshly washed, looking every bit the second in command of a powerful border clan.

Provoking him would only cause her more trouble. She shouldn't do it. But whether it was the wine or something else, Clara knew what she wanted.

She wanted to be with Alex.

He'd given her a taste, and she wanted more. Pretending otherwise was for virgin brides with marriage prospects. Or ladies old enough to understand desire but too young to have the chance to act on it. She was neither.

She'd seen camp ladies flirt, something she was perfectly capable of mimicking. Clara had simply never felt the need to do so. Until now. And so instead of popping the final bite of wine-soaked pear into her mouth, she extended the moment.

Before picking up the cloth to clean her fingers, she licked the sweetness from them as slowly as possible without being so overt Emma would notice.

But Alex definitely did.

Clara never let her eyes leave his, and she knew he'd seen her every move as he stood before the dais. Though he averted his gaze to make his apologies to the lord and lady of Kenshire, a fire had been lit, and Clara prepared herself to get burned.

His apologies made, Alex walked to the empty seat next to hers —the one reserved for *him*. Emma admitted to having rearranged their seating earlier, though at the time it had not seemed to matter.

But he was here now.

"My lady." Rather than look at him directly, Clara chanced a glance at Emma, who tried to hide her broad, mischievous smile by starting a conversation with Sara.

Clara turned to Alex as if she had not a care in the world. "I thought perhaps you were not hungry."

His eyes darkened as a servant poured him wine. He nodded his thanks to the cupbearer, seized his cup, and brought it to his lips.

"Quite the opposite."

His look sent a shiver to her very core. The pull that had been there from the start seemed to grow with each passing day.

Clara refused to look away.

"Look," she said, pointing to the servant who walked their way with a tray containing remnants of their earlier meal. "It appears your appetite will be sated soon."

They watched the food as it was placed in front of him.

Alex raised his brows, his lips twitching as if to fight a smile.

"I can assure you, my lady, this—" he nodded to the food, "—will not help."

Clara had caught herself in her own game. She swallowed, remembering what he'd done to her on the beach. Her body remembered too, and tingled in anticipation.

Alex leaned toward her, lowering his voice. "I know what you're thinking."

The tingling sensation grew, demanding her attention. She turned away, but Alex did not relent.

"I would do it again, a thousand times if you'd let me."

Oh God, she should not have started this.

Alex leaned forward to look across the table, smiling at Lady Sara, who'd glanced their way.

"Besides—" he leaned back, "—we need to talk."

She tried to calm her beating heart.

"We're talking now." She tried to make her voice sound casual, but Clara was sure she'd not succeeded.

"Nay, love, this is called flirting, not talking."

Love.

"You're not very subtle," she chided.

"I don't intend to be."

With that, he turned his attention to the food before him. Normally, she loved Alex's directness. But sometimes, namely this evening, it could be a tad off-putting. She supposed she deserved it for setting such a sensual tone.

"Aren't they delicious?"

Emma had posed the question about her beloved pears, but Alex took it upon himself to answer.

"I haven't tasted them yet. But I look forward to doing so."

His meaning was abundantly clear.

The very thought made her squirm in her seat.

When Emma turned away once again, she braced herself. Sure enough, Alex leaned toward her.

"Aye, love. That is exactly what I meant."

Clara's entire body tensed. She could not endure this any longer.

"You're a devil," she told him, sincerely.

"To tempt you so? I won't disagree. But Clara. . . " He took a bite of roasted duck, chewed it, and sat back, smiling. "You started this."

So he *had* seen her.

She'd been in complete control, and somehow she'd allowed him to take it from her.

Clara took a deep breath and stared straight ahead. She concentrated on the retainers finishing their meals and the servants weaving through the packed trestle tables. When she was ready, she leaned toward him once again.

"Aye, I started it, and when you come to me this night, I assure you that I will finish it."

She was proud of how strong her voice sounded, and a quick glance at his face made her burst out laughing. She just couldn't hold it in.

The others looked over at them, but Clara couldn't regain any semblance of decorum. She'd managed to disarm him, and he still had not recovered. He laughed along with her, drawing glances from those in front of them.

"Your mood seems much improved," Emma observed.

"Indeed," she answered coyly. What else could she say? That she'd just offered her virginity to a man who was not her husband? And if his expression at this very moment were any indication, he'd be taking her offer this time.

She had nearly killed him tonight.

He really should open the door. The hallway around Emma's bedchamber, now occupied by Clara, was isolated. But guards were stationed everywhere, a remnant, Geoffrey had told him, from the days when Sara's life had been in danger. Alex should not be lingering. . . and yet he was.

Just open the door.

He hesitated, thinking about her words.

"I will finish it."

He'd enjoyed seeing this saucy side of Clara. Every day she spent out of her Alfred disguise, she became more and more comfortable with herself. For his part, he thought about her every moment when they weren't together, which was the exact reason he'd stayed away from the meal. Until he could figure out what their future looked like—he certainly couldn't imagine her back in his command as a squire, and she seemed unwilling to consider marriage—he needed to distance himself.

In the end, he hadn't been strong enough to stay away. Cursing himself, he'd hurriedly prepared for dinner—and then proceeded to do the exact thing he'd told himself he wouldn't do. When he saw her eating that pear, it had only taken him a moment to realize that his not-so-delicate Englishwoman was actually flirting with him.

Where had she learned to do that?

Being seated next to her hadn't helped. And then, that comment. He may have deserved it, but the image he'd immediately conjured of her lying naked under him had forced the lightness from their conversation.

They did need to talk, but this was likely not the best time and place for a discussion about their future. Now that his mother had been found, it was time for him to make decisions. He wanted her to be a part of those decision since her future was also at stake. He hoped.

I'll talk to her tomorrow.

Almost against his will, his hand pushed the door open.

Damn.

He planned on restraint. He'd not dishonor her by taking her virginity. And yet he found himself closing the door and crossing the room in just a few strides. Clara stood in front of the fire, the outline of her shift clearly defining every curve. When she turned, he was lost.

Alex pulled her into his arms and kissed her, and Clara immediately responded. Their tongues tangled together, his knee separating her legs so they could be even closer.

There were too many layers between them.

He tore off his tunic in one easy motion, then lifted the borrowed shift over her head. She didn't stop him. If this continued, they would make an irreversible mistake.

Nay, not a mistake. He and Clara had been pulled together from the first by some unnamable force. She tried to cover herself, but he wouldn't let her. Alex took both of her hands in his, memorizing the perfection in front of him. He'd seen her from afar, but now, standing so close, he was in awe.

"You're perfect," he said, and meant it.

She hadn't appeared nervous until that moment. Her mouth lifted at the sides, but Alex reminded himself to slow down. He'd never wooed a virgin before, and this was no ordinary woman. It was Clara.

As for the consequences, they would face those later. Together.

He let go of her hands and began to remove the remainder of his clothing. She didn't turn away this time. Indeed, she watched him so intently that he sprang to life immediately.

"Um, Alex."

Her eyes were so wide, he couldn't help but laugh. "Trust me, Clara," he said.

"Can I. . ." She took a step toward him. God help him, Clara was going to touch him. He may have nodded but wasn't sure. She reached out and tentatively placed her hand on him. Alex closed his eyes and prayed for the strength he'd need to do this right.

Gently. Slowly.

When she wrapped her hand around him, his eyes popped open.

"Clara." He reached for her, but she wouldn't be dissuaded.

And while she was the first virgin he'd been with, Alex would wager she did not act like most women who hadn't yet experienced the joy of lovemaking.

This was a woman who'd spent six years disguised as a boy. Afraid for her life. Living among men and camp followers in one of the most brutal settings on either side of the border. Tournaments offered gold and jeweled prizes, and their stands glittered from spectators in fancy clothes, but the reality of what went on behind the scenes was harsh and raw—and she'd been exposed to all of it.

"Show me," she said, looking at him appreciatively.

He mistakenly looked down at her hand wrapped around him, and while he'd enjoy nothing more than for her to continue, he couldn't do it. Not before he gave her pleasure.

He guided her hand away from him.

"Later," he said, his voice thick with desire.

He pulled Clara toward him, their bodies slamming together, skin on skin, his column pressed against her. He kissed her deeply, their tongues melding together, as he ached from a need so powerful it terrified him.

He refused to think about that now and pressed against her, allowing her to grow accustomed to the feel and size of him. She returned the pressure, grasping at his back, trying to get even closer. He knew what she wanted, but he'd promised her something else first.

Without warning, Alex picked her up and carried her to the bed. He tore the covering completely off and tossed it onto the ground, laying her down as gently as possible. He shoved the trunk at the foot of the bed, standing in the place it had vacated.

"Come toward me," he told her, no longer able to see her expression now that they were farther away from the fire.

"I don't understand." Her voice faltered, and Alex knew how she felt. The need to be inside her nearly consumed him, but he had vowed to make this night about her. She deserved pleasure after so much pain. And he was going to give it to her.

He pulled her toward him and toward the edge of the bed, where he knelt below her. Just a little closer.

"I made a promise that I intend to keep," he murmured, lowering his head toward her.

And that's when she nearly screamed.

21

At dinner, she'd thought he was surely jesting, but he really did intend to. . .

All thoughts of stopping him fled her mind. At the first flicker of his tongue, she grabbed the coverlet and decided never to let go. She squeezed it and arched her back toward him. The sensation was similar to when he touched her there, but much, much more intense. She raised her head and immediately wished she hadn't. The sight of his head between her legs, the muscles of his shoulders moving as he did indeed taste her. . .

"I. . . can't," she murmured.

She wasn't even sure what that meant.

He stopped just long enough to prod her legs apart. No, it wasn't anything like the time he'd pleasured her at the beach. This was so much more primal. He teased and tormented, and her grip tightened. The pressure was almost unbearable.

"Not too loud, love."

Had she made a sound? "Please don't stop."

When Alex chuckled against her, the sound so familiar and yet unexpected at this particular moment, another feeling took hold.

One deep within her that made her feel more connected to this man than anyone in her life.

Dear lord. . . how had she allowed herself to fall in love with this Scotsman?

And that was when her entire world shattered. She arched toward him and tried not to cry out while every muscle tensed and exploded. It was as if she was being torn apart from the inside, but in a good way. Nay, a magnificent way. Clara couldn't breathe. She lay motionless, trying to understand what had just happened.

Except Alex didn't give her time to understand. He moved around to the side of the bed and she shifted up toward him. Clara was surprised she was able to move at all.

He positioned himself above her, and she looked down.

Oh dear.

"Clara, are you sure about this?"

"Not at all. I understand that is supposed to be inside me, but. . ." She felt foolish to say it aloud, but would it really fit?

Though his features were obscured by the shadows, his broad smile reassured her a bit.

"That's not what I meant, lass."

She was about to ask if he was all right—his face, though extraordinarily handsome, also appeared a bit pained. But then she remembered what ailed him. She remembered because he had taught her.

"Desire," she blurted.

He cocked his head and drew his brows together.

"You look a bit like you're in pain. But I remember what you told me."

That smile again.

"This will work just fine," he said, nodding downward. "Are you sure you want to do this? You can lose your maidenhood but once."

"Oh." She was perfectly aware of that. "I'm sure, Alex."

He reached down between her legs while warmth began to spread through her again. "I want to do the same to you."

It was the wrong thing to say. Or perhaps just the opposite. Either way, something snapped in her previously composed Scot. He withdrew his hand, made a sound that reminded her of. . . Well, she'd never heard such a sound. But she liked it.

And then he entered her, just a bit. It felt different. His manhood guided inside her easily until it stopped.

"Clara?"

Her maidenhood. It was useless to her.

She reached up and pulled him toward her. With that same guttural sound, he pushed again, and this time there was pain. Alex was lying atop her, his arms holding his body over her. He lowered his head and kissed her. But it wasn't the insistent kiss from before. This one was soft and tender. His mouth guided hers open, his tongue coaxing, gentle.

Clara kissed him back and only remembered the pain when he began to move again. But it had already dissipated, replaced by an entirely new sensation.

"I like this," she said.

He pulled up to look at her.

"Like? Then I'm not doing my job correctly."

He moved a different way then. Using circular motions, he pushed into her and then pulled away. She mimicked his movements.

"Alex?"

It felt so good. *He* felt so good.

"Clara?"

He looked at her with such intensity that she completely forgot what she had intended to say. She moved her hands from his arms to his backside and forced him even closer.

He smiled.

She loved that smile.

She loved him.

And she especially loved the way he was moving against her—into her—right now. As if sensing that she no longer felt any pain, Alex pushed a bit deeper, withdrew a bit more. That same pressure began to build, and this time, Clara knew what was coming. She closed her eyes in anticipation.

His hands covered her breasts, caressing them while he moved. She matched his thrusts, pushing harder, wanting more.

"I want to feel that again," she said.

"You will." His voice, thick with desire, made her feel so powerful. She arched her back and mimicked his circular movements. . . only to be caught in her own net. The pressure built and built until her buttocks squeezed with the release that flooded through her.

"Oh God, Clara."

With a final push, he tensed and cried out. She pulled him toward her, wanting to feel his entire body atop her. They were still joined, and she was glad for it.

The words she'd thought of earlier caught in her throat. Had she really been about to say 'I love you?' It was true, but it wouldn't matter in the end. Clara would not risk another man she loved. She simply would not.

But those thoughts were for the morrow.

"Well," she said instead. "That was quite nice."

"Nice?" He pulled up enough to look at her. "Hell, woman. It wasn't anything of the sort."

"It wasn't?"

He moved so quickly Clara didn't have time to react. Somehow, he was now underneath her but still inside her.

"I'll hurt you," she said, practically lying atop him.

He grasped both sides of her head, pulled her toward him, and kissed her so thoroughly that Clara completely forgot about her position. In fact, when she became aware of it, she could feel his manhood stirring inside her.

Surely that wasn't possible. . .

Then Clara became aware of several things at once—his legs intertwined with hers, her core pressed against him, his hands splayed across her buttocks. Alex squeezed, ever so gently.

"Yes," she said, knowing what he was asking.

This time, there was no pain. He moved just slightly, and she immediately understood that she needed to move with him. She met his movements and matched them with her own.

His wicked grin made her realize that she was in control this time—he'd known it all along and had been waiting for her to figure it out.

And she did, quickly.

"Clara. . ."

Her name on his lips was the sweetest sound she'd ever heard. She moved with him until the pressure became too much to bear.

"I need. . ."

He circled his hips beneath her, somehow understanding, and once again Clara lost herself to the pleasures that he awoke in her. He called her name again, thrusting into her as she shook and squeezed and shuddered.

She wanted to tease, 'Not too loud,' as he'd done before, but she couldn't talk. She couldn't breathe. She allowed her whole body to go limp atop him. It was as if she were frozen in place.

This time when he broke contact, he rolled them both onto their sides.

"You spin me around like I'm a kitten," she said.

"A kitten?" He laughed. "Nay, a full-grown cat, ready to pounce. No wee kitten here," he said, kissing her nose.

The intimate gesture made her smile.

"Nice?" he asked.

"Perhaps I could have used another word," she admitted. "How many times can—"

"As many as you'd like."

"Really?"

"Aye." His voice had suddenly grown serious. "But every time we make love, the chance you're carrying my babe grows."

She would have been excited by the prospect, even unmarried, if she could offer a babe any kind of normal life.

But she could not.

"You've done that before?'

He didn't flinch, but instead pulled her closer to him. Wrapped in his arms, Clara could imagine all would be well. That she wouldn't ever have to say goodbye to him. She'd never felt so safe, or sated, in her life.

"Aye."

"And you have no babes?"

He sighed. "I do not. There's a way to avoid it."

She waited.

"I could have, should have, pulled myself from you at the end to prevent it."

"Pulled yourself?" Though she knew how a woman became pregnant, she'd never thought about how to avoid it.

"Aye."

He watched her as she thought about what he was saying. "Why did you not do so?"

"That's not so easily answered, lass."

Actually, she thought it might be, but didn't dare say so aloud.

"Have you ever been with a vir. . ." She stopped. She really didn't want to know.

"No, I have not. You are the first."

But he didn't seem happy to admit it.

"Which is why, of course, we will marry."

It took her a moment to understand his words.

"Marry?"

That was how he would propose marriage? Nay, they would not marry, but the look on his face told her that he was earnest.

"Alex, we will not be getting married."

"Clara—" he mocked her tone, "—we will."

And the stubborn Scotsman actually believed his own words. As if she would ever put him in such danger.

Another, more alarming thought occurred to her.

"The bed? Alex. . ." She pushed away from him and looked down but could see nothing. She pushed at him until he moved, and sure enough, drops of blood stared back at her.

He looked amused.

"'Tis not funny. I didn't think. . ."

"The sheet can be replaced." Alex pointed to the silken coverlet that he'd torn off the bed earlier. "That, not so easily."

"You thought of that before. "

He reached for her and ran his finger gently down her cheek. "I thought of everything."

"Including—"

"Aye, including the fact that you could become pregnant."

She stared into the face of the man she loved.

"I don't regret it," she said.

He smiled and pulled her toward him. Nestling her head in the comfortable and familiar crook of his arm, Clara closed her eyes. She wasn't sure she could sleep pressed against him this way, her hand draped on the ridges of his stomach. Those ridges were the last thing she remembered. When she woke, it was morning, and he was gone.

The first thing she noticed, of course, was his absence. The second was a folded sheet at the foot of the bed. How the devil had he managed that? Besides which, the fire still raged when it should have died out during the night. He'd stoked it without her noticing, and he'd clearly also seen to the candles at some point in the night, for they were not much shorter than they'd been the evening before.

He truly had thought of everything.

Clara sprang from the bed, the cool air reminding her of her state of undress. Locating and tossing the shift over her head, she tore the coverlet, pillows, and sheet from the bed and began to redress it with the fresh sheet Alex had left behind. She really had missed sleeping on a feather mattress. At Bristol, the large linen bag stuffed with wool was an improvement on the pallets she'd often found herself on moving from tournament to tournament, but it was nothing compared with this bed. She shuddered at the thought of sleeping on the ground once again.

The bed freshly made, Clara only had to determine where to hide the offending sheet. Moments after she shoved it under the bed, a knock landed at the door, followed by a familiar voice.

"Clara?"

It was Emma's voice. She struggled to stand, but her friend opened the door before she could manage it.

"What are you doing down there?"

She stood and, seeing her friend fully dressed, realized it was much later than she'd thought. "When Faye said you were still asleep, I thought I'd—"

Emma closed the door behind her.

"What's wrong?"

Clara's plan completely fell apart. Instead of hiding the truth, she told Emma everything. Including her true feelings for Alex.

If Emma was shocked, she didn't show it. Instead, she sprang into action.

"Find something to wear," she ordered.

Clara moved to the trunk to do just that.

Emma reached under the bed and pulled out the sheet. She calmly walked to the fire and tossed the evidence into its flames. Why had she not thought of that?

"I'm so sorry, Emma. I—"

"Sorry? For being with the man you love? For allowing yourself to feel something other than pain and sorrow?"

Emma pulled out a fresh shift and simple pale blue gown. The color matched her mood. What had seemed so exciting and romantic the night before was now wrought with complications.

Once dressed, she moved to put her boy's clothes back into the trunk, their freshly washed state courtesy of Faye, when Emma held out her hands.

"Give them to me."

Clara was poised to do just that when she realized what the other girl intended. She was going to toss them into the fire.

"No, you can't!"

"Clara, you don't need them. Surely you realize you'll never be Alfred again?"

Emma must have sensed the panic that welled up inside her. She could not get rid of her disguise. Susanna was temporary. Alfred was her future.

"Of course I will," she said. "I will not be marrying Alex."

She'd told Emma everything except the fact that she had refused his offer.

"Clara, what are you saying? You love him. 'Tis obvious. And 'tis just as obvious he feels the same way."

"I doubt that."

Emma ignored her.

"Did you tell him of your decision?"

"I did. Although," she admitted, "I don't think he believed me."

Emma rolled her eyes. "Well of course he didn't. What possible reason could you have—"

"I will not be responsible for his death."

Her words must have penetrated because Emma stopped talking.

"Everyone I love has died trying to protect me. I will not allow Alex to do the same."

"Clara, you don't know what will happen if—"

"I will not take that chance." She tried to be firm without hurting her new friend. "Please understand. After my father died, I never expected to have my own life again. I didn't allow myself to think about a future. This—" she waved to the bed, "—felt right. I love him, and perhaps selfishly, I wanted to know what it would be like."

Emma shook her head. "I don't agree with you, Clara, but I would never presume to tell you how to live your life. But please, please just think on it a bit more. At least until you leave Kenshire. I could tell Sara and Geoffrey, perhaps—"

"No." Clara softened her tone. "I should not have told you. Promise me, Emma. Promise you will never tell anyone."

Emma hesitated.

"Please?"

The look on her face indicated she didn't like it. And Clara was sorry for having involved her. But it felt good to have an ally. A friend.

"I will not tell, but—"

Clara dropped the clothes and hugged her.

Emma hugged her back, and at that moment, Clara vowed to do anything this woman asked of her.

"But," Emma pushed her back slightly, "only if you promise to consider, just consider, his proposal. Think about why you fell in love with him. Trust that his words to you are true."

She agreed.

"Good," Emma said, turning to leave. "Let's eat."

Clara had never seen anyone who loved mealtimes so much. And yet she stayed so slim.

"Wait," she said, holding back.

Emma looked back, curious.

"Alex," she said simply.

Would she be embarrassed to see him? What would she say?

"Is gone," Emma replied.

"Gone?"

"To speak to his mother." She turned once again to leave the bedchamber, but Clara didn't follow.

"But. . . I thought he didn't find her?"

Once again, Emma turned. This time she looked confused.

"He didn't tell you?"

"Nay. Tell me what?"

"A man was here yesterday, some lord of something. He knows Alex's mother and heard he and Geoffrey had been to Elkview looking for her. Apparently, the merchant was correct and she was there the whole time."

He found his mother? And didn't tell her?

"She is actually the lady of Elkview. Apparently she remarried, though her husband is now dead. How can you not know this already?"

"We were, uh, slightly busy. I supposed he never had the chance to mention it."

"Never had the chance? How busy could you possibly have—"

Emma stopped, her eyes widening even more. "You must have had quite an evening."

Clara had never been more mortified in her life. Even though there was no judgment in her voice, both of them knew giving your maidenhead to a man who was not your husband was wrong. It was a sin and simply wrong. And she'd done it in the bed of the woman who'd befriended her. Somehow, she had not felt ashamed until now.

"Oh Clara, please don't misunderstand me."

A single tear fell down her cheek as her chest constricted. Emma rushed to her side and took both of her hands.

"Listen to me."

It was the first time she'd heard her friend speak so sternly.

"You will not feel sorry for what happened here last eve. I meant it when I said you've been through too much sorrow to not enjoy some modicum of joy now."

She spoke as if from experience.

"I will take back my vow unless you stop feeling badly, imme-diately."

How could she argue with such a demand?

"Done." She made the vow, but it was, of course, not so easily accomplished.

Emma continued talking as they walked. "The most extraordinary women I know found themselves in similar positions. I don't think poorly of them and will not allow you to judge yourself harshly either."

She meant Catrina and Bryce, of course.

But she'd said. . . "Women?"

"My brothers, well, not Neill, have both gotten themselves into, shall we say, delicate situations before they were wed. And yet they continue to lecture me as if I should be the one Waryn to do things the conventional way."

"Sara and Geoffrey. . ."

Emma's grin confirmed it.

"You see? So stop worrying about last eve and start worrying about tonight instead."

"What's happening tonight?"

Emma turned to leave once again, calling over her shoulder, "I don't have much experience in this area, but I hear 'tis something you, and likely he, may want to repeat."

2 2

*A*lex and Geoffrey hardly spoke on the way to Elkview. The castle loomed before them, consisting of a small keep with just a few outbuildings and a village less than half the size of Brockburg. Their uneventful ride had been punctuated with conversation, but Geoffrey must have sensed his mood, for he'd eventually stopped trying to talk to him.

They'd agreed to meet at sunrise, though Alex had been ready well before the sun made its first appearance. Finding clean sheets without raising suspicion had been more of a task than he'd anticipated. Trying not to wake Clara, Alex had stoked the fire and relit the candles. But before he could leave the room, she made a noise. Wanting to be sure she wasn't having it a nightmare, he returned to the bed.

Standing beside it in the darkness, he watched Clara sleep. Her lips slightly parted, Alex could imagine she was dreaming of him. He'd certainly dreamed of her—then awakened to feel her body pressed against his own. He nearly reached for her, but it had been her first time, and she would likely be sore.

He was the first, and only, man she'd been with.

And he would be the only one.

Alex was forced to concede he'd been wrong about taking a wife, and just as wrong about blaming English women for what his mother had done. He would endure his brothers' jests and admit his folly. But he was still determined not to claim Dunmure. How could they hope to make a future in a place steeped in the past?

He wasn't concerned that she still had reservations about marrying him. Clara could be stubborn, but no more so than he. She held back only out of fear, but he would never allow anything to happen to her.

"Are you ready, Kerr?"

Just as before, they gained entrance easily. None would deny Sir Geoffrey Waryn, the new Earl of Kenshire, and Alex was glad for the man's company.

They dismounted and led their mounts to the stables. Alex thought of how he'd greet his mother, discarded the idea, and considered a new one.

"They'll never allow us entry with that scowl," Geoffrey quipped. "Summon that legendary wit of yours or we'll be riding back to Kenshire without an audience."

"Wit, my arse. I could no sooner smile at that woman than willingly chop off my right arm."

After handing their reins to a groom, they made their way to the front entrance of the keep.

"You could at least not look as if you plan to kill someone at any moment."

Alex's answering expression was meant to convey exactly whom he planned to kill if Geoffrey wouldn't stop talking. But his brother-in-law simply laughed.

"Greetings, my lords," the steward said from the steps of the main keep.

The man was hiding something. And this time Alex knew exactly what it was. He would not be put off by feeble excuses.

"I want to speak to her," he said simply.

The steward, large in both height and in girth, barely flinched.

"I'm unsure to whom you refer, my lord, but I can assure you—"

"We are not leaving without speaking to Lady Margaery." The name was bitter on his lips, but he would not be put off. "Tell her—"

The man looked up so quickly, Alex nearly missed it. He followed his glance to an arrow slit just above them. She was there.

He took a few steps back and glared directly at the tower and the woman he knew was watching him. Alex would not leave Elkview until he spoke with her. Rage boiled inside him as he continued to look up. He ignored Geoffrey and the steward and waited. Two guards joined them, but still Alex stood, unmoving.

The door to the main keep finally opened, and his mother emerged. She walked toward them and placed a hand on the shoulder of the steward, who stood aside.

She had not changed much. She was still a beautiful woman who looked much like an older Catrina.

He hated her.

"Leave us," she said, obviously expecting to be obeyed. Her men did so, but Geoffrey moved toward them. He was looking for Alex's permission to leave, which he gave with a nod. Geoffrey left him alone with the woman who had abandoned him and Reid and Catrina and Toren when they'd needed her most.

She looked nervous.

Good.

"You are despicable."

He'd dreamed about this moment for years—imagining what he'd finally say to her when he saw her next. He supposed it was as good a greeting as any.

"Good day, Alex."

Her lilting voice, so serene, sounded exactly as it did in his memories.

"Good day? I would think not. Not for you. Nor for me."

"You're angry—"

"Angry?" He took a deep breath, his hands shaking with rage. "What could I possibly have to be angry about, *Mother*."

"Let us speak privately—"

"So your new family does not overhear?" He looked around. "I understand you remarried. Do I have brothers? Sisters? You weren't so old when you left your first family—"

"Alex, please."

Alex could see her hands tremble ever so slightly. The fear in her eyes was real. He should not care. Did not care. But something about the way she looked at him made him relent.

He bowed, mockingly, a gesture for her to lead the way. She did not lead him into the hall, as he'd expected, but around the tower where he'd first seen her. A narrow passageway led them to a dirt-floored area surrounded by stone walls. An odd choice to host a long-lost son.

Or perhaps not.

"I should not be surprised that you would choose to hide me in the shadows."

He wanted to turn around and leave—the bitterness of this moment, all of the moments since she'd left, threatened to choke him. But he had one question he would not leave without asking.

"Why?"

He refused to be moved by the tears that formed in her eyes and threatened to spill onto her cheeks.

"Since my husband died—"

"Which one," he asked, not caring that his voice sounded cruel to his own ears.

"My English husband," she replied, wiping a tear from her face with a small white strip of cloth from her pocket. "I wanted nothing more than to come to you. To all of you. And explain. But his son. . . and your hatred of me. I should have come, but—"

"Why—" he ground his teeth together, "—did you leave?"

"What is the only acceptable reason for a mother to abandon her children? Her grieving children who just lost their father?"

"Acceptable? Surely you jest, there is no—"

"Is there not?"

The resolve in her voice startled him. It was the same tone Catrina used when she knew she was right. He'd forgotten that about their mother. When she set her mind to something, she was immovable.

"Alex, before I met your father, I was already betrothed."

"Betrothed? To whom? Did Father know?"

Her wistful smile almost appeared genuine.

"Of course. 'Twas the reason we married in secret, the reason we never visited my family in England. My parents never forgave me. Sir Godfrey, the man I was supposed to marry, was so angry that he refused to meet with your father. Refused to discuss compensation."

"How could we not have known this?"

She shrugged. "It was easier to pretend your father hated all things English, which was very nearly true. Though he would certainly have visited had my parents welcomed me home."

"What does this have to do with—"

She ignored his interruption. "Sir Godfrey never forgave me. He was old enough to be my father, and though his holdings are not large—" she looked up at the keep near which they stood, "—he was well-connected."

"You left four children behind." He ground out his words. "Why?" He did not care about the circumstances around his parents' marriage or his mother's second marriage to this Sir Godfrey. He wanted an answer so he could get the hell out of—

"He found me. And threatened my life. Or, more importantly, yours."

Alex looked into his mother's tired eyes, trying to understand her words.

"He learned of the battle, of your father's death. Somehow, he gained entrance to Brockburg. I woke one morn to a knife at my throat and a threat that could not be ignored. I could either leave, return to England as his wife, or he would kill every one of my children."

Alex laughed. "You expect me to believe—"

"He was cunning enough to be there, in my chamber, alone. The bastard vowed to find a way to do the same, whether that day or months, even years, later to you. And Toren, Catrina, and Reid. I believed him." She swallowed. "And knowing him as I did later, as his wife, I believe him still."

He shook his head. "You had three sons, any of whom could have—"

"Defended me? Defended themselves? You were so young. And the man found his way into my private chambers and held a knife to my throat. He was evil and cunning, a dangerous combination. I would not take that chance." She stood a bit straighter. "And I would make the same decision all over again."

He stared at her, unsure of what to say.

"So you left to save us," he said mockingly. "Married this monster. And then he dies. You could have come to us then. Told us—"

"I was scared."

Her simple words stopped him, penetrated his hate. She *was* scared. Had been since the moment he'd confronted her. He looked at her shaking hands, her tears, and this time he saw her behavior for what it truly was.

Raw, unmitigated fear.

"Did he hurt you?"

She didn't answer. She didn't nod or shake her head. His mother simply continued to look at him, to watch him.

He *had* hurt her. Alex would kill the man.

And was reminded that he was already dead.

"When we came here looking for you. . ."

"The man you met earlier is one of many loyal to me. But there are others loyal to the new lord, Godfrey's son, who is just as cruel and cunning as his predecessor."

"Is he here?"

She shook her head. "Nay, but he will return in a few weeks."

"Does he—"

"He leaves me alone, for now," she said. "But I give him no reason to remember that I exist."

A prisoner in her own home.

"You can question anyone here. Everything I've told you is true. Most know my late husband for the cruel man that he was. But their fear hasn't ended with his death. And they worry, as I do, that his son will be just as bad. Or worse."

Alex didn't know what to say. He'd hated her for so many years, resented her, it was hard to think of her in any other way. Could he really have gotten it so wrong?

And then the tears spilled down her cheeks in earnest. "I've missed you so much. Alex, you have no idea what it's like for a mother to lose her own children. I've dreamed of travelling to Brockburg, of what you and your sister and brothers would say. I knew you'd hate me. I hated myself for so long."

Alex went to her and engulfed the mother he had thought he despised in his arms. "After he died, I became careless." She wrapped her arms around him. "Started bragging about my children, wanting people to know. I asked everyone who passed by here if they had word of you."

He believed her.

The raw pain in her voice was real. He had never, not once, considered the possibility that she still loved them. That there might be a genuine reason for her abandonment. But he had no doubt Elkview's retainers would validate her story. For now, he tried to forget the years of hate and misunderstanding that stood between them.

She cried for what seemed like hours, and he held her still. His mother. Who loved her children so much she'd done the unthinkable to protect them.

"Shhhh, Mother. I'm sorry for how I treated you—"

She held his face in her hands, her tears finally subsiding. "I do not blame you, son. It's exactly the reaction I expected. When I heard you'd come looking for me. . . I was going to come to Kenshire, but I was so afraid that you would hate me for what I'd done. And John. . ."

He placed his hands over hers.

"The son," she explained. "He's never treated me as poorly as his father did, and I know you are grown men now. . ."

When her voice trailed off, Alex finished her sentence.

"We will protect you."

She was coming home, to Scotland. She would never have anything to fear again. And if the new lord of Elkview thought to threaten his mother or his siblings, he would start a war, if necessary, to end that threat for good.

She nodded and tried to smile.

"I'm glad you found me, son. I love you so much. I've thought of nothing but you and your siblings, every day and every night, since I left." She began to cry once again.

He held her in his arms, his mind still struggling to reorganize the past into this new frame. That was when it occurred to him. She'd lost a husband and four children all at once. And had been forced to marry a cruel, abusive husband.

He squeezed a bit tighter. "I love you, Mother. And I will never let anyone hurt you again."

23

They returned just past the midday meal. Clara was preparing for a ride to Kenshire's village with Emma and Sara when Geoffrey walked into the stables to announce the arrivals.

"You can remove my wife's saddle, and tell Eddard I must speak to him at once," Geoffrey told the stable hand. He was out of view, but it was unmistakably him. Sara planted her hands on her hips, and when her husband entered, she glared at him.

"I'll thank you not to order me about, husband. I was just about to—"

He reached around the countess's expanded waist and silenced her with a kiss, followed by whispered words for her ears only.

"I'm so sorry, ladies," Sara said by way of apology. "Do you mind terribly if I do not accompany you?"

"Actually," Emma said, looking toward the entrance of the stable, "I may come back with you."

Clara followed her glance toward Alex, who filled the entrance with his large frame and imposing presence. His grin stretched from ear to ear, and the way he looked at her. . . Clara knew she was lost. She had promised herself not to seek out any additional contact with him. Until she figured out what to do next, being with Alex was not wise.

And yet, that smile drew her in. Something had changed in him. His smile was broader, his steps lighter, as he entered the increasingly crowded space.

"I'm very sorry to hear that, Emma. But surely you won't leave —again—because of me," Alex teased.

Emma was already beginning to follow her brother.

"Nay, 'tis not you at all." She held her hand to her head, implying that she'd suddenly acquired a horrible headache.

"Shall I unsaddle your mount as well, my lady?" the beleaguered stable boy asked Clara.

"Aye."

"No."

The poor boy looked from her to Alex, confused.

"I will gladly accompany you to the village, Lady Susanna," he clarified.

If he was surprised she intended to go there without her disguise, he didn't show it.

She pretended to be shocked. "Unaccompanied? Why, my lord, I could not consider such a thing."

His laugh made her forget everything but this very moment. It was a hearty and careless laugh, one that filled her soul with joy. As if eager to escape their banter, the stable boy led her horse outside.

"I assure you, fair maid, I am quite harmless."

"That, my lord, is a lie," she said, allowing him to escort her out of the stables. He held up his hand, and she took it, mounting the chestnut mare easily, even inhibited by the folds of Emma's gown. Once seated, he continued to hold her hand just a few moments longer than was necessary.

"Did you have a particular destination in mind, my lady?"

Once he was satisfied that she was well settled on the mare, he mounted his own horse and they began to ride. They continued the pretense of formality through the inner bailey and beyond the gatehouse.

"Enough," she relented as they wove their way down the incline that led away from Kenshire Castle.

Suddenly shy, she didn't know what to say. She wanted to know what had happened on his journey but also why he'd left so suddenly—and without telling her about the latest news regarding his mother. Thoughts about *that* night, which had filled her every waking moment. prompted her to look ahead rather than at the Scotsman riding next to her.

"We found her," he said.

"You did?"

Alex looked around them and nodded ahead to a thicket of trees. He sped up, and she followed. Moving away from the dirt road, they entered a grassy clearing between two massive oaks. He dismounted, tied his mount quickly and efficiently, and came to assist her. Clara took his lead and did the same, reminding him she was quite capable of handling both herself and the mare he had lent her at Brockburg.

"What are we doing?" she asked.

"This."

He pulled her into his arms, and Clara immediately wrapped hers around him. She inhaled deeply when an afternoon breeze blew a tendril of hair between them. He moved it away and brought his lips to hers so tenderly, she forgot to close her eyes.

He pulled away just enough to see her face.

"We found her," he repeated. And the rest of his words rushed out. Alex told her of his initial anger—and how it had wilted in the face of his mother's explanation of the events that had unfolded after his father's death. When he spoke of her English husband, he broke contact, likely not even realizing it. His fists clenched as he paced back and forth, clearly infuriated by his mother's mistreatment.

When he mentioned the look in his mother's eyes—the fear

and sadness—Clara's chest tightened. She was shocked when she realized Alex's eyes swam with unshed tears, and she went to him, holding him close, eager to ease some of the pain.

"You didn't know, Alex. How could you have known?"

"I should have kept looking for her. We could have protected her."

She lay her head on his chest and listened to the rapidly beating heart of a man in pain. She willed it to slow, for Alex to begin to heal after believing for so long his mother didn't love him.

"I'd convinced myself it was my fault she left," he said quietly.

Clara didn't move.

"Toren was always the bravest and strongest. Surely she wouldn't leave her first-born son. And even now she and Catrina look so much alike. There is no doubt they are mother and daughter." His voice cracked. "Reid was the baby, innocent and beloved by everyone. But I..."

Oh, Alex!

"But I was none of those. A second son who had to spend every waking moment training to be as good. . ."

Though he stopped, Clara knew he had been about to say, 'as Toren.' Alex loved his brother dearly, but he clearly felt lesser than him. Though she could never understand why. To her, Alex was perfect.

"She loved us, me, all along."

That simple truth had clearly changed everything for him.

She looked at Alex, her gaze unflinching. "You are as strong, as honorable, and as witty as you've been since the day we met. Any person would be honored to know you. Any mother would be honored to have you as her son."

She nearly added, 'Any woman would be lucky to love you,' but something stopped her. She'd vowed to Emma to consider a life with Alex, and she'd been thinking of naught else. But she could not forget the risks. If he came to harm while protecting her, she would never recover. She understood, all too well, his mother's decision to leave her children.

Clara and Alex stood like that for a long while, wrapped up in each other's arms. If only she could spend the rest of her life in this wooded spot, somewhere between her home and the one she was not brave enough to make with Alex. . .

But eventually, he pulled back.

"I promised you a ride to the village, though I must admit, it was a bit of a shock to learn you'd agreed to go there at all."

Clara would have been content to call off the trip entirely. She'd only relented after an entire morning of goading by Sara and Emma. They both believed that Alfred was firmly a part of her past. Sara had made some discreet inquiries, she'd said, and there was every indication the peace agreement between the king and his errant barons was being honored.

Even so, Clara was hesitant. She'd tried to explain what Gilbert had told her, but neither woman wanted to listen. They were so convincing that Clara had finally agreed, though she was adamant they continue to call her Lady Susanna in public.

"Sara and Emma convinced me it was safe."

"Geoffrey told me the countess has been making inquiries."

She didn't wish to discuss Alfred right now. . . or her family's past.

"Alex—" something had just occurred to her, "—your mother. Where is she now?"

They walked toward their horses and mounted them.

"She agreed to return to Brockburg, or Dunmure, with us but asked for a few days to prepare."

Dunmure Tower. She was pleased he considered going back. "So she is coming home with you?"

He turned that irresistible smile on her. "Aye, lass. As are you."

With that, he spurred his horse forward, and Clara had no choice but to catch up. She had no opportunity to answer.

Which, she supposed, was just as well. She still wasn't sure what to say.

It was settled.

Alex would return home with his mother and the woman who would be his wife.

He never imagined this journey would have led to either development. The revelations about his mother also opened a new possibility. He'd been opposed to claiming Dunmure because of the memories it held, sweet turned bitter, but now he could allow himself to honor and enjoy those memories.

His mother had not abandoned them.

Which changed everything.

Unfortunately, the woman who rode beside him now did not altogether share his enthusiasm about his plan. They headed back to the castle after a very short trip to the village. While he was surprised Clara had agreed to make the visit as herself, he was less so when, after spending just a few minutes there, she had begged him to leave. She wasn't ready, she'd said.

He had tried to discuss the previous evening and their future, but she changed the topic to his mother. Alex could understand her reluctance. She'd endured much over the past years. But as comfortable as she'd become at Kenshire, there was a part of her that still clung to Alfred. That still clung to the perceived safety that disguise had given her.

"Walk with me," he said as they dismounted in front of the stables.

She looked at him as if he would devour her, which he was sorely tempted to do.

They handed their reins to the groom and Clara followed him toward a set of stone stairs that led to a parapet overlooking the sea. They stood side by side, silent, for a long while.

"There's something calming about the ocean," he said.

"I've only seen it once before. I begged my father to accompany him to a holding not far south of here. He hardly ever agreed to take me with him, but on this occasion, he relented."

As he watched her talk, Alex wondered how he ever could have believed her to be a boy. Standing against the bright rays of a setting sun, she was every bit a woman. . . a noblewoman. The vestiges of Alfred were becoming more of a memory every day.

"Though I was awed by such a sight—" she gestured to the sea below, "—it was the lady of the castle who most impressed me. She was so confident and assured, much like Lady Sara, that for years I thought about being just like her."

He understood.

"I've not met a more confident woman than you, Clara. You will get along well with my sister," he said suddenly. "We can visit Bristol."

She didn't answer him. They needed to openly discuss the future, but he could tell it still frightened her to do so.

"Once my mother is ready for travel, we'll leave for Brockburg forthwith."

Still, she said nothing.

"Where we will marry."

Clara simply continued to stare out to the sea, as if he'd made a comment on the weather, not their future life together.

"Say something, Clara."

When he saw her expression, he almost wished he hadn't prodded her.

"I don't know what to say."

"You don't..."

He took her by the hands then and spun her toward him. "Clara, what we did last eve. . . it cannot be undone. I will keep you safe, always. Do you really believe I'd let anyone harm you?"

Her hands felt so small in his own.

"Nay, but what if I'm discovered? What if they come for me? What if—"

She stopped, but he knew what she was going to say.

"You need to listen to Sara. She's one of the most powerful and influential women in England. If she says the king and his barons brokered peace, you need to believe her. And you'd be in Scotland anyway. Believe me when I tell you that no one will ever take you from me. Do you understand?"

He loved her.

But he hadn't told her that yet. Maybe it would make a difference.

"Clara, I—"

"My lord. My lady."

Geoffrey's young squire, Reginald, a competent lad who'd trained with them a few days earlier, called to them from below.

"Lady Sara wishes to see you."

Alex attempted to put him off. He wanted Clara to know how he felt. "Please tell—"

"Pardon, my lord, but 'tis Lady Susanna she wishes to see. Immediately."

Clara, of course, lifted her skirts and excused herself.

"Apologies," she said as properly as the queen. "We shall speak more later?"

If it was truly a question, she didn't wait for an answer. His skittish Englishwoman hurried back to the keep. He turned toward the sea, not quite content to listen to the call of the seagulls above him.

Alex wasn't sure if he'd be content until they were back in Scotland and his mother and future wife were safely installed at Brockburg. Or Dunmure.

Kenshire was beautiful, and given that he was a former enemy to the Waryn family, he was treated quite well here. But it was not Scotland.

And he wanted to go home.

24

"We have visitors," Reginald explained, words that made Clara's skin crawl. Who could it be? Would they know her?

Reginald escorted her back to the keep in silence. Faye awaited her there, and she led the way through a dizzying array of passageways.

They ended their journey in a part of the castle Clara had not seen before, and when Faye opened the door to a room on the second floor, the grandest of solars awaited her.

Sara and Emma both began talking at once.

"Lord Edmund and his wife are passing through. . ."

"You should not be concerned. . ."

Clara stopped them. "Who is Lord Edmund?"

"He and his wife are frequent guests at the keep," Sara said. "His family is old. . ."

"And he is even older," Emma finished.

Sara tried not to smile.

"He is harmless. But he's also a staunch supporter of the prince, so I thought you should know he and his wife—"

"Lady Susanna will not be making an appearance this evening."

Again, both women spoke at once, but this time it was Emma whose appeal was louder.

"Trust us, please," she pleaded. "Do you think we, and Geoffrey, and Alex—" she emphasized that last name, "—would ever put you in danger? Tell her, Sara."

The countess's smile calmed her just a bit. "You know I've made some inquiries," she said. "And by all accounts, you've nothing to fear. In the last three years, none of de Montfort's supporters have been taken into custody or. . ." She swallowed. "Killed since the provisions at Marlborough."

It was hardly a comfort given that several of the man's supporters had been killed and imprisoned in the first three years of her self-imposed isolation.

"Furthermore," Emma added, "you aren't even using your real name. There's no danger, and no question that you—"

"I'll do it," she said, surprising both of them—and herself.

Although she was terrified to go against Gilbert's advice, she trusted Alex. And these women.

"You will?" Emma hugged her as a relieved-looking Sara smiled.

"I will," she repeated. "But there is another problem."

Before her new friends could become too concerned, she added, "I will never find my way back from here."

"Follow me," Emma said. "'Tis a bit of a surprise. I rather thought you would insist on not joining us tonight."

She remained quiet as they walked, Clara allowing Emma to lead the way.

"I'd much prefer to dine in the hall."

The swish of Emma's gown as they turned the corner caught her attention.

"Thank you for allowing me use of your wardrobe while I'm here."

Emma waved her hand dismissively. "I've more gowns than I need. When we first came here after living quite simply with our aunt and uncle, Sara insisted on them."

"Have you ever thought of returning home?"

Perhaps one of the reasons she and Emma got along so well was their similar histories. Both had been forced from their homes.

"When Geoffrey and Sara wed, Bristol was still. . ."

She stopped, and Clara knew why. "In the hands of the Kerrs," she prompted.

They rounded another corner, reaching a part of the castle that Clara recognized.

"Aye," Emma said. "Geoffrey convinced me to stay here. Though fortifications have since been added, Bristol is quite close to the border."

"I can't imagine Kenshire being taken," Clara agreed.

"When her father died, Sara was in real danger here. From reivers, the Scots—no disrespect to Alex, of course—or monarchs too busy overseas to care much for Northumbrians. The borderers will always be in danger."

"But you are able to go outside the walls alone," Clara said. "Travel to the village. Or even farther."

They'd arrived at her bedchamber, or just outside of it.

"Geoffrey doesn't like it, but if I didn't, I'd be no more than a prisoner. What kind of life would that be?"

What kind of life indeed?

Emma could have been talking about Clara's life as Alfred. She was undeniably safer as Alfred, but safe was not happy. She had been *living* as a squire. As a person without ties to anyone or anything. Mayhap it was time for her to start listening to the people she trusted. She would attend this meal, speak to their visitors, and then to Alex.

There was something different about Clara.

She sauntered into the great room as lovely as ever, greeting him with a smile that held more promise than Alex could have hoped for.

Although he thoroughly enjoyed seeing her so relaxed, he was surprised to find her here at all. When he'd learned of Lord Edmund's visit, he'd assumed she would panic. Instead, Lady Sara had informed him that Clara would be attending the meal.

They needed to settle things between them, and he would not be put off any longer. But it seemed his worries were unwarranted. Just after they sat down at the dais, she leaned over to whisper, "Tonight?"

The simple question, so poignantly asked, sent blood coursing to every part of his body, making it difficult to sit still. By the time the meal ended, Alex was left with no doubt about her meaning.

His English vixen had flirted with him from the first course to the last, and while he anticipated their night together, he looked forward to their future even more. He was eager to take Clara as his wife—the sooner, the better.

After the meal, she and Emma slipped out of the hall, but Clara gave him a little wave that promised she would return. Some of the hall's occupants had begun to disperse. The lord and lady remained, though they moved to a table in front of the massive fireplace. Alex stood not far from the dais, deep in thought.

"So you are the brother of the man who took Bristol?"

Alex turned to find the aging Lord Edmund at his heels. Clara and Emma, he saw from the corner of his eye, had just returned to the hall. Where had they gone, anyway?

"I am," he said, not sure how to respond to that.

Lord Edmund was just as Geoffrey had described him. If his grey hair didn't proclaim the man's age, his slight hunch certainly did. The man seemed less than bothered by his wife's open flirtations with a knight who, by Alex's estimation, would not be sleeping alone that night. Much younger and more attractive than

Lord Edmund, Lady Maude seemed to be the last thing on her husband's mind.

"Yet here you stand, an honored guest and well-treated, I'm sure, if I know Lady Sara."

Though his words insulted, his tone did not. Alex chose to be amused by the old man.

"You know the lady well—"

"And her father before her. Less so her husband." He gestured toward Geoffrey.

"He's the best sort of enemy a man could have," Alex said.

"Former enemy," quipped Emma. She and Clara had just reached them and had obviously overheard the latter part of their conversation.

"Former," he agreed, smiling not at Emma but at Clara.

Tonight, she wore gold. A gown meant to dazzle. . . which gave him an idea. While there'd be no time for gowns to be made before they left, Alex could surprise her by sending word ahead to the only tailor brave enough to visit Brockburg on occasion. Neither he nor his brothers made use of him often, but Catrina had used his services before moving to Bristol. She would know how to reach him.

He would surprise Clara with a new wardrobe as his wedding gift. He'd speak to Emma about it as they were the same size.

"My ladies," Lord Edmund bowed his head and brought Emma's hand to his lips, then Clara's. It was a wonder the lord's wife was not better charmed by her husband. Alex tried not to laugh at Emma's expression. While Clara remained passive and polite, Emma did everything but pull her hand free.

"I must speak to Lady Sara about the wretched seating arrangements," he said, evidently referring to the location of his seat, which had been at the very opposite end of the head table from the two visions before him.

"What brings you to Kenshire, my lord?" Alex asked, attempting to distract him from the women.

"Ahh," he said. Waving a hand toward his wife, he made a face that Alex supposed was intended to convey his answer.

"What of you, Lady Susanna?" Lord Edmund said, turning to Clara. "You're a friend of Lady Gillian's then?"

Without hesitation, Clara nodded. "Aye, my lord."

"And who is your father?"

While it was common, at least in England, to establish precedence, and the question was not unusual, Alex still took a step toward Clara.

"He is—"

"A minor baron from the north. You would not know him, my lord." Emma cut Alex off, clearly as protective of her as he was.

"How long are you staying, Lord Edmund?"

Emma tried to appear casual when she asked the question, but he knew her better. Alex wasn't the only one who'd noted Edmund's slight change in demeanor after they avoided his question.

Lord Edmund deigned not to answer but asked his own question instead.

"I suppose marrying across the border worked for your family?"

And while his tone was as light as it had been earlier, Alex was no longer amused. Clara's nervousness made him more defensive than he should be.

"We are allies with Waryn, of course."

"Allies are good," the older man allowed. But then he shrugged. "Until they are not."

They all looked at him, unsure of how to respond.

"Take de Clare, for instance. I say an ally like the Earl of Gloucester is worse than an enemy."

Both Alex and Emma looked at Clara, whose face had gone white. The careful look of neutrality she'd kept thus far had vanished.

Alex took a step away from Clara, forcing the lord's attention to him.

"Not the only man to change sides," he said, referring to Gilbert de Clare's famous alliance with Prince Edward. Though a staunch de Montfort supporter, the Earl of Gloucester later switched sides and was rewarded for his efforts.

Attempting to change the subject, Alex turned toward the front of the hall.

"I've been to Kenshire before but am always amazed by its splendor," he said, all too aware that his brothers would laugh at such a pretty speech. But Lord Edmund was the kind of man to appreciate such things, and he needed to make him stop talking about Gloucester.

But the stubborn old fool would not be dissuaded.

"One man gets the hand of the king's niece. Another, his head chopped off. And now rumors of a renewed effort to dissuade de Montfort's supporters despite the treaty."

Alex shot a quick glance at Clara, who, as expected, looked visibly upset.

"Excuse us, gentlemen," Emma muttered. He watched as she and Clara left the hall without bidding a good evening to anyone.

Lord Edmund, fortunately, didn't seem to suspect anything.

"Women," he muttered, obviously bemoaning their inability to tolerate such political talk.

Alex wanted to go after her, but that would appear too suspicious. Instead, he listened to more of the elder baron's *many* opinions until Lady Sara made her way over to them.

As if speaking to an older uncle whom she'd taken care of for most of her life, Sara chided Lord Edmund and guided him toward Geoffrey.

"My husband is eager to speak to you," she said with a wink at Alex as they walked away.

If he hadn't been so worried about Clara, Alex would have laughed at Geoffrey's expression. He appeared none too pleased to be entertaining a man with strong opinions and an even stronger odor of ale upon him.

Poor Geoffrey.

But he had no time to worry about the Earl of Kenshire. He needed to find Clara.

Now.

25

Clara paced back and forth. The night before had been a disaster. After resolving to bury Alfred forever, she'd been so excited to speak with Alex. To ensure he felt the same way about her. Though he'd never used the word 'love,' neither had she. She'd finally felt ready to be completely open with him—and to plan for the future.

And then, Lord Edmund.

His words had been a stark reminder of why she'd spent so long in disguise. She'd put everyone in danger, and why? Because she wanted to wear a gown again? Her vanity would lead to her discovery, and though Alex and the others thought it safe, she wouldn't risk their safety.

"Lady Susanna?"

Emma's voice. She didn't want to speak to her, but neither could she remain locked in her bedchamber all day. Especially since it was, in fact, Emma's room.

She thought of the night before, after Emma had escorted her back to her room. As expected, he had come to her within the hour. But she'd not answered his knock. Not willing to wake everyone and alert the entire castle to his presence, he'd left after a few persistent knocks and pleas to open the locked door.

She'd successfully avoided Faye earlier, but Emma would not be put off so easily.

Opening the door, she offered her friend a hesitant smile. "Yes?"

Emma pushed open the door, closed it behind her, and planted her hands on her hips.

"Alex is worried. I am worried. Clara—"

"I can't."

She didn't know exactly how to put it into words, but she knew that she couldn't face Lord Edmund again. "I can't present myself with him here."

"Can't," Emma challenged, "or won't?"

"It hardly matters—"

"Clara, it matters more than you realize. I asked you to reconsider, and you did. I was so pleased, as were Alex and Sara and Geoffrey—"

It only served as a reminder that far too many people had become involved in this.

"I'm so sorry," she said, meaning every word. "I never meant for you, for them—"

"Clara, we care about you. Come down with me. We can—"

"Okay," she said, startling Emma. If she gave Emma any reason to suspect her plan, her friend would have Alex up here immediately. It would be easier to see him with others around. Clara didn't know if she was strong enough to face him alone.

He might not love her, but her feelings for him were not ambiguous. The thought of leaving him, walking away knowing she may never see him again. . .

She could endure a disguise. She could endure a life on the run. She could even endure the crude comments and high-handedness of those who would hire her to squire. But life without Alex, without his easy smile and gentle touch. That, she did not know if she was strong enough to endure. But what other choice did she have? As long as she stayed here, Clara was in danger of discovery. And as much as Sara proclaimed otherwise, no one could ensure she—and those who'd knowingly harbored a traitor's daughter—were safe.

It was the only certain way to protect them.

But she'd need to find a way to leave without anyone suspecting, and if that meant venturing below stairs with Emma, then she would do it.

Still surprised, Emma pulled her along until they were in the great hall. The tables were already being cleared.

"Are you hungry?" Emma asked. "I can ask Cook—"

"Nay." She looked around but didn't see anyone other than servants.

"He's already in the training yard," she said. "Shall we go there—"

Clara shook her head. She was surprised he had not looked for her this morning. It would be easier not to see him again, but part of her was disappointed. She would need to change and gather her few belongings. . .

"Lady Susanna."

The voice was one she knew well. Clara spun around and watched Alex walk toward her from the back of the hall.

"I'd thought you and Geoffrey—" Emma started.

"I came back to speak to Lady Susanna."

He did not smile nor jest. His expression was grim, and Clara's breath caught when his gaze found, and held, hers.

He could not know. If Alex suspected her plans in any way, he would not stop until he had changed her mind. Which she absolutely could not do.

"Oh?" she said. Clara gave Emma a look that clearly told her to stay.

"It seems every time you are near, I have urgent business to attend to," Emma said to Alex, completely ignoring Clara's pleading looks.

With that, Emma walked away.

Always trying to help her, even when she didn't wish to be helped.

Thank you, my friend, Clara thought. *I will miss you.*

Clara turned to Alex. She couldn't do it. Looking at him, she couldn't bear the thought of leaving him. The sweat and dirt on his loose-fitting tunic only made him more appealing. More vulnerable.

"You asked me to come," he said.

Hurt, disappointment. . . oh, she knew the feelings well.

"I wanted to speak to you, but—"

"Clara," he pulled her into the same anteroom where they'd sat just a few nights before. "Lord Edmund doesn't know you."

"But if he did?"

"If he did, it would hardly matter. He's speaking of something that happened—"

"That saw my father killed and my home taken from me."

He let go of her arm.

"Alex," she said, suddenly realizing how her words might be taken. "That was different. Your brother was ordered to take Bristol—"

"Stop."

This was a side of Alex she'd never seen. And though she didn't like it, Clara did not attempt to pacify him. If he was angry with her, it would make it easier for her to leave.

But she would not provoke him either. She *knew* the pain etched in his face. Better than she wanted to.

"I think we should speak later," she said.

Clara held her breath, hoping he would agree. Wishing he would take her in his arms but knowing that it could not happen. This was the best way.

"Fine."

With that, he turned and walked away.

Clara wasted precious moments sitting here, but her legs would not move. Her body felt limp as if it had lost the will to propel her forward.

She'd been such a fool. Gilbert had never relaxed his vigilance, and since his death, she'd broken every rule he'd ever made for her. If it were safe to travel about as a lady, even one with a new name, certainly he'd have told her so.

It had felt so good to be herself, or at least mostly herself, that she'd ignored the inner voice telling her to be careful. A voice smothered by her love for a man she'd never see again.

Unless, of course, she sat here feeling sorry for herself. Surely he would realize what she planned. Or mayhap she'd angered him so much he would not care if she left?

She couldn't even make herself believe it.

With incredible effort, she forced herself to stand, to retrace her steps and make her way back to Emma's chamber. Once there, she quickly tore off the gown, glad for its simplicity, and under-garments. She laid the gown out on the bed, wishing she could leave Emma a note. Her tutor had wanted to teach her how to write, but her father had possessed rather ancient notions of a lady's abilities. Her skills were more aligned with running a household or entertaining guests.

Until, of course, she fled her home with Gilbert. Since then, she'd acquired an entirely different set of skills, and she intended to put them to use now.

Once dressed, she pulled her sword out from under the bed, fastened it in place, and began to arrange one of her least favorite parts of the disguise. After fumbling with the pins, she placed the hat atop her head, Alfred once more.

She knew now, after a few days of exploring, how Alex had gotten past the guard at the top of the stairs that first night. If she could make it to the other end of the hall without being spotted, Clara could take the secret passageway down to a doorway just outside the kitchens. From there, she simply had to make her way outside and slip away unnoticed.

Only a few people knew of her disguise. She'd worried at first that some of Kenshire's folk might ask about Alex's squire. But Lady Sara had assured her they would not, and indeed, she'd attracted far more attention as a visiting noble than she had as Alfred.

She just had to avoid the few people who knew the squire existed.

Pushing thoughts of Emma and Alex aside, Clara concentrated on the task of getting out of Kenshire without being recognized. Once outside, she put her head down and looked for two things: dirt and a bit of privacy. Finally finding both in a secluded corner, Clara completed her disguise. Smearing the dirt onto her face, she breathed in the scent of baking bread streaming out of the kitchens, wishing she'd been able to take a meal with her.

As she'd done at Brockburg, Clara would be forced to leave on foot. Though Alex would forgive her stealing the mare he'd lent her for their travels, she could not risk getting it out of the stables without raising an alarm.

With every step she took away from the courtyard, she knew her plan was more and more likely to succeed. No one would question a boy, and it was much too early for her friends to start looking for her.

But they would, eventually.

Grateful to have found people who cared for her, Clara might have taken comfort from the knowledge they would certainly search for her. . . except it meant they would be endangering themselves, which was exactly what she hoped to prevent.

So it was with great relief that Clara found herself outside the castle walls and on her ways to Kenshire's village. She had the coin earned from squiring for Toren, which was enough to sustain her for longer than most stretches in between tournaments. With it, she could afford shelter and food until she found the next tourney to attend. She'd need to find a merchant to ferry her, but in the meantime, she'd do best to stay off the main roads.

For Alex would come, and for his sake, he could not be allowed to find her.

———

He'd found his mother after six years. He was regarded as one of the best trackers along the border. And yet, he could not find one woman, on foot, and though he was ashamed to admit it, Alex was beginning to worry. From the horrifying moment he'd realized Clara was gone, the dread that plagued him continued to intensify.

"You look like shite."

He darted a glance at Geoffrey before dismounting.

"I don't like it," he said, not for the first time.

"Alex, darkness fell hours ago. We've knocked on every door in the village. Spoken to more people here than in Elkview. She's not here."

"Then I know where we're headed next."

"Tonight?" Geoffrey asked.

"If Sara were out there somewhere. . ."

He untied his mount from the post in front of the tavern where they'd intended to stop for a meal. There was no need for him to wait for an answer; Geoffrey had already re-mounted. Their agreement was silent—they'd eat when they found her.

"If Sara were out there," Geoffrey said as they rode away, "someone would have already noticed a countess travelling alone, on foot, even if she did wear her breeches."

Lady Sara tended to dress. . . unconventionally. . . at times, something his sister, Catrina, and Lady Juliette, no doubt, had begun to emulate. He was surprised he'd not seen her in such attire during their stay.

He'd once thought it unusual for a woman to wear breeches. If he found Clara, Alex would never again give a thought to what she wore. She could dress as Alfred every day for the rest of their life if it suited her. He just wanted her back.

His mind travelled back through the long, torturous day, looking for any clues that could help him find her. For any hope. After parting from Clara, he'd trained for the remainder of the day, though his mind had never strayed far from his love.

At first he'd dismissed her fear. Lord Edmund, or anything they met for that matter, could talk about the rebellion all they wanted. It was over. No one was looking for Clara or any of the others who'd sided against the crown.

But then he'd forced himself to imagine what it must have been like for her, a girl of only ten and eight, to watch her father murdered in front of her—the helplessness of it. He'd thought of the years she'd spent on the run, hiding, worried about losing her life if discovered.

He had been wrong to push her. If Clara needed more time, so be it. They could wait to be married until she felt safe. Or until she began to show a babe in her stomach. He loved her enough to go along with any plan she devised.

Except, of course, for this one.

The moment Emma hurried out into the yard, he'd known. . . he'd run back to the keep to verify what she'd told him, and as he stared down at the gown Clara had worn earlier that day, fear crawled through his body.

"Alfred's clothing is gone," Emma confirmed breathlessly, answering his next question.

Sara and Geoffrey followed them into the room, and after Emma relayed the previous evening's conversation, they all understood that she'd run away.

"I never imagined—"

Sara looked especially pale, and Alex knew she blamed herself.

"How would you know that pompous old man—"

Sara's narrowed eyes cut Geoffrey's thoughts short.

For the briefest of moments, Alex thought back to the horror he'd experienced upon learning his mother had left them. But she'd done so for a good reason, as had Clara. How could he have missed the signs? She'd refused to see him last night, and this morning she'd pushed him away, knowing all along that she planned to leave.

"She talked to you today," Emma began, the panic in her voice not making him feel better about the situation.

"Aye," he said, not willing to divulge much else. "She didn't say anything to you about leaving?"

Emma shook her head as she looked around the room. "Nothing of import. I know she was still upset about last eve but. . . oh Clara, I'm so sorry," she said.

"We'll find her," Alex said.

Geoffrey and Sara began to leave, but Emma stopped Alex before he could follow them.

"She's trying to protect us."

"I know."

Years of training forced him to remain calm when he wanted to do anything but.

"Alex?" Emma looked as if she wanted to say more, but her mouth opened and closed a couple of times without any words coming out.

"Do you know where she is? Where she could have gone?"

"No, I'm sorry, I do not."

He waited, hoping she would tell him something, anything, to help him find her.

"You need to find her. She loves you."

That was not at all what he'd expected to hear.

"Did she tell you that?"

They'd never talked about love. He'd meant to tell her how he felt, but something had always interrupted him.

"She didn't have to. Her feelings—your feelings—are obvious. Please. . . please find her," she begged.

She left the room, and he stood alone for a moment, thinking of Emma's words.

The thought of never seeing Clara again brought him physical pain—the kind of ache that would never go away. Aye, he loved her, and he would find her and convince her she was safe. That *they* were safe. He didn't care how long it took.

Gilbert had kept her alive, but being alive was not enough if she spent her entire life running.

Now, riding atop his horse next to Geoffrey, something finally clicked into place. *Gilbert.*

"Gilbert told me if anything ever happened to him, I should go to Keston House," Clara had said, after telling him she'd left Keston before long, worried she'd put the owners in danger.

"Geoffrey, we go to Keston House."

26

Clara bounced up and down with the motion of the cart, thanking God for her good fortune in finding not just any merchant, but a fur trader willing to accept her coin. The cart was much more comfortable than she'd expected, and although the elderly trader would not be of much assistance against potential threat, he and his young nephew navigated the roads well.

They had just been stopped for a tax collection, having passed through a new lord's border. Clara assumed the man would then stop for the night since darkness had already begun to fall, but he did not.

She had spoken to no one in Kenshire's village, assuming Alex would start looking for her there. She'd tried not to feel too badly about taking a loaf of bread since she had left the baker ample compensation.

So far, her disguise had worked well. Clara had kept her head down and taken only what she needed. Standing at the edge of the village, she'd waited for someone, anyone, to leave—and she'd given the fur trader double the usual amount for his trouble. There was a chance he'd attempt to rob her, knowing she had that much coin on her, but it was a chance she had to take.

The man and his nephew had been kind thus far, so when the wagon creaked to a stop and she heard the raised voices, Clara did the one thing Gilbert had trained her never to do. Get involved in a confrontation. Usually she was more careful about choosing her riding companions, and she favored those who could provide her with protection.

Damn fool reivers.

She couldn't tell if they were English or Scottish, but that was the danger of travelling by moonlight.

"We don't care about your guild, old man. Show us the goods."

Clara jumped out on the opposite side of the would-be attackers—there were two—and hid behind the large wheel, knowing surprise was her best defense.

She could tell the merchant was nervous, likely because of her. The merchant's guild might offer some protection, but this trader needed either an older nephew or plenty of coin to keep himself from harm.

"Pay us in coin or in fur. You decide."

"I've not got more than I earned at Kenshire."

So he didn't have a bribe. How did he plan to stay alive?

Clara moved around the side of the wagon and held her finger to her lips when the boy looked down to her. The poor lad was terrified.

"Please," the merchant begged. "My sister and her husband are both dead. The boy only has me to look after him. Without that fur—"

As soon as the second man dismounted from his nag, she moved quickly, taking advantage of the opportunity before her. Clara kicked the lance from the first man's hand and held her thin sword to his back.

"You have choices," she grumbled. "Leave us in peace and rob some other unsuspecting victim, or lose your partner for a few pelts of fur."

She only had one chance to get it right, to convince him her words were true. Her training, it seemed, had not deserted her.

"Move," she muttered to the man, who smelled like a mixture of dirt and dung, "and die."

He could overpower her easily, but she wouldn't give him the chance to learn that.

"I've no wish to see anyone die," the second man said.

It wasn't at all what Clara had expected to hear.

"Can't overlook the opportunity for extra coin," he continued. "But we'll be on our way."

This was the most dangerous part. Once she took the sword away, she would be vulnerable.

She tried to think of something to say, hoping for some time for the merchants to arm themselves. Even an old man and a boy would know enough to carry weapons. She peered around her captive to see the old man did indeed hold a knife in his hands.

But it would provide very scant protection against these men unless they truly believed her a threat.

She'd been in difficult situations before, but this was one of the trickiest. Not even a full day had passed, and her life was already on the line.

Alex and Geoffrey were forced to slow down without much moonlight to guide them. They rode side by side, their horses kicking up pebbles and dust. At least it had not rained in a few days, making the road easily passable.

Unable to calm himself, Alex found himself thinking of all the horrific things that could befall Clara on her journey.

"Tell me about your brothers," he said to Geoffrey, hoping the conversation would help distract him.

"You've met Bryce, of course," Geoffrey said. "He's always been the quiet one."

"Quiet," Alex chuckled. "I suppose that's one way to describe him."

In truth, Bryce glared more than he spoke. His silence was unnerving at times, and Alex still wondered how Catrina could have fallen in love with such a man. She was his opposite in so many ways, and yet there was no denying they were happy together.

"And Neill. . ." He was quiet for a moment. Alex allowed him time to think. "He takes after his eldest brother in his good looks and charm."

Alex laughed aloud then. "I doubt that."

Geoffrey ignored him.

"But he's as headstrong as Emma. He oft acts before he thinks."

Alex thought it was a good description of Geoffrey's sister as he knew her.

"But I see Bryce in him too. Though I believe he uses silence more to his advantage than anything else. With us, he's never too shy to give an opinion."

"That sounds like Catrina," Alex said.

"A fine woman," Geoffrey complimented his sister. "Bryce could not have found a better one."

"She is very much like the mother I knew from my childhood."

Geoffrey didn't answer, and Alex could have kicked himself. No matter how friendly they became, the subject of Geoffrey's parents would never be a comfortable one for them, and he did not wish his. . . friend any discomfort.

"As is Emma," Geoffrey finally said. "That my mother was killed attempting to attack one of your men was not a surprise to me."

There was no malice or condemnation in his voice. Alex didn't know how he managed such a thing.

"I feel sorry for the man who attempts to tame that hellion," Geoffrey said. "I love my sister dearly, but she's never once listened to anyone. Perhaps with the exception of our father. But

I'm not the only one who couldn't control her. My mother and my aunt and uncle had no better luck."

Alex thought again of Catrina. Of Clara and Sara and all the other strong women he knew. "Maybe you should all stop trying."

"Ha!" Geoffrey slowed his horse. "What of when she sneaks off in the dead of the night to 'watch the waves ebb and flow,' giving the entire household a scare? I could tell you stories that would make your protective instincts flare."

Those same instincts made him aware that they weren't alone. Geoffrey had slowed for a reason, and he could hear that reason just up ahead. Not voices, yet—these were more like whispers in the wind. He moved his hand to the hilt of his sword and waited, as did his brother-in-law.

They didn't have to wait long for the threat to reveal itself.

27

There were as many different kinds of reivers as there were men. Some were of noble birth, even lawmen, who thought of reiving akin to a sport. Others, like the ones they met on the way to Kenshire, were more ruthless and mercenary than the most disillusioned of men. Most fell somewhere in between, reiving as a means for survival.

The reivers slowed, finally having spotted Alex and Geoffrey. Waiting for their approach, Alex flexed his hand—ready to determine if words would be enough to see him and Geoffrey on their way. He had no desire for bloodshed, but neither did he appreciate this delay. Clara was out there, alone and afraid, and he needed to find her.

He couldn't see their faces yet, but if Geoffrey's position were any indication, he was also preparing for a possible fight. Having been a reiver himself for a time, he knew their ways better than most, and Alex allowed him to take the lead as he edged his horse forward.

"Greetings, men," one of them said. "You can relax your... Waryn?"

They were close enough now for Alex to get a good look at the men. They were neither large nor small.

Geoffrey jumped from his mount, as did both reivers. To Alex's surprise, the lord embraced them one at a time. The reunion lasted but a moment before they all turned toward him.

"Alex, come meet these men."

He dismounted and walked toward the group.

"Aaron and Robert Dunn, meet my brother-in-law, Alex Kerr."

Their smiles faded and the Englishmen, which their reaction revealed them to be, looked as if they wanted to kill him.

"Geoffrey— " the light-haired one named Robert began.

"Yes. He's a Kerr. And a good man, so you can stop staring at him like that unless you want your skull cracked in half."

The other reiver looked toward Geoffrey. "By who? Certainly not you? We've heard you're a great earl now. Likely you can't even use that thing," he said, pointing to Geoffrey's sword.

Geoffrey moved quickly, grabbing the lance from Robert.

"Who needs a sword?" Geoffrey said. "This will do quite nicely."

Aaron laughed. "That's twice tonight you've been taken unaware, brother."

Geoffrey finished the introductions. "Aaron and Robert are friends of my aunt and uncle who took us in after Bristol."

The men exchanged another surprised look, likely because Geoffrey had spoken so calmly about his home being attacked.

"They introduced me to reiving."

"And Hugh. Where is your uncle?"

Geoffrey handed the reiver back his lance. "He's visiting Lettie and Simon with his wife."

It took Alex a moment to place the names until he remembered they were the aunt and uncle whom Geoffrey had referenced a moment earlier.

"Wife?" the lighter-haired one grimaced. "The poor woman."

"What are you doing this far east, Aaron?" Geoffrey asked. "And at this time of night?"

The reivers looked at each other and then at Geoffrey. "We're headed to you."

"Me?" Geoffrey's surprise was evident. "Is something wrong?"

"We didn't know you needed us, Waryn," Aaron said. "Rumors of Bristol reached us too late. We'd not have you thinking your reiving family had abandoned you."

Geoffrey put his hand on Aaron's shoulder. "If I'd needed your help, I'd have found you."

The men both looked at Alex again. "But clearly you did not," said Robert.

"Much has happened since we last met." Geoffrey walked toward Alex, evidently as a display of allegiance. "Bristol is secure, and the Scottish king who ordered Clan Kerr to take it—" he emphasized the word *ordered*, "—has relinquished their claim. And —" his tone hinted at the finality of his words, "—my brother, Bryce, is married to his sister."

Robert shrugged, apparently satisfied. "Whatcha doing out here? Are you missing your reiving ways?" he asked.

Geoffrey nodded to the road ahead. "We're looking for someone."

Robert moved toward his mount. Without asking any further questions, he displayed the legendary reiver loyalty to family and clan, and said, "Then we'll help you find them."

Geoffrey didn't seem surprised, and Alex was just glad to keep moving.

"Where are we going?" Aaron asked.

"To Keston House," Alex answered.

"Who are we looking for?" Robert stroked his mount's mane with care, another indication that, reiver or not, he was the kind of man Alex would be glad to travel alongside.

"A lad," Geoffrey answered. "A squire by the name of—"

"Alfred?"

They all stopped to look at Robert.

Alex understood immediately. "Were you taken unaware by a lad named Alfred?"

"You should have seen it," Aaron boasted. "He was as small as his sword, but the lad held it so quickly to Robert's back I thought I may have one less brother this eve."

"And you're sure his name was Alfred?" Alex held his breath, waiting.

"Aye, that's what they called him. He travels with a merchant and another young boy."

"When?" he and Geoffrey asked at the same time.

"A few hours past," Aaron answered.

"Did they say where they were going?" Alex asked eagerly. Though he swelled with pride, the vision of Clara arming herself against these men terrified him.

Aaron shook his head. "On this road? 'Twould seem the same place you are. Not much besides Keston House between here and—"

"He is okay then?" Alex interrupted.

"You should be asking my brother that. I didn't get a good look at him."

"Aaron?" Geoffrey prodded.

"Aye, better than that. He is a feisty lad. It was only when we mentioned we were headed to Kenshire that he took his sword from Robert's back."

"Please tell me you didn't rob them?"

"Rob?" Aaron apparently was appalled at such an idea. "Tax them, more like. This is our territory."

"Aaron!"

"Nay, Geoffrey, we did not take anything from them. Certainly not after the boy pulled his sword."

The relief that coursed through Alex's body almost felled him. He was in love with Clara. The thought of seeing her, of holding her in his arms. . .

To hell with the danger. They knew now his guess was accurate. Clara was headed to Keston House. He sped up and led the group, not caring if the other men followed.

He would get there by daybreak, and when he found her, he'd never let her go.

"Alfred?"

Clara leapt off the cart and ran to the woman who had kept her safe after Gilbert's death.

Albri was a plump but fierce middle-aged woman whose hair had long ago gone grey. A woman who was known to harbor smugglers and slit the throat of any man who crossed her. Her ruthlessness was matched only by her husband's. Edgar, the son of a wealthy merchant who once made a living as a mercenary, was large, scary, and incredibly kind. At least to Clara.

They were the kind of people she never would have gotten to know as Clara, but to whom Alfred owed much.

"I am a boy," Clara reminded her. Albri released her, and luckily, none seemed to have noticed the overly-long embrace.

"What took ye so long to come back?"

And before Clara could answer, she kept talking. "It's hardly daybreak. You travelled all night?"

"Albri—" she gestured to the fur trader and his nephew, "—they need a room."

Albri watched them bring the cart to the nearby stables. From the decisive nod she gave them, it was clear she knew they'd helped Clara. "The best Keston has to offer," she said, turning away. "Come, lad." She chuckled, reminding Clara of the other reason she'd not remained here longer. Albri was not very good at keeping secrets.

These were Gilbert's friends, and they had treated her like a daughter when she needed it most. But Clara still had trouble understanding how a man like Gilbert—a man killed for refusing to involve himself in illegal activities—could call Edgar and Albri friends.

"Albri," she called out to her hostess, knowing that she would soon be whisked into the wattle-and-dab structure known as much for its penny-a-night rooms as it was for harboring smugglers. Though it was further inland than most smuggler establishments, it was close enough to gain the attention of evil-doers looking for safe passage to both sides of the border.

"Before you feed me—"

"Ha, gone for months and she—pardon, *he*—thinks he knows ol' Albri."

Clara watched her wrinkled face scrunch up, leaving no doubt as to where the lines on her face had originated.

"Well? When's the last you've eaten, boy?"

Clara would have laughed, but she remembered she was no longer Clara. Masking her feminine laugh was something she'd never been able to do successfully.

"Just so," Clara said. "But I need to speak with you first. It's important."

Whether Albri took heed of her impatient tone or saw the look of panic in her eyes, Clara couldn't be sure. But rather than bring her inside, the older woman pulled her to the side of the inn.

"Are they after ye?"

Clara smiled. Albri was fond of saying exactly what was on her mind.

"There are men looking for me," she started, pausing to search for the right words. How could she convey the importance of misdirecting Alex without unintentionally putting him in danger? If Edgar and Albri thought he was a threat to her, they would not rest until that threat was eliminated.

"Well, of course there are—"

"Nay, Albri, different men. A Scot. Not a bad man," she rushed to explain. "In fact, he is a very good man. But. . ." She hated to do this, but it was the only solution she could think of. "I just don't care for him. In that way."

She did not want him to be harmed. And if Albri had any indication of her true feelings for Alex, he'd be welcomed into Keston House like a king.

Albri's eyes widened. "He knows?"

Clara nodded, looking down the road as the sun rose higher in the sky. "He does. And please—" she emphasized her next words, "—*please* do not do him any harm. I just. . . he is not someone I care to be with."

Albri scrutinized her face, and Clara prayed she looked sincere.

Please, please believe me.

"If you're sure—"

"Yes! I am sure. Oh Albri, thank you. Bless your heart. I promise one day. . ." She could not help her now, but if she was ever in a position to repay the woman for her kindness, Clara would do so.

"Come then."

Clara followed her inside, where most of the inn's visitors still slept. The two-floor building, along with a separate kitchen and stable, featured more than one depiction of a magpie. From the sign hanging outside to the large tapestry that hung inside the common room, the good omen seemed to have worked thus far. Despite its location along the border and its questionable reputation, Keston House not only remained standing, but it continued to thrive, making its owners wealthy.

They climbed the stairs and Albri drew out a key from her pocket. "I've only got one room. Your merchant will have to sleep in the stable. I'll go outside and tell him as much."

So much for the 'the best Keston has to offer.' Albri handed her the key with a warning. "If yer worried about being caught, stay away from the window."

Clara understood immediately when she opened the door. The

room was front facing with a view of the entrance below. Not an ideal situation, but it would have to do.

"Leave the rest to me."

With that, Albri closed the door behind her. Clara had just begun to undress when the older woman returned with a bowl of stew and two thick slices of bread.

"Eat. And don't you worry about your Scot."

Despite the warning, Clara peered out of a crack in the shuttered window. She watched as Albri, now accompanied by her husband, forced her companions to bring their cart around to the back of the stable. Of course! If Alex saw it, he would surely question them. A few moments later, they emerged once again, and Albri handed the man and his nephew two loaves of bread. She pushed the merchant's hand away. She wouldn't take his coin.

Clara smiled. She'd come to the right place. Now, if she could just remain hidden. . .

The room was much smaller than the one she'd occupied at Brockburg. And nothing like her chamber at Kenshire. But it was clean, and that was all she cared about at the moment. That, and keeping Alex and her friends at Kenshire safe.

She ate hungrily, listening to the sounds of the inn coming to life around her. A bang here and there. Voices outside her room.

After she finished her meal, Clara lay down, not even bothering to turn down the blanket. She was exhausted.

She'd just begun to drift off to sleep when she heard it. Nothing about the voices should have woken her, but nevertheless she knew.

He was here.

Springing up from the bed, she did the one thing she knew she should not do. Closing the shutters so that barely a slit remained, Clara looked out.

And immediately began to cry.

2 8

"How long ago was she here?"

Alex looked at Geoffrey, whose expression showed the same skepticism he was feeling.

"At daybreak, mi'lord."

If Geoffrey's descriptions of the innkeeper were true, she was more biddable than he would have thought.

He and the others stood in front of the infamous inn, having ridden through the night to get here. It had never occurred to him that he would miss her; he'd assumed she would at least stay long enough to rest. Alex had spent the last hours fueled by the thought of holding her in his arms again. Making love to her again. Telling her over and over that he loved her.

To be told she was not here. . .

"But she was here, and she was well," Geoffrey said.

"Aye," the innkeeper answered. Too quickly?

"Then it appears we move on," Alex said to the men. "Shall we break our fast first?"

If Geoffrey and the reivers thought it odd he wanted to stop now after racing here like the most desperate of men, they didn't show their surprise.

There should be no reason for him to doubt the woman's word, and yet. . .

"Very well," the innkeeper replied. "I am Albri," she said.

"We've met," Geoffrey nodded to Albri and her husband. "My uncle and I stopped here on our way to Kenshire."

"To Kenshire?" Albri asked.

Alex attempted an introduction. "May I present Sir Geoffrey Waryn, earl of—"

Before he finished, both innkeepers bowed, obviously embarrassed not to have recognized one of the most powerful men in Northumbria.

"A hot meal is all we require," Geoffrey said, prompting them to stand.

Alex grinned as they made their way inside the inn. "Why do you insist on appearing thus?" he asked Geoffrey, having wondered the same on their visit to Elkview. The earl looked more like a reiver than he did the lord of Kenshire. His shield was hidden, and no mark on his surcoat identified him. Typically, the English were fond of their armorial bearings.

"Perhaps there is still a bit of reiver in me," he quipped.

No doubt that was true.

Entering the common room, one more well-appointed than most, Alex looked around but saw just one female besides the innkeeper. Reminding himself he was looking for a lad, Alex squinted, adjusting his gaze to the dim lighting.

"She's not here," Geoffrey said beside him.

"Nay." He turned to Robert. "I want to keep an eye on the innkeeper," he said quietly as they all sat. "Something seems amiss. Can you search for the merchant's cart?"

Robert stood up and left without questioning him, a testament to his loyalty to Geoffrey.

They ate, unspeaking, watching those around them. For a reputed smuggler's den, Keston House was well-kept. The patrons were better dressed and more well-mannered than those at The Anvil Inn.

It was, of course, early in the morn.

"Nothing." Robert was back already. "I searched inside the stable and didn't see any sign of it."

So the woman spoke the truth. Did he just want her to be hiding something? The alternative was unacceptable. It meant Clara was still on the road. Still in danger.

"I know we've been travelling all night—" Alex began.

"We'll keep going," Geoffrey said.

The innkeeper walked by, and Alex stopped her. "You know Alfred," he said flatly.

"Aye," she responded warily.

"Then you know she could be in danger."

According to Clara, the inn's owners were Gilbert's friends, and they'd wanted her to remain with them. Which meant they cared for her.

"How could you have let her leave so soon?"

It was what had been bothering him since the moment they arrived.

"Have ye met her then?"

He didn't need to ask what she meant. Clara knew he was coming for her. And she was trying to avoid him.

Dammit, Clara!

"Where is she going?"

"She didn't tell me."

That, at least, Alex believed. It was the first time he'd sensed truth from the woman. But apart from tearing the inn to shreds, he had no choice but to believe her.

"But I'd guess looking for a tourney," she added.

Alex handed the woman enough coin to pay for their meal.

"Thank you for your hospitality."

Alex stood, and the others followed.

"Where are we going?" Robert asked.

Alex gave the room a final glance before heading for the door.

It was a question he couldn't yet answer.

29

$\mathcal{A}$nd then he was gone.

For a few heart-pounding moments, Clara expected a knock at the door. She'd seen them enter, surprised to see the reivers she'd encountered travelling with Alex and Geoffrey. But they had said they were travelling to Kenshire to see Geoffrey, so she supposed it made sense.

What did not make sense was the disappointment that flooded through her as she saw the men emerge from the inn. She hadn't wanted him to find her. This was best for him.

And yet, she was a fool to deny that part of her had hoped and hoped for a different outcome. That Alex would somehow learn Albri was lying. That he'd break down every door in the inn to find her. She had imagined it so thoroughly she could almost feel his arms around her.

Before he left, Alex stopped and turned back toward the inn. Was he looking at her window? Did he suddenly suspect?

Impossible.

He looked devastated. In that moment, she knew Emma had been right. Alex loved her—just as surely and as inescapably as she loved him.

261

When he turned away, Clara slumped to the floor. She buried her face in her hands, too busy tending to her tears to notice that she was no longer alone.

"Hush, girl. What's the matter then?"

Albri closed the door behind her and sat next to her on the floor. She held her in her arms, and Clara continued to sob. She could no sooner control the tears than she could worry about Albri's reaction.

"You lied to ol' Albri."

She didn't deny it, but the words brought Clara out of her misery. . . if only for a moment. She sat back and wiped her face with her sleeve.

"I'm so sorry. I knew if I told you—"

"I've a mind to fetch that handsome boy—"

"No!"

She grabbed Albri's arm in panic. "You cannot. Albri, he will fight for me."

"And protect ye, no doubt."

Clara didn't care if the innkeeper thought she was mad. Every time she doubted her decision to run, she needed only to close her eyes to see her father's body dropping to the ground. The great knight, a warrior who'd loved his country as well as anyone. Dead before she could even yell out a warning.

"No," she said. "I will not allow Alex to be killed. Or you."

She stood, and Albri stood with her.

"I can't stay here."

Clara began to gather her belongings when Albri intercepted her.

"Fool girl, you need to rest."

Clara moved to an opening in the shutters and peered out.

Nothing.

They were gone.

"You will stay here, or I'll send someone after 'em to tell the Scotsman just where—"

"Okay," Clara relented. "But promise me, Albri, you will not send for him?"

Albri frowned.

"I will not be responsible for another death."

Finally, after a few agonizing moments, the innkeeper agreed. "But ye'll stay here for at least a few nights."

"One."

"Three."

Clara smiled despite herself. "Two nights." As if the word 'night' reminded her she hadn't had any sleep, Clara yawned.

"Lie down then, ye stubborn lady."

Albri pulled back the blanket for her, and this time, she listened.

"If ye truly don't want to be found, then ye best stay here. Your Scot spoke to every man below. Offered them coin to find you, I'm thinkin'."

Of course he did.

"Thank you, Albri."

She tried not to think of Alex when she closed her eyes. But his face, so full of pain, was the last thing she remembered before giving in to the weariness that overcame her.

"I'm sorry, Alex."

They'd parted ways with the reivers earlier. Geoffrey had spoken to his friends quietly before they left. After two days of searching, there was still no sign of Clara. They searched roads, farms, and villages. They had spoken to hundreds of people and paid nearly as many with the promise of more if they found her and sent word to Kenshire.

"Perhaps she went back?"

That slim possibility was the only thing that made him agree to return. That and the hope that someone may have seen her—or at least the boy she pretended to be.

"We'll stop at Elkview first."

His mother would be waiting for him. Alex would have to tell her they wouldn't be heading back to Scotland just yet, but he wanted her out of that place. She could stay at Kenshire while he looked for Clara.

They rode in silence, the mood as somber as it had been since they'd left Keston House. Turning back felt like a defeat, and it was not a feeling to which Alex was accustomed. Nor did he enjoy it. But what else could they do? Travel the English countryside looking for a woman, dressed as a boy, who had spent years learning how to disappear? He pictured Clara with her sword held to the reiver's back and smiled.

She was a remarkable woman, and a beautiful one too. His mind was full of Clara. Disrobing by the lake. Snuggling up to his backside for warmth in the tent they'd shared. Giving herself to him with abandon. . . Och, he'd been a fool not to tell her how much he loved her.

"Someone is ahead," Geoffrey said, which Alex had already surmised.

Alex watched the lone rider approach. There was a grave look in the man's eyes that he recognized all too well. He looked as if someone he loved had died.

"Good day, my lords," he said, his voice flat.

An Englishman. He was finely dressed, though his clothing appeared well-worn. A large man, his brown hair and beard mixed with grey, he was almost as tall as Alex and his companion.

"Good day," Geoffrey replied back.

The man made no move toward a weapon and didn't appear to be a threat.

"Travelling alone?" Alex asked. "A dangerous proposition." It made him think of Clara, out there all alone, and he nearly turned his horse back around.

"I've little coin to steal," he said, slowing as he caught up to them.

"Where are you headed?" Geoffrey asked.

"In search of a troubadour's tale," he answered.

Alex raised his brows and waited.

"Keston House," the man replied. There was something kindly about him despite his size. "You?"

"To Elkview. And then Kenshire," Geoffrey said.

The stranger nodded as if that made more sense to him. "You are lord there?" he guessed correctly.

"Sir Geoffrey Waryn, at your service. And this is my brother-in-law, the Scot."

Alex laughed at that introduction. "Otherwise known, back in my country of heathens," he joked, "as Alex Kerr of Clan Kerr."

"Ahh, a border clan."

"A borderer by birth and choice," he said. "And home to you is?"

He hesitated and looked ahead. "I have a home no longer."

A chill crept up Alex's spine.

"What is your trade?" Geoffrey asked.

"An armorer." The man shrugged. "Or I was once."

An armorer. Without a home. Heading to Keston House.

It could not be possible. Gilbert was dead. And yet. . . Alex had felt a connection to this man from the start. Every hair on his body seemed to stand up.

Would he even give his name? Of course, it was Clara who was in hiding, not him.

"And what do you call yourself?" Alex asked, the humor from his voice gone.

The English armorer, now in front of him, looked back as if contemplating whether or not to give an answer. But he did.

"Gilbert, my lord."

———

"You're welcome here any time, my... Alfred." Edgar was no more skilled than his wife when it came to keeping her secret.

"Many thanks," Clara said. "I hope to see you again and pay for your charity in kind."

Though the morning threatened rain, which had very nearly delayed her departure, the clouds outside had just begun to clear. The knight whom she'd hired would take her two days south, and from there, it would be up to her to find a way west toward the edge of the borderlands.

"I say yer makin' a mistake," Albri said, not for the first time. Refreshed and laden with enough food to feed Alex and all of his men, Clara was grateful for Albri's care. But she didn't agree with her about Alex, and they would have to part ways on those terms. Albri had spent every waking moment of the past several days attempting to change Clara's mind, which reminded her a bit of Emma. Still, she would not be swayed. Gilbert had told her to trust no one. And while she wasn't sorry to have broken that promise a wee bit at Kenshire, she had renewed her silent vow to him, one that had kept her alive for years.

"I know you believe so," she said. They stood just inside the inn's entrance, but Clara knew she was wanted outside. The knight waited on her. He was a frequent visitor to Keston, and Edgar and Albri had assured Clara of her safety with him. She couldn't chance letting such a man leave without her.

She hugged the older couple, wishing she could stay but knowing it was not possible.

"And remember what to say if he returns."

"I know what ye told me to say."

Clara chuckled. That was exactly why she had not divulged her exact destination to them.

"Take care of yerself," Albri said as her husband moved aside to open the door behind Clara. "And if yer ladyship arrives again at our humble door, she will always be welcome."

"And I love you both for it," a voice behind her answered.

It cannot be!

Clara spun around and stared at the man who blocked her way out.

"Gilbert? You are dead!"

Gilbert, *her* Gilbert, stood there, very much alive. How was it possible?

She took a step toward him and threw her arms around him. Gilbert. Alive?

"Ahh, Alfred."

She didn't care about strange looks or how strange it must appear for a young squire to have his arms wrapped around an armorer. Somehow, Gilbert was alive.

"How it is possible? What are you doing here?"

She let go long enough to look at his face once again. It was, indeed, Gilbert.

"You're dead!" She glanced at Albri and Edgar, who appeared just as stunned as she felt.

Gilbert, who looked just as she'd last seen him, held up his arms. "Not dead, as you can see. At least, not now that I've found you."

Clara's hands were shaking. She didn't understand, but neither did she care. Nothing mattered except that Gilbert was alive.

"Yer big bulk is blockin' the door," Edgar said to Gilbert jokingly.

He walked inside and nodded to an empty table.

"Do you still have the best ale in all of England?"

Albri and Edgar brewed and sold their own ale, and while they sat, Albri waved her hand to a serving maid.

"Ale for all," she called loudly, and everyone who sat in the great room cheered. Money flowed through Keston, and its loyal customers would benefit from this happy occasion.

"Gilbert?" She hardly knew what to say. What to ask.

"I was left for dead— "

"But I heard them. They talked about tossing your body in the river."

"That much is true," he said, taking a mug of ale from the serving wench. "And if I hadn't been yanked out like a trout, I'd still be in there rotting away for the fish to feed on."

He drank deeply, and Clara and the others waited.

"I woke with the gash in my side wrapped, the lump on my head pounding, and the knight who'd dragged me from that river loomin' over me like a nursemaid."

"A knight saved you?"

"More like he took a piss and happened upon my bleedin' body. But, aye, he saved me. And allowed me to remain in his tent until the tourney was over, and I was mended. Or mostly mended."

"But—"

"You were gone. I cursed that I'd told you to run. Just a day later I awoke, but there was no sign of you. I reopened the wound and had to crawl back, much to the consternation of the squire who helped tend to me. But I had to search for you."

Clara understood the pain he must've felt at losing her, because she'd felt it herself. Twice before. And now three times.

But he was really here. She wasn't alone!

Alex.

Gilbert would not be happy when she told him how many knew of her secret.

"Gilbert," she started, wanting to get it over with. "I've something to tell you."

Edgar and Albri stood as if a string pulled them up together. They left, muttering something about tending to new guests.

She was grateful to be alone with the man who had saved her life.

"And I you. There's someone who waits—"

"Me first, Gil. I need you to know. I'm so, so sorry." She took a deep breath and lowered her voice. "I told someone." She bit her lip. That wasn't exactly true. "I told a few people, actually. But before you chastise me, let me explain! I was so scared after you left. And alone. But I did okay, Gil. You'd have been so proud of me. This one time. . . never mind that. A man by the name of Toren Kerr, Chief of Clan Kerr, hired me. And he was so kind. I didn't let on at all. I stayed in disguise, I promise. But. . ."

"His wife discovered your secret, they took you to Brockburg, where you met Toren's second, who took you to Kenshire because, for reasons I'll never understand, the man thought it appropriate for you to accompany him on his quest to find his mother here in England."

As he spoke, Clara shook her head. No. He couldn't know any of this. Unless. . . had he followed her this whole time? As he talked, Gilbert glanced toward the front door and nodded. Why was he. . . ? It couldn't be. . .

It was.

Alex was there, filling the door to the inn as surely as he had the stables in Kenshire. He looked. . . relieved? Angry? She couldn't be sure.

Clara looked back at Gilbert, gawking in shock.

"I met him on the road on the way here." Gil took a swig of ale and glanced at Alex, who was walking toward him.

"I'm sorry, Gil. I. . ."

"Listen to me." He looked at Alex again and shook his head. Alex stopped. "You've nothing to be sorry for."

She pulled her attention back to Gilbert.

"Nothing. Alfred, do you hear me?"

For so long that name had been her own, but now it sounded foreign on his lips.

"But you told me so many times. . ."

"I told you to trust no one. To tell no one. Aye. But that's when you had me. You did the right thing. He's a good man."

A good man? Nay, he was better than that.

"But I'm in danger still. . ."

"Perhaps. Perhaps not. But you're not alone any longer."

She looked at Alex, who started toward them again. When he reached the table, he spoke as if they were the only two people in the inn.

"I was worried about you."

The expression she couldn't reconcile earlier was easily discernible now.

Alex was scared. Or had been scared. And she had done that to him. She hated that she'd caused him pain.

Clara glanced at Gilbert, who said, "Go. I'll be here when you return."

She wanted to reach across the table and squeeze his hand. Gilbert was alive, and he was here. At Keston House.

"You better be," she said, standing.

The look Gilbert and Alex exchanged was a conspiratorial one. Not only had the men met on the road, it seems they had formed a bond, which, knowing Gilbert, was not surprising. He might appear scary to some, but to her, he was like a second father. Her savior.

Clara followed Alex from the hall, and when they reached the door, he held it for her. She walked through it with one last glance at Gilbert. Alex continued walking, so she followed. Past the kitchen and the stables, he walked to a path that led downhill.

Like most inns, especially ones this remote, Keston House was built along a river. She'd discovered it on their very first visit. Rivers tended to have mud, which was a necessary component of her disguise.

He didn't stop or even speak to her along the way. So he *was* angry. Well, she couldn't blame him. But he could at least tell her that himself.

"Alex?"

He continued walking until he reached the river bed. She turned and could no longer see the inn. They were quite...

"Oh!"

He pulled her toward him so quickly she nearly lost her footing. His lips were on hers before she could say another word. She wrapped her arms around him and clung on as if she would never let go. His tongue slid into her mouth and she met his movements with her own. Urgent and frenzied ones that said more than words ever could have.

He'd been scared for her, but no more scared than she'd been for herself. To be in his arms again. . .

She never wanted to leave.

3 0

𝒶lex had never been more relieved in his life. Seeing her through that window, knowing she was truly safe. He needed to be closer. He needed to feel her, love her, show her that they were never going to be separated again.

He started with the cap. Having taken it off her before, he knew where the pins were located. After tossing them to the ground, he removed her boy's clothing next, which, admittedly, was much more malleable than her heavy lady's gowns.

His heart soared when Clara attempted to remove his tunic, and he helped by raising it over his head.

"Clara," he murmured against her lips. Her answer was to untie the laces of his breeks. He tore off the remaining vestiges of her clothing and didn't even hesitate. His cock was hard, ready, and he knew she was just as primed. Checking to ensure it was so, he hardened even more at the feel of her slick folds and the sound of her soft moan.

Alex lifted her then, not wanting to waste time even to lay her down.

"Wrap your legs around me," he instructed as he held her with one arm and guided himself into her with the other. His face was buried in her neck, her hair teasing him from above. But Alex only wanted one thing, and he was about to have it.

"Oh," she said as he entered her. He slid her down atop him gently and then wrapped both arms around her buttocks, bringing his mouth to hers.

Alex kissed her with all of the built-up passion, the longing he had endured not knowing if she was safe. He moved against her, trying to go slowly.

She wouldn't let him.

The vixen slid her tongue against his suggestively and lifted herself up just enough to slide down once again. He groaned, increasing the pace and the pressure. He needed this, needed her. They matched each other's intensity until she broke away from him, tossed her head back, and climaxed, allowing him to do the same.

He thrust into her, leaving no doubt that she was his, now and forever. He held himself there, wanting to bind them together for eternity.

Alex tightened his grip on her backside as he leaned toward her to whisper in her ear.

"You are mine, Clara. And I am yours. We will never, ever be parted again."

If she said aye or nay, it hardly mattered. So long as she wanted him, so long as she loved him, he would spend a lifetime looking for her. He'd spend his days trying to convince her with words and his nights doing the same with deeds.

As the throbbing slowed, he pulled back to look at her.

"I will keep you safe, always. And before you say another word," he knew what she would say next, "'tis my choice to do so. Sara believes there's no longer a threat. Gilbert approves. But more importantly, I'm going to spend the rest of my life proving to you that you're safe and showing you how much I love you."

Her eyes widened.

"I love you, Clara. And if you think I'll let the woman I love walk away from me again—"

"I love you too, Alex."

Her warm, soft eyes peered into his soul. And he held her gaze, glad for it.

"And you won't have to come looking for me again. I will not leave you."

Reluctantly, he lifted her off of him. She tugged his hand toward the river's edge, and he followed. Kneeling beside it, she dipped her hand into the water and brought it to her face, washing the smudges there.

He watched, mesmerized, hoping it meant what he thought it did.

Alex followed her lead and helped her wipe every bit of dried mud from her cheeks until they were clean.

"He is gone."

And then she stood, giving him a full view of the glorious body he had first spied when she washed herself at the lake. But this time, she would not be putting her boy's clothes on. Instead, she picked them up from where he had discarded them, walked back toward him, and promptly tossed every piece into the river.

He roared with laughter as she made a second trip for the cap. He stood as she marched back to him as proud and tall as an ancient water goddess.

"It will be okay," he said.

He ran his hands along her sides, her back. She was beginning to feel cool to the touch.

"Clara," he said, holding her face in his hands.

Clara's fingertips glided down his arms. "Aye," she murmured.

"What do you intend to wear back to the inn?"

Her eyes widened.

"Aye, lass, I'm sorry to have mentioned it."

"Alex, 'tis not funny. What will I do?"

He ran his thumb along the outline of her lip.

"I will find something, love."

Her expression changed from concern to. . . something else.

"I could get used to hearing that."

He caressed the length of her body until he reached her hands, which he clasped, squeezing them gently.

"I will say it every day. All day."

"You complained about your brother and Lady Juliette," she reminded him.

"I did. But I expect to act just the same. . . when we see them."

"What do you mean?"

He leaned forward and kissed her on the nose.

"We will live at Dunmure," he said.

"Dunmure? But Alex, I thought—"

"It is mine, and 'tis time for me to claim it. My mother can live there, or Brockburg—I leave that for her to decide. If it pleases you."

"Of course it pleases me. I'm just surprised."

"No more surprised than I was to watch you toss your boy's clothes into the river."

"Don't you dare laugh at me. I just. . ." She smiled. "I just wanted to get rid of them. I wasn't quite thinking of anything else."

"I see that," he said, his gaze appreciative. He was unable to keep the laughter from his voice.

"But Geoffrey and I scoured the countryside to find you. And now—"

"And now, I am Clara. I thought I had to choose, and I was so afraid to choose wrong. But I'm not afraid anymore. Alex?"

"Aye, love."

"There is a bit of Alfred in me still. And I don't know if I'll ever be Clara completely again. Not after all that has happened."

She said it by way of an apology, but there was nothing to apologize for.

"As long as you're by my side and not holding a sword to English reivers, it matters not to me."

"You should have seen me," she said, clearly proud of her efforts. "And I still wish to train."

"Then you shall."

"And mayhap wear leggings as Lady Sara sometimes does."

"Wear this—" he gestured down to her beautiful body, "—I care not." He then thought better of it. "Well—"

"And one other thing if you are to be my husband. . ."

She turned serious, so he attempted to do the same.

"There shall never be any secrets between us. I abhor them."

"Well then. . . " he said. But he ruined the seriousness of the moment by running his hands from her hips to brush against the side of her breasts. "We should get started. I do have a few secrets to share that I think you'll be pleased to learn."

EPILOGUE

*D*unmure Tower, Scotland

"Alex, your mother will be here any moment!"

Clara swatted his hand from her backside as they stood in the entranceway of the keep that she now called home. Her mother-in-law was visiting from Brockburg. She'd chosen to stay at the larger holding in her own quarters so as "not to disturb either set of newlyweds." But she had promised to visit often, and she and Toren and Juliette were due to arrive at any moment.

Three months had passed since they'd married and moved to Scotland—the best months of her life. Alex could not wait to show his mother the improvements they'd made to his ancestral home, including the waterfall he had constructed in the garden. He remembered what she'd said about the soothing sound of the waters back at Barrington.

"Then let her come," he said, pulling her toward him once again and kissing her in full view of the servants who hurried from building to building looking for warmth. "You do remember the promise I made at Keston?"

Oh, she remembered. He'd not let her forget it.

"Which reminds me, I'm planning something special for Emma when we next visit Kenshire."

She and her friend wrote often, thanks to Father Simon's tutoring. When Alex had discovered she was unable to read or write well, he'd begged his tutor to reside with them for a time, and Father had happily agreed.

"Do you have any ideas?"

She pulled her cloak tighter around her shoulders, the cold just beginning to seep through.

"Come, we'll go inside." Alex took her hand and tried to pull her into the keep.

"Nay," she said. "I love it here."

The view was spectacular. Like Brockburg, Dunmure was positioned high above the surrounding landscape. She still could not believe this was her home.

Alex wrapped his arms around her.

"So what do you have planned for Emma?"

Clara nodded toward the armory, knowing Alex would understand.

"Gilbert?" Alex smirked. "You plan to marry Emma and Gilbert?"

Clara laughed. "Of course not. I've asked Gilbert to make her a sword like my own."

Though the threat she'd worried about for years was becoming more and more of a distant memory, Clara continued to train most days. She remembered Emma admiring her sword and thought it would make the perfect gift for her friend.

Alex tightened his hold when she shivered.

"She'll love it," he said. "Though not as much as I love you."

Though he told her so every day, Clara would never tire of hearing it.

"Will Gilbert engrave the Waryn motto on Emma's sword?"

She nodded. "I've made sure of it."

Clara looked up at the man who was now her husband, the Scot who'd learned her secret and stolen her heart, and smiled.

"*Non ducor, duco,*" she said, and was about to translate when Alex responded.

"I am not led. I lead."

She thought for a moment he would be serious, but should have known her husband better than that.

"I would like to lead you inside," he said, his hands beginning to stray.

She pointed to the approaching riders, well beyond the gates but distinct nonetheless.

"They're here!"

Alex groaned. "And we shall greet them happily. But tonight—"

"Tonight," she promised, "and every other night, you shall know me well. For I fear you still have a secret or two you've yet to reveal."

In answer, Alex smiled. A slow, sensual, genuine smile that confirmed she was right.

The Ward's Bride: Prequel Novella

English knight Sir Adam Dayne, to keep peace along the border, must accept a betrothal to the Scottish Marcher warden's beautiful daughter. Lady Cora Maxwell hates everything English. When Adam proposes a unique challenge, Cora is forced to face her greatest fears and the burgeoning desire he has awakened.

The Thief's Countess: Book 1

The son of a baron, Sir Geoffrey has been reduced to stealing the resources he needs to reclaim his family legacy. Lady Sara is distraction he resents. With her betrothed coming to claim her hand in marriage and a distant cousin intent on usurping her earldom, the countess feels beset by controlling, unwanted men including the reiver sent to protect her. As the threats continue to mount, Sara must decide what's more important—her duty or her heart.

The Lord's Captive: Book 2

After reclaiming his brother's inheritance, Sir Bryce is faced with an unwanted distraction—the sister of his greatest enemy. Divided loyalties pull the English knight and his Scottish captive, Lady Catrina, apart even as passion ignites between the unlikely pair.

The Chief's Maiden: Book 3

The Scottish king gives Toren Kerr a dangerous but important mission—kill the English Warden. But when he travels to England to participate in the Tournament of the North, he's immediately drawn to Lady Juliette Hallington. The English noblewoman longs to escape her sheltered life, but learns the very thing she wants most might consume everything she holds dear.

BECOME AN INSIDER

The absolute best part of writing is building a relationship with readers. The CM Insider is filled with new release information including exclusive cover reveals and giveaways. Insiders also receive 'Border Bonuses' with behind the scenes chapter upgrades, extended previews of all Border Series books and a copy of *Historical Heartbeats: A Collection of Historical Romance Excerpts* from various authors.

CeceliaMecca.com/Insider

ABOUT THE AUTHOR

Cecelia Mecca is the author of medieval romance, including the Border Series, and sometimes wishes she could be transported back in time to the days of knights and castles. Although the former English teacher's actual home is in Northeast Pennsylvania where she lives with her husband and two children, her online home can be found at CeceliaMecca.com. She would love to hear from you.

Stay in touch:

info@ceceliamecca.com